INFERNAL RISING

NOVELS OF THE MARVEL UNIVERSE BY TITAN BOOKS

Ant-Man: Natural Enemy by Jason Starr
Avengers: Everybody Wants to Rule the World by Dan Abnett
Avengers: Infinity by James A. Moore
Black Panther: Panther's Rage by Sheree Renée Thomas
Black Panther: Tales of Wakanda by Jesse J. Holland
Black Panther: Who is the Black Panther? by Jesse J. Holland
Captain America: Dark Design by Stefan Petrucha
Captain Marvel: Liberation Run by Tess Sharpe
Civil War by Stuart Moore
Deadpool: Paws by Stefan Petrucha
Morbius: The Living Vampire – Blood Ties
Spider-Man: Forever Young by Stefan Petrucha
Spider-Man: Kraven's Last Hunt by Neil Kleid
Spider-Man: The Darkest Hours Omnibus by Jim Butcher, Keith R.A. Decandido, and Christopher L. Bennett
Spider-Man: The Venom Factor Omnibus by Diane Duane
Thanos: Death Sentence by Stuart Moore
Venom: Lethal Protector by James R. Tuck
Wolverine: Weapon X Omnibus by Mark Cerasini, David Alan Mack, and Hugh Matthews
X-Men: Days of Future Past by Alex Irvine
X-Men: The Dark Phoenix Saga by Stuart Moore
X-Men: The Mutant Empire Omnibus by Christopher Golden
X-Men & The Avengers: The Gamma Quest Omnibus by Greg Cox

ALSO FROM TITAN AND TITAN BOOKS

Marvel's Guardians of the Galaxy: No Guts, No Glory by M.K. England
Marvel's Avengers: Extinction Key by Greg Keyes
Spider-Man: Miles Morales – Wings of Fury by Brittney Morris
Spider-Man: Hostile Takeover by David Liss
Spider-Man: Into the Spider-Verse – The Art of the Movie by Ramin Zahed
The Art of Iron Man (10th Anniversary Edition) by John Rhett Thomas
The Marvel Vault by Matthew K. Manning, Peter Sanderson, and Roy Thomas
Marvel Contest of Champions: The Art of the Battlerealm by Paul Davies
Marvel's Spider-Man: The Art of the Game by Paul Davies
Marvel's Guardians of the Galaxy: The Art of the Game by Matt Ralphs
Obsessed with Marvel by Peter Sanderson and Marc Sumerak
Marvel Studios: The First Ten Years
Avengers: Endgame – The Official Movie Special
Avengers: Infinity War – The Official Movie Special
Black Panther: The Official Movie Special
Spider-Man: Far From Home – The Official Movie Special
Spider-Man: Into the Spider-Verse – The Official Movie Special
Thor: Ragnarok – The Official Movie Special

MARVEL

MIDNIGHT SUNS

INFERNAL RISING

BY S.D. PERRY

Based on *Marvel's Midnight Suns*, developed by Firaxis Games in association with Marvel Entertainment, published by 2K Games Inc.

TITAN BOOKS

Marvel's Midnight Suns: Infernal Rising
Print edition ISBN: 9781789097726
E-book edition ISBN: 9781803360560

Published by Titan Books
A division of Titan Publishing Group Ltd
144 Southwark Street, London SE1 0UP
www.titanbooks.com

First Titan edition: November 2022
10 9 8 7 6 5 4 3 2 1

FOR MARVEL PUBLISHING
Jeff Youngquist, VP Production and Special Projects
Sarah Singer, Associate Editor, Special Projects
Jeremy West, Manager Licensed Publishing
Sven Larsen, VP Licensed Publishing
David Gabriel, SVP of Sales & Marketing, Publishing
C.B. Cebulski, Editor in Chief

Special thanks to Brian Overton

FOR MARVEL GAMES
Amanda Avila, Associate Manager, Integrated Planning
Bill Rosemann, Vice President, Creative
Haluk Mentes, Senior Vice President, Business Development & Product Strategy
Jay Ong, Executive Vice President
Peter Rosas, Senior Manager of Product Development & Project Lead
Tim Hernandez, Vice President, Product Development
Tim Tsang, Executive Director, Product Development

Cover design by William Robinson

Marvel's Midnight Suns developed by Firaxis Games in association with
Marvel Entertainment, published by 2K Games Inc.

© 2022 MARVEL

A CIP catalogue record for this title is available from the British Library.
Printed and bound in the United States.

For Steve and Dianne

PROLOGUE

SATANA Hellstrom was bored.

It wasn't the party, the party was fine. Better than fine, obviously; she had the most interesting guests in any Hell dimension, period. Artists and musicians, addicts and gamblers, famous suicides and forgotten monsters mingled in her throne room, laughing and talking and plotting against one another at her feet. They drank the finest spirits and enjoyed fantastic fusion cuisine, flawlessly provided by one of her countless soulless servants... who also provided entertainment, as needed. Nothing to liven up a dull moment like a spontaneous evisceration. She'd recently completely redone the chamber in shades of plum and rose, perfectly entrail-themed, and arranged her best trophies into fun athletic poses on the walls.

And yet it's the same as the last party. And the one before, and the ten thousand before that.

Satana sighed, letting the frenetic energy of a hundred vibrant conversations wash over her. The players changed regularly, but the smell was always the same—desperation, envy, ego. All of them endlessly jockeyed for favor with her advisors, whom she only kept so that nobody bothered her with their stupid requests. Did any of them understand all that she did for them, the pains she took to make everything so amazing? Did they realize how lucky they were, to have come to her realm, where there was fun and art and beauty, instead of landing in a torture prison or a lake of fire? Of course not. They fawned over her, groveled before her, stabbed each other in the back to get a step closer to her, but not a single one of them *appreciated* her. She was a competent and capable ruler with exquisite taste, better than any of them deserved.

She shifted against the throne's stone back, artfully carved to provide good back support, and the conversation lulled as a score of guests turned to watch, their eyes greedy. The theme for this party was *scandal* and Satana had dressed for it, her tight black bodysuit cut to reveal plenty of creamy skin, her thigh-high stiletto boots a deep shade of crimson. She'd done her hair cherry black and piled it into a loose knot between her horns, a few wispy tendrils artfully teased out to give her a tousled, sex-kitten vibe.

Okay, so she didn't hate those hungry looks, but she was a succubus; everyone wanted to touch her, it was a given. How did that validate her in any way, besides the super obvious? It wasn't fair that everyone around her got to experience the delight of her company *and* her ever-changing, dynamic realm, and all she got back were variations on how hot she was. Where was the recognition of her work?

Maybe it's time for a change. She'd completely remodeled her slice of Hell a dozen times in the last few decades, thrown herself into each transformation with enthusiasm and creativity. She'd raised cities and castles of gold, bone, obsidian, ice, gone through multiple palettes for environment and interior design, changed the weather, the light levels, even the design of the vermin that scurried around the crumbling edges of the infinity pits. Her guests wore knock-offs of clothes and jewelry she'd created—she'd spotted a dozen bad copies of the ouroboros necklace she'd adorned herself with just the night before—but trend-setting was old news, and no matter how engaging each re-creation was, she always ended up vaguely dissatisfied in the end.

And the end comes faster and faster. First night of a grand unveiling, and here she sat, itching for relief from all the sameness... But what was the cure? She could dump her guests and minions into one of the eternity pits south of her palace and burn every structure in her domain to ashes, then rebuild as it suited her. Again. She could take a vacation, open herself to inspiration, but she'd done that, too, lots of times. The party scene *was* getting tired, but nothing she could think of sounded better than what she had.

There were a dozen-plus admirers hoping to talk to her, gathered at the low stone steps of her platform and held back by the glowering Krek brothers, a matching pair of rock demons she'd lately been using as security. The Kreks were mute, ten feet tall and thicker than the walls of her best castle, plus their natural charcoal color went with everything. Satana scanned the waiting faces, mostly mortal, looking for anybody who might be worth her attention. A heavy-metal pill overdose with delusions of grandeur, a brilliant physicist with chronic halitosis and a tendency to get handsy, a handsome but dumb actor who went on and on about his instrument…

Satana's upper lip curled. There was that starlet who drank too much and always pushed "us girls" narratives—ugh. The blonde wore a trashy red dress with spangles and, when she realized she'd been noticed, dropped Satana a broad wink.

Satana had grown up in Hell and was the ruler of her own domain; her soul had once been bonded to the arch-demon Basilisk; she'd traveled through space and time, saved or doomed worlds as suited her, and been slain and resurrected more than once. Yes, it was *exactly* the same as being in a movie. They were practically *sisters*.

On a whim, Satana pointed at the winking actress and sent her to one of the pits, with no fanfare or public announcement. Even a year ago, she would have come up with some horrifying spectacle that ended with the actress as a trophy on her walls, fun for everyone and a friendly reminder not to be too familiar. These days, Satana didn't even bother waiting for their expressions to change when they realized they were uninvited. And the people behind the starlet just crowded into the empty spot, each of them convinced that they were special, different, worth tolerating...

Satana took a deep breath, causing another conversational dip, and then let it out slowly. Her advisor Veren, a mostly useless idiot, had said something about celestial alignments the other day. There was one of those once-in-a-millennium, darkness-rising deals coming up within the year. Satana hadn't really paid attention. Alignments happened all the time and she kept her realm stable, but perhaps it was making her restless. In any case, there was nothing for it but to quit the party before she burned everyone alive.

If you still want to burn them tomorrow, fine, but don't be reactive, she told herself, and rose from her throne. Maybe she was in a rut, but good for her. Recognizing her mood and checking her own behavior, that demonstrated maturity and—

Satana's thoughts cut off as she felt something push at her dimensional wards, magic that wasn't hers. The far wall, across from her throne platform, trembled and flickered.

The partygoers made *ooh* and *ahh* sounds, and were suddenly five times louder, shouting and calling to each other as the wall continued to shake.

"Shut *up*," Satana hissed, throwing up a hand, and froze the party. Her guests were stuck in mid-shout, some still pointing at the shimmering wall. In the new silence, Satana could hear the rock particles shifting. The wall's structure flickered again, the motion localizing to a narrow, jagged sliver by the floor, emitting an ugly green light. Whoever it was, they were weak, their magic puny. She could hear a whisper of chanting through the stone and tilted one delicate ear toward the sound.

"…nos voca nomen eius et Satanas, obsecro, audi nos…"

"Oh," Satana said, and sat down on her throne again, crossing her legs and sitting up straight, adjusting a few of her assets. Someone was reading a very old, very powerful spell, respectfully begging an audience with her specifically. The flavor of the magic was unfamiliar, secretive. Had she gained new worshippers? The invocation was strong enough to worm into her wards, but whoever was reading it apparently wasn't robust enough to make it work properly.

She waited. The almost-portal just kept flickering, which was irritating and embarrassing for the spell-caster, so Satana opened and stabilized it with a wave of one hand, creating an archway. The electric-green light intensified, spilling from the realm on the other side; it clashed with her décor and smelled man-made. She also smelled meat.

Human. She didn't bother unfreezing the Kreks, or anyone else. If the spell-caster couldn't even make a hole, she had nothing to worry about.

A man stepped into her throne room and held up his hands. He wore a kind of bulky bracelet that threw off the same green backlighting him, a soft glow like decay, like graveyard gas on a moonlit night. He was tall and pale, with slicked-back red hair and a full beard with mustache, neatly groomed. He wore tiny rectangular glasses and was dressed in an impeccably tailored brick-colored suit that fit him like a glove. The color was fabulous.

"Glory unto you, Satana Hellstrom, that you deign to acknowledge this worthless form," the man called. His voice had a nice rasp to it and sounded European, one of those brisk, practical countries.

Satana beckoned, shoving a few of her frozen guests out of the way, and the mortal appeared in front of her platform, blinking at the sudden transition. Up close, she could see that he was almost handsome in an angular, wolfish kind of way, closing in on middle age. He had light-blue eyes with the twitchy, too-wide stare that always accompanied zealotry of one kind or another.

"I'm listening," Satana said, and arched a brow, leaning toward him. The mortal blushed deeply, sweat popping across his wide forehead. He was uncomfortable! How sweet.

"My name is Fenn, and I seek vengeance upon Mephisto, who destroyed my family," the man began.

Satana snorted. "So, you've got a death wish. Hey, how'd you get in here, anyway?"

"One of many formidable spells I've collected, and this," Fenn said. He held up his left arm, showing off his glowing bracelet. It was all cheap black Velcro and tiny buttons, except for the green light, which pulsed with some kind of inherent energy. Radiation, maybe.

"I'm an inventor, of sorts, an engineer. I design machines. And I don't have a death wish. I've found a way to control Mephisto."

"Oh, really? Do tell."

"An amulet, called the Varkath Star," Fenn said. "An azure stone the size of a sparrow's egg, created from the direct energies of the lost dimension Abalosom and set into silver forged from the bones of Abalosom's angels. The Star's creation required all of the dimension's reality. It's been hidden away for centuries. The wearer can command any demon."

Satana laughed. "Yeah, right." This *was* entertaining.

"Varkath was a powerful sorcerer from Earth, long ago," Fenn said. "The eldest of the Thaumaturge Trivium. His magical prowess was legendary, before he was possessed by the evil entity known as—"

"Sure, sure," Satana broke in. Backstory was a drag. "But how do you know it works? It's been out of circulation for a while, right?"

Fenn smiled tightly. "I wouldn't dare bother Your Highness without certainty, or pursue my vengeance against Mephisto based on wishful thinking. I've done my research."

Huh. He had a point there; if he was lying or mistaken, he'd be more than sorry. Mephisto held grudges. And, she'd been known to incinerate stalkers. She'd never heard of the Varkath Star, but that didn't mean it wasn't a thing. "So, why are you talking to me, and not out there getting your vengeance on?"

"The amulet is part of a small collection, hidden and sealed away by powerful wards," Fenn said. "I believe I know where it's secreted, but will need help pinpointing the location and breaking the protections."

There it is. Nobody ever dropped in with a free gift, did they? "And you thought I would help you, because…"

Fenn blinked. "With the power to cast Mephisto from his throne—really, to unseat any demon ruler, in any dimension—I thought… That is, why *wouldn't* you be interested in expanding your magnificent realm? Planets and dimensions are coming into an alignment that will destabilize magic everywhere, an ideal time to redefine power dynamics, and Mephisto must pay for what he's done. I was only five years old when he took my mother's soul and…"

Fenn kept talking, but Satana tuned him out. *Expansion.* If the amulet was real, if Mephisto was unseated… There'd be a major power vacuum, and who was more qualified than her to step up?

You've outgrown this place, that's why you're never satisfied anymore. You need room to create a thousand perfect domains, to be recognized as the wise and powerful ruler you've become and—

"… and that's why I'm putting together a team," Fenn said.

Satana scowled inwardly, but batted her lashes and made a pouty mouth, leaning in closer. "You, me, and who else, Fenn?"

"Zarathos," he said, pointedly staring at his feet and sweating more. "He's Mephisto's prisoner, and I believe he can break the seals on the collection."

Elder Gods, he's going to make me ask again. Satana just managed to keep her tone even. "If Zarathos can get you the amulet, why are you *here?*"

"Even with my technical assists, the spells I have access to won't get me to him," Fenn said. "But you can. Free Zarathos, and the three of us will become the Triumvirate, dedicated to ending Mephisto's tyrannical rule. I only ask for the boon of immortality when the deed is done, so that I can torture Mephisto until the end of time, for what he did to Mo— to my mother."

Zarathos? Really? Zarathos had once rivaled Mephisto in terms of raw power, but he wasn't half as smart, and he absolutely wasn't going to share anything once he got involved; the demon was a complete narcissist, believed himself born to rule. Zarathos had blown his shot at taking down Mephisto once already. A loser.

Fenn stared up at her hopefully, his zealot's gaze twitching and crackling. Satana strongly considering melting his face. The *audacity.* Fenn actually wanted Zarathos, and was inviting her along just to get to him. Satana was used to being underestimated by anyone with a libido, but Fenn had come into *her* throne room and invited her to be a useful, pretty key without even *considering* that she might not want to prop up some entitled—

A deeper thought drowned out her wounded dignity. *Yes, he sees you as a key. To get to an amulet that controls demons. Any demon.*

Zarathos wasn't half as smart as *her*, either. She could run rings around him on her worst day. And Fenn was a human male who would faint if she flashed real skin at him.

Satana smiled, really putting her heart into it, turning up the pheromones, and Fenn raised his hands again and backed up a step, swallowing. In the quiet of her frozen gathering, she could hear his throat click.

"Triumvirate," she said, slowly, and licked her lips. "You know, I love a good threesome. Let's go for it, Fenn. Let's do it."

Fenn made a strangled sound but bowed deeply. Satana chuckled and dialed the sex back so that he could start filling in some of the blanks. She also took a second to acknowledge that she was really, truly excited for the first time in ages, space and light blossoming in her chest, a flutter of bubbles in her stomach. She hadn't been born to rule, but she was more than ready for the challenge. And it seemed her own keys to get there had just fallen into her perfect lap.

1

BLADE crouched atop the roof of a dilapidated warehouse, a warm end-of-summer wind rustling discarded city trash past the alley three stories below. The setting moon was a sliver in the hazy night sky, hanging over New Jersey like a tarnished sickle; its soft light glimmered across the sluggish crawl of the Hudson, a block west. The warehouse was old, nothing inside but boxes of rusting boat equipment and his target's squatter setup tucked into a corner—a tattered sleeping bag, some clothes, food debris, a jug of water. A couple of freshly used needles nearby. Blade had checked it all out when he'd arrived. The oily, bitter flavor of dark magic hung around the guy's stuff, a low note of sulfur, the tingle of void lending a sharp note to the stale, stinking air of the forlorn structure, but whatever he was holding, he'd taken it with him.

And his stuff's still here, so he's coming back. But there's no way our friend Pendragon got his hands on a Darkhold page. With a name like Malachi Pendragon? Anybody trying that hard who was also a heroin addict was unlikely to have stumbled across one of the cursed immortal pages. Not that it was *impossible*—the pages had been scattered and lost a long time ago and could be anywhere—but *Malachi Pendragon*?

A corner of his mouth lifted at the thought but settled quickly. It wasn't actually funny. Caretaker put up a cool front, but with the Midnight Sun coming, she was jumping at shadows. Lately, when she wasn't training the kids, she'd been glued to the mirror table, obsessively searching for trouble. This was the fourth time in a week he'd been sent out on recon, and only the vampire nest in Texas was even worth knowing about. This Pendragon was a low-rent Satanist artifact dealer who specialized in supernatural trinkets; he claimed to have one of the cursed Darkhold pages for sale, but what were the chances? Caretaker had heard about him through one of her obscure channels, and just the rumor was enough for her to send him to check it out.

It's the alignment. She's worried. Between that and losing Agatha…

He took a deliberate breath and counted it out, letting the thought fade. Whatever Caretaker was going through personally, she'd find her way. He needed to be present and lose his assumptions about this guy. A real Darkhold page was a powerful thing, and Pendragon had hold of something, Blade had sensed it.

He heard solitary footsteps incoming from the east a block away, hurried, athletic shoes scuffing pavement. Blade inhaled deeply through his nose. Yes, magic, with a hint of brimstone, but not one of the immortal pages. A page from the legendary Darkhold, penned by the Elder God Chthon himself, would stain the air around it black. Pendragon was carrying something much, much lighter.

He's scared, too. The guy's heart was pounding, his sweat reeked, his breathing was fast.

The target stepped around the corner one building over and hunched a heavy pack up on his shoulder, shooting a look back before heading for the alley. Malachi Pendragon was thin, white, late twenties, with greasy long hair and a greasy long beard. They'd both been dyed black about six months before and hadn't been trimmed; his inches of mouse-colored growth gave him a diseased look. He had a pinched, narrow face and worried eyes.

Blade watched him enter the building—the side entrance to the warehouse had a busted lock—his own perch trembling as the door slammed closed with a screech. There was a broken skylight to Blade's left, but he didn't need to look to know what was happening inside; he kept his eyes on the street, waiting to see if the man's paranoia was justified, his other senses occupied with the junkie magician.

Pendragon put his pack down and immediately set to shoving a heavy equipment box in front of the door. At least a dozen rats were disturbed by the noise and movement, chirping and scattering as Pendragon panted and dust squealed beneath weighted wood, the sounds echoing in the mostly empty room. Pigeons rustled in the rafters, the soft dander of their wings slightly muting the sharper stink of fresh rat urine wafting out through the skylight.

Door blocked, Pendragon picked up his bag and stumbled straight to his scruffy camp, plopping down heavily on his sleeping bag. He lit a cheap candle, unzipped his pack and rifled through it: paper, leather, tarnished pewter. A small, enameled ceramic something *ting*-ed off the old metal. The leather definitely smelled like Hell, but the dark magic of it was small; Blade sensed wispy, misty tendrils of its strength, about as menacing as an old, fat housecat. The ceramic was a protective charm, and gave off the gentle blue feel of the mildest of breezes, but it wasn't strong enough to hold off much more than that same cat. The other items, whatever they were, had no magic at all. Mr. Pendragon had been telling fibs.

Outside, the river slopped sullenly at the rocks, and a coyote caught a rat under one of the rotten piers a few hundred yards south. More random trash scuttled around on a wind that was just starting to lose its summer richness, which in this part of the city was a truly violent amalgam of odors. Rotting, burning garbage was the most prominent scent, wafting across the river from the landfills in New Jersey, but the body odor of millions and the toxic sewage riding the Hudson added to the humid, gaseous mix. There were people around—in the city there were always people around—but nobody close was moving.

Pendragon was paranoid, and Blade wanted to get back

to the Abbey. He'd been running extra classes in the wee hours; they were just getting into close knife work, and the kids would pout if he didn't show soon.

You could just leave. There's no threat here. Left to his own devices he would bail, but he could already see Caretaker's eyes narrowing when he explained that a guy like Pendragon wouldn't have known anything useful. The fine lines around her mouth would tighten, and she'd throw off something casually brutal, like, *I suppose we'll never know, as you didn't bother asking.*

Sighing, Blade stood and wrapped his long coat around his body, not wanting to snag the leather on the broken skylight, then jumped through the hole.

He landed on the patched concrete and turned to the southeast corner. Pendragon was still sitting on his sleeping bag thirty feet away, staring wide-eyed into the dark abyss of the warehouse, panicked by the sound of Blade's trench coat tapping the ground. He couldn't see past the glow of his candle. He'd gone from pale to ashen.

"Who's there?" Pendragon tried to sound commanding, but his voice shook. "Show yourself!"

"Don't panic, I just want to talk," Blade said. "I—"

"I have weapons, knives!" Pendragon shrieked, clutching his bag of stuff to his chest. Overhead, the pigeons fussed at the echo, a few feathers raining down. "I'm a powerful sorcerer. Get out or I'll shoot!"

Wow. Blade tried again. "I'm not going to—"

"Who are you? How'd you get in? Leave, get out, begone!"

On the second interruption, Blade decided to give up on the gentle approach. He put himself in front of the shouting Pendragon on *begone*, hoping the sudden appearance might shock him into silence.

Pendragon let out a scream and immediately thrust his left hand toward Blade, grubby fingers spread. A crooked pentagram with blown lines was tattooed on his palm.

"Relinquam in nomine domini vestry, daemonium!"

Blade had to smile. *Leave in the name of your master, demon.* That was the intent, anyway. "You use an online translator? You're not saying what you think you're saying, and I'm not a demon. Now shut up so I can talk to you."

Pendragon slowly lowered his hand. "You dare not kill me, creature. I worship your master, Satan. Your punishment will be merciless and—"

"What did I *just. Say?*"

The guy shut up. Finally. He stared up at Blade, lips trembling.

"I've heard you have a Darkhold page for sale," Blade said, calmly. "May I see it?"

A ray of hope flashed into Pendragon's terror-mad gaze. "Yeah, of course! Absolutely!"

He started flinging stuff out of his pack. "It's the real deal, you know, I can sense its power. I've got a protection amulet, too, and Aleister Crowley's snuff box, charms for money and sex. I've got all kinds of stuff. I was asking for at least—You know what? You can have it, okay? It's a gift for your master. For you!"

Pendragon held out the Hell-scented scroll and Blade took it. Not even real parchment, just plain cowskin. The dark energy tingled against his fingertips as he unrolled the ancient leather and scanned the words. Latin, medieval German. It was a curse for somebody's livestock to die, signed in blood. A minor demon had apparently granted the request, lending the scroll its potency, but it would only be dangerous to a man named Gunther who owned eight pigs and three goats.

"Where did you get this?" Blade asked.

"From the deepest Egyptian catacomb, sealed beneath a priest's tomb—"

"No, really," Blade said, leaning in a little, letting his teeth show.

"Estate sale in Hillsdale. But it *is* from the Darkhold."

Blade held out the scroll. "No, it's not. No offense, but you should stick to charms. It's dangerous, running around telling people you've got big magic."

"It's not even real?" Pendragon stared at the worthless scroll, his expression baffled. "So why is everyone following me?"

"Who's following you?"

"I found it last weekend and tried to sell it to a couple of places, okay? But nobody wanted it, not even for, like, a hundred bucks." Pendragon sniffled. "And then yesterday, I saw these guys... Different places, you know? Different guys, but everywhere I went. At least three of 'em, maybe more. They were watching me, following me. I thought they were after that."

Pendragon nodded at the scroll, still not reaching for it. "You can keep it, okay? I don't want nothing else to do with it."

Hmm. Paranoid, drug-fueled fantasy, or was someone else tracking Darkhold pages? Blade was leaning toward fantasy. Nobody seeking a piece of the Darkhold would be fooled for a second by Malachi Pendragon's barnyard curse. Blade dropped the scroll, tired of holding it, and was about to split when the junkie sniffled again, his dirty brow furrowed with self-pity.

Not your business, he's a grown man, he thought, but found himself opening his mouth anyway. "You know, you don't have to live like this. You could get clean, take up palm reading or something. There's a free clinic in Harlem, on Second Avenue."

"Kill me or leave, demon," Pendragon snarled.

Whatever, Blade was done here. He was going to have to have a talk with Caretaker about priorities. He flashed to the side door and kicked the box out of the way—

—and heard a car coming in, fast, from the north.

"Somebody's coming," he called. "You expecting company?"

Pendragon shot to his feet. "No! I told you, it's those guys!"

"Sit down where you are and don't move," Blade said, and slipped out the door just as the speeding vehicle squealed to a stop on the waterfront, a block away.

Blade quickly climbed back to the roof, dancing between

Pendragon's hideout and the fire escape of the condemned tenement next to it. He landed in a crouch and looked west, where a battered black SUV idled, roughly parallel to the warehouse, its back end blocked from view by a stack of shipping crates. The driver was turned toward the back seat. Blade could only see a tan neck and a short blond hair.

"Come on, come on," the driver breathed, hand clenched on the wheel, and Blade's eyes narrowed.

He's soulless. The part of the man that made him human was gone.

A deeper voice in the back grunted, then a back door opened. Blade side-stepped across the roof to see, just as he heard a heavy clang of metal, the deeper voice talking fast. "In three—two—"

A second soulless man was leaning out of the back door on the passenger side, young, dark hair combed to a rockabilly pompadour. He was pointing an RPG at the warehouse, the heavy launcher steadied on the vehicle's roof rack. He fired on *one.* Smoke and light exploded from the launcher.

Damn! Blade dove through the skylight and flew for the southeast corner—*shield his body*—seeing that Pendragon wasn't there, even as the grenade blew through the sheet-metal siding and exploded.

Blade whipped himself into a tight ball and hit the empty corner as the blast hit, the explosion slamming him into the metal wall, hard, his ears popping painfully. The concussive force blasted a dozen crates into the walls and took a hefty chunk out of one of the main support pillars, the warehouse moaning and screeching like it was in pain. Hot shrapnel and splintered wood and rusted heavy metal rained down on the concrete. Panicked birds fluttered through the bitter smoke. Outside, the SUV peeled out and sped away.

Blade leapt to his feet, ears ringing, ready to follow— but Pendragon groaned, and the chance was gone. He lay in a tumbled, broken heap against the north wall, splashed with blood. It looked like the guy had been on his way to the exit and had ended up crushed against it.

Blade was at the dealer's side in a flash, but there was nothing to be done; he could hear Pendragon's stuttering, failing heart amid the slosh of his ruptured guts. He wasn't conscious, at least, and didn't wake up for his last choking exhale.

What a waste. And for what?

That was a good question. Less than a mile away, a fire engine went lights and sirens. Blade stood up in the creaking, broken room and took out his cell. Time to get back to the Abbey and find out if Caretaker knew the answer.

○————————○

NICO and Robbie met in the training yard at 0230 dressed in sweats and tees as they'd been doing for a full month now, twice a week, but Blade didn't show. They ambled around, stretching, enjoying the sound of the waves and the night air, always brisk at the Abbey, the ocean winds scented by ancient stone and Caretaker's roses. The Abbey was in its own pocket dimension, but it could have been any giant, weird Gothic castle on a towering sea cliff in witch-haunted

Massachusetts. It was like living on a Vincent Price set—crazy high ceilings, stained glass, gargoyles, and shadows everywhere you looked. Nico loved the aesthetic, which extended to the training yard—arches of slate-gray rock framed the sunken grassy yard, weight benches and heavy bags were tucked under groined wooden ceilings, swords and daggers decorated the walls.

Swords and daggers that I would like to use, and also learn to defend myself against, please and thank you. They all did martial arts. Blade taught a couple of different styles every day, plus boxing, but that was hand-to-hand stuff. Magik didn't need extra weapons classes—no one could beat her with a sword—and Robbie could go Ghost Rider if someone ran up on him. Nico had magical power, sure, but it wasn't like the Staff of One always gave her exactly what she wanted, and magic was already getting glitchy as the Midnight Sun approached; she *needed* more extensive combat training. Of all the Suns, she was the most physically vulnerable.

Robbie glanced at his phone with his pretty, mismatched eyes and stood up from the stone step he'd been lounging on. He ran a hand through his short, dark mop of hair with its shining silver blaze at the crown. "Twenty minutes no prof, class dismissed! I'm gonna go raid the kitchen, you in? There's pie."

"Just a few more minutes," Nico said. "Where'd he go this time, anyway?"

"Magik sent him to New York about four hours ago. And she said he wasn't happy about it."

Another one of Caretaker's mysterious look-sees; she'd sent Blade out a bunch of times in the last few weeks. With Agatha gone, Caretaker had become more tight-lipped than ever.

Nico exhaled heavily but didn't burst into tears, which was a nice change. She'd seriously considered leaving the Abbey, after the accident. Agatha and Wanda had been working on some private, high-level training, invoking powerful magic, and Agatha had been killed. Which was horrible enough, but then Caretaker had freaked out and blamed Wanda, said she wasn't safe to be around, and banished her from the Abbey. Caretaker had sealed Agatha's wonderful library for an indefinite mourning period, and still refused to talk about any of it.

Nico sincerely respected and admired Caretaker, but she was so different from Agatha Harkness. The pair of women had run the Abbey, had reassembled the legendary Midnight Suns to prepare for the big alignment. Agatha had been wise and thoughtful: she'd taught spells and baked cookies. Caretaker, of the long-lived Blood, devoted her time and energy to keeping everyone on task—training, school, tactics, more training. That or she worked in one of the Abbey's many gardens, hacking at weeds. In her softest moments, Caretaker told brutal war stories about battles of the past, when the great and glorious Hunter, a *real* hero, single-handedly beat back the tide of evil.

Blade had pulled Nico and Robbie and Magik together after Agatha's memorial, and spoke about staying focused on the mission while everyone took time to "process," which was fine, but half of what Nico was processing was that accidents weren't allowed in the Midnight Suns, you would be blamed and sent away, and that their team was way weaker because of Caretaker's temper. And now she was sending Blade out on mystery missions and keeping the rest of them in the dark.

"I mean, why would she get us together and then not use us?" Nico asked.

"You're doing that thing again," Robbie said. "Where you skip parts?"

"Caretaker," Nico said. "The big alignment is barely six months out, and that's literally why we're here, right? How come Blade is being sent out by himself?"

Robbie chuckled. "You think *Blade* needs backup?"

"No, duh, but she could still tell us what's going on. We're not children."

"Says Minoru the teenaged witch," Robbie teased, and Nico hopped up a step to punch him. He knew she was twenty.

"Jeez, elder abuse," Robbie said, rubbing his arm. "She's... She's Caretaker, you know? She'll tell us when there's something to tell. Come on, there's *pie*."

"Ugh, you're such a guy," Nico said. "I'm going out to the dais."

Robbie was already heading for the main door connecting the courtyard to the Abbey. "Pie is the answer to all your questions, little one, seek and ye shall find," he called, and disappeared inside.

Nico grinned. Robbie cracked her up, and he was so laid back it was almost pathological. She'd nursed a crush for a whole week before they'd naturally fallen into an older-sister–younger-brother dynamic, even though technically he had three years on her, and his own kid brother. Robbie had been a car mechanic and street racer before he'd been possessed by a murderous ghost, then adopted by the Spirits of Vengeance. When he was Ghost Rider, he was terrifying, all grinning techno-skull and chains and Hellfire. As Robbie, he liked messing with his Charger, videogame tourneys, and pie.

Nico set off south, where the Abbey's small chapel faced the crashing sea. The portal dais was set on the edge of the cliff that dropped to the water a hundred feet below, and Magik might be out there waiting for Blade. Dry, windswept grass crunched beneath Nico's high-tops, and she rubbed her arms against a chill. Summer was fading fast.

Past the training yard on the Abbey's west side was the grotto, a shady pool spanned by a low stone bridge and overshadowed by the high, slate cliffs and wind-bent old-growth forest that mostly surrounded the Abbey grounds, north and west. Nico skirted the stairs that led down to the semi-cave, catching a scent of the cool mossy rocks that banked the water. When the Abbey had been relocated from Transia a few hundred years back, its topography and outbuildings had come along with it.

Nico passed the Abbey's west entrance, then its barracks, which made up a good third of the Abbey's length. She brushed her left hand along the pale stones as she walked, liking the cool smooth feel of them. There was enough space to house a couple dozen fighters inside, give or take, even with the showers and kitchen stuck in; at the moment, the space housed four, if you didn't count pets. Caretaker's room was on the other side of the foyer, separate from the rest of them.

As Nico stepped out of the trees, she faced the beautiful, lonely altar that Caretaker had dedicated to Agatha, overlooking the ocean and backed by the Whispering Woods. The torches flanking the memorial's steps burned brightly, the magic that kept them alight giving off a soft incense-y smell. The familiar scent was comforting in a bittersweet way, reminding Nico of the day Agatha had taught the spells for smokeless fire to her and Wanda. The three of them had wandered the Abbey's halls one morning, extinguishing and relighting the chandeliers. Nico could still hear the old witch's soft, brisk tone, encouraging, see Wanda's delighted grin.

Across the open south lawn at the edge of the ocean-front cliff was the dais, and Magik stood there alone, silhouetted against the velvet night sky and the weak glow of a crescent moon.

Magik could make portals anywhere, usually, but the encroaching alignment had started to mess with magical energies. Caretaker had set up a circular, railed platform overlooking the crashing ocean and stabilized it as a focal point for dimensional travel. Until the Midnight Sun was past, it was the only secure way in or out of their tiny dimension.

Magik had manifested her Soulsword and held it high, which meant Blade was probably incoming. Her silhouette was almost demonic, the armor that the mutant grew when she used the sword all sharp edges and horn-like spikes. Her straight, pale-blond hair rippled in the wind as she slashed at the air with the shining blade and the diffuse, fiery light of Limbo fell across the grass in a ragged, disc-shaped patch.

Magik stepped into the round, shimmering portal and then back out again, with Blade at her side. Time passed differently in Magik's Limbo. The opening winked out behind them, and they started for the Abbey. Magik's sword was reabsorbed, disappearing as she slid it over her shoulder, her armor going with it. Blade was brushing at his coat.

Nico cut across the lawn to greet them, noting that Blade was walking like he was in a bad mood, leaning forward a little, limbs stiff. His sunset-red eyes announced the same—intent with just a hint of frown. If she didn't know him, he'd look dangerous.

"What happened in New York?" Nico asked, joining the pair as they walked up the wide stone steps. Blade smelled like smoke. "Why were you there, anyway? More vampires?"

The front door opened before he could answer. Caretaker stood in the foyer, all in black, her head high, her cool blue gaze glittering. Her short, silver-white hair looked rough, like she'd been running her hands through it. For Caretaker, that was practically a panic attack.

"I saw what happened," she said, addressing Blade, her creaking voice perfectly crisp and level. "We can speak in my study."

Caretaker turned to lead Blade to her rooms, but Nico

couldn't stop herself. "Can we *all* talk about it? We're a team, right?"

The old woman didn't answer, just kept walking. Blade shot Nico a *not-now* look and followed her, their steps in the foyer echoing through the dimly lit halls that branched in either direction. They took a right at the main hall and then Caretaker's door opened and closed.

Nico lingered on the steps, looked at Magik. "What's going on? Why wouldn't she tell us?"

Magik shrugged, a gesture she'd clearly been practicing. Illyana Rasputina was the Mistress of Limbo, a heavy hitter with responsibilities outside the Abbey and a dark, complicated past. She was generally polite—her dark side was literally a demonic entity that she kept under tight control—but she didn't talk much and often struggled to relate to regular human stuff, like movies or nuance.

Magik's precise Russian accent went well with her terse response. "I believe Caretaker looks for trouble and sends Blade to see if we're needed."

"I mean, probably, but she could make an announcement or something. Are the rest of us going to just train the whole time?"

"We are always training, every day," Magik said. "With or without the Midnight Sun."

Nico sighed. "I want something to *do*."

Magik frowned. "Earth's realm is protected by the Avengers. If this dark season passes and we are not called, be grateful."

Figures, Magik would be all pragmatic about it. She wasn't wrong, but Nico wasn't afraid of what might happen: she just wanted to be a part of it. Or at *least* know what "it" was. Being on the understudy team was fine, but how were the Suns supposed to step in to take care of business without *knowing* anything?

"I'm going to walk Charlie, if you'd like to come with us," Magik said.

The mutant was trying to help, in her way. Nico loved the hellhound, but she didn't want to be soothed, she felt self-righteously thirsty for info… and hanging in the hall outside Caretaker's office could be just the thing, if she hurried. Magik and Robbie might be chill about the state of affairs, but Nico was betting that Blade had something to say.

"Thanks, but I'm gonna go lurk for a bit," she said. "Have fun, though."

Magik nodded and smiled, a shy curve of her Cupid's-bow mouth. Wanda had talked Magik into short bangs when she'd complained about always having to tie her hair back, and they made her look extremely non-threatening, and younger than Nico. "I will, thank you."

They stepped inside together and parted ways, Magik turning toward the barracks—Charlie hung out in the kitchen, mostly—Nico kicking off her shoes as soon as the other girl was out of sight and sock-sliding across the foyer's glowing wood floors toward Caretaker's study. Blade would know she was there, he could hear everything, but no way he'd rat her out. It was Nico's right as an independent worker to understand the conditions of her continued employment. That's what she'd say, if she got caught. Or she could pretend she was on her way to the common room to grab a book.

Yeah, definitely the second one. Nico turned into the arched corridor that ran north and considered the best place to hide.

○———————————○

CARETAKER opened the door to her study for Blade and closed it behind him. She motioned at the stuffed leather chair next to the bookcase, but he didn't sit down. He started to pace as soon as she sat at her desk. She turned her spindly legged chair to face him.

"The page wasn't real," Blade said. "I'm surprised you didn't catch wind of that. He was shopping around what he had. An old farm hex—nothing."

Caretaker waited. She didn't have to explain herself; she'd heard the claim and sent Blade to investigate. Darkhold pages were too powerful to ignore at the best of times, but especially now.

"So why would two soulless men blow up a junkie artifact dealer?"

"Fellow Satanists, I'd imagine," Caretaker said. "Maybe Pendragon wouldn't sign his soul away. They kill each other fairly often, as I'm sure you're aware."

Blade shook his head. "Usually not with grenade launchers. Pendragon tells everyone he's got a Darkhold page and ends up dead inside of a week. He said he was being followed. If the men tailing him thought the page was real, they'd have bought it or tried to take it. If they thought it was fake, why bother killing him?"

Caretaker spread her hands. "An internal dispute, perhaps. It doesn't matter. We must keep careful watch. When we investigate these kinds of things, it frees the Sorcerer Supreme to focus on strengthening Earth's defenses."

"Strange and Scarlet Witch," Blade said, watching her.

Even the name stung, but Caretaker held his sharp red gaze. Wanda Maximoff was reckless, unable to control herself; the Midnight Suns were better off for having sent her to Stephen Strange. The team didn't like it, and that was fine. Children never liked what was best for them.

Come now, Agatha whispered in Caretaker's mind. *Children need love, too.*

The exact words Agatha had used three-hundred-plus years ago, about Hunter. They'd raised the orphaned warrior together and buried the child far too soon. Agatha had always been the gentle voice of reason, of compassion... and now she was dead by the hand of her own favorite, the careless witch, leaving Caretaker to hold everything together, to manage the headstrong, powerful young Suns by herself, to make them ready for whatever was coming. Love came and went, a fleeting dream. Discipline and training were what mattered in the perpetual war against chaos.

"Why a grenade and not a gun, or a knife to the throat?" Blade continued. "Did they want to destroy the fake for some reason? He had an amulet, too, but just a trinket, nothing worth dying about. Were they trying to shut him up about Darkhold pages?"

That was an angle Caretaker hadn't considered. If someone *was* collecting pages privately, they might want to keep even the whisper of it out of the air. She immediately added it to her list of ongoing concerns, which grew by the minute. She could feel energy shifting, darkness gaining strength as the alignment crept closer.

"They didn't look military." Blade scruffed at his close, neat beard. "The RPG was military grade but they were in a used car, just the two of them."

Caretaker glanced at the single stem of pale pink foxglove in the vase on her desk. Agatha had cut it for her, on her last day alive. Caretaker had used a spell to keep the delicate cascading bells from wilting; the thought that they would fade, shrivel, disappear from her life, made her feel like she couldn't catch her breath. She knew what it all meant, she'd lived too long not to recognize the mechanisms of grief, but knowing that she grieved changed nothing.

Caretaker stood up. She was letting herself be distracted by Blade's interest in what had turned out to be nothing. "A Satanic militia, perhaps. I'll watch for them. Thank you for going to New York."

Blade didn't move. "*Could* someone be putting together the Darkhold?"

"I doubt it," she said. "Even a few pages together would create a disturbance that I would see in the glass." She had good reason to believe the book couldn't possibly be reformed.

"Have you seen other soulless lately?"

"No more than usual," Caretaker said, and waited for him to leave. They both stood there, Blade studying her, and instead of irritation, she felt the great weight of her age. Gone were the days when her word was law and her fighters listened and bowed and obeyed without hesitation.

She glanced again at the lovely pale foxglove on her desk and found something to add. "You're the best at protecting yourself, that's why I send you. I'm never afraid that you won't return."

Blade watched her eyes. "And if you thought a real fire was cropping up, you'd tell me."

"You'd know, because you're the one looking," Caretaker said, neatly sidestepping the question.

Oh, how you deceive. Was it Agatha's voice, or her own? No matter; she'd tell the Suns what they needed to know as they needed to know it, not before. They were a fine group, and she'd worked with them for long enough to know their strengths: Magik was extremely powerful, Blade was focused, Robbie had a brave heart and the Spirits of Vengeance at his back, and Nico was gaining more control over her energies every day... But they were still a collection of independent fighters, not a team, not yet, and they were all so achingly young. She'd keep forging them, keep the Abbey running, keep watching the mirror table for signs and searching the otherwheres for portents and omens...

And you'll do it all alone, with these summer children. No one to talk to who understands what you fear, no one to soothe you when your darkest memories rise. No Agatha Harkness, who loved the Suns as she loved Hunter. As she loved you.

Caretaker mentally slapped herself. Self-pity was beyond worthless, and not at all like her. She needed to rest, to get hold of her thoughts. She stepped past Blade to open the door—

—and saw a flicker of movement in the corridor, a rustle in the red banner that draped the wall to her left. A beat later, Nico stepped into the hall and walked toward her. The girl tucked bits of her long mohawk behind her right ear, playing casual to the hilt. The dim chandelier light sparkled off her many steel piercings. Her brown eyes were wide and innocent, framed as always with smudged, heavy black eyeliner.

"Hey, is Blade still here? He's not in the common room."

Blade stepped out. "What's up?"

Nico kept up the pretense. "I was just wondering about the knife class…"

"Good night," Caretaker said to both of them, and closed the door.

2

ZARATHOS sailed the black voids between dimensions on muscular ebony wings, not thinking, only existing in the vast silence. Once, he'd seen only Mephisto, and destroyed him again and again, unleashing his rage and reveling in the demon lord's destruction, but those dreams had been lost in the apocalypse of his torture, the fire and ice and pain. Finally deafened by his own screams, Zarathos had left Mephisto's Hell and lived in the abyss, where there were no burning chains holding him down and no one shrieked in agony.

Zarathos.

Infinity spoke his name, her honeyed voice like strange music in the nothingness. The sound was a butterfly of light, a speck in her infinite, formless—

Zarathos! Hel-lo, you in there? Wake up!

Zarathos was reborn into agony, the void ripped away. His broken body still hung from shackles; his hands were dead lumps of meat, and the wounds from his last flaying were still fresh. He cracked one feverish eye; the other was swollen shut, or missing.

A beautiful demoness was in his cell, floating above the spiked floor. A succubus. He could smell her aura of attraction, and her garb was tight and revealing. Everything about her worked to inspire hunger.

"There he is!" the succubus said, smiling. "I was starting to think you were a lost cause."

Zarathos could barely speak, his voice a choking whisper. "Who are you?"

"Satana Hellstrom. You want to get out of here?"

Zarathos closed his eye. It was another of Mephisto's torments, to trick him into hope, to keep him from the lonely perfection of the void where he was free and—

"Wake *up!*" Satana shouted in his ear, and he opened his eye again, groaning.

"To portal us both out of here, I need you awake and willing," she said, as if speaking to a child. "It was hard enough to get in."

"Leave me be, temptress," Zarathos choked out.

Satana snorted. "Zarathos, Corrupter of the Blood, the Locust-Breather, the Soul-Devourer. I gotta tell you, I was expecting a little more zip. We're going to need you to actually give a crap about taking Mephisto down."

Zarathos forced his eye wider. "Take Mephisto... down?"

"Steal the throne. Force him to your will. Set him up for eternal torture. It's a whole thing. I'll let Fenn tell it, but first we need to get out of here. That is, if you *want* to leave this cell and seek vengeance upon Mephisto. I'm sure the Triumvirate can find another third, if you're not interested."

Zarathos struggled to focus his thoughts. "If this is a trick—"

"You'll do what? Keep hanging in this nasty little room, getting beaten?"

Zarathos sagged from his chains. Truly, he could do nothing. He was a shell of what he once was.

Satana stepped close and fixed him with a soft and shining gaze. "You will rule all of the Hell dimensions, Dark Lord, as is your right, if we can find an amulet of power hidden on Earth. You will lead the Triumvirate, dedicated to Mephisto's destruction. But we have to go, now, before your tormentor's break is over. Sound good?"

Zarathos didn't understand *Fenn* or *Triumvirate*, but the rest of her words stirred him. He remembered his dreams of revenge, of Mephisto broken by Zarathos's hand, pleading for death.

"It sounds good," he whispered.

○————————○

AFTER his talk with Caretaker, Blade had showered and then rested in his room. Not sleep, exactly, only a drifting, empty time, thoughtless, his senses on low. He slowly reconnected to consciousness, using the languid, liminal space to observe his tensions and release them. When he was ready, he brought his senses back up, breathing deeply and opening his eyes. He could see by the angle of the light through the small, high window that it was late morning. It was Saturday. The kids would be hoping for pancakes.

He rose from his cushioned floor mat and went to the dressing table, where he took a syringe out of the autoclave. He unlocked the heavily warded cabinet next to the table and took out one of a hundred small glass bottles, loaded the syringe, replaced the bottle, and then relocked the cabinet. Making a fist with his left hand, he injected into the vein that popped up, sighing as the miracle coursed through him, chasing away the memory of hunger, waking him up, keeping him alive. The serum wasn't as satisfying as blood, but not having to kill to eat won over every other consideration. The injection site was already healed by the time he dropped the syringe back into its steam bath.

He got dressed: black tee and cotton pants, thin-soled workout shoes. Nico had made him promise to do weapons after breakfast. She was in the kitchen already—he could smell coffee, and the only other Sun who drank it was Robbie, who was still asleep across the hall and down two doors; Blade could hear the younger man's slow, steady heartbeat and breathing.

He grabbed his shades and hooked them on the collar of his shirt as he started for the kitchen, past the copper Shiva statue. The Abbey was littered with statues, mostly religious or magical, standing in corners, balancing on pedestals, set into alcoves and reflecting off the polished wood floors of the long, shadowy corridors. Caretaker and her sister, Lilith, had raised the structure in Transia back in the Iron Age to train fighters in the eternal war against the Elder God Chthon. It seemed like Caretaker had been collecting statues ever since.

Better than becoming the Mother of Demons. Lilith had thrown in with Chthon and caused a lot of trouble before her demise, after the Abbey was moved to the States back in the late 1600s. Caretaker could be set in her ways, but she'd always fought the good fight.

Blade hesitated at the entrance to the foyer, listening. Caretaker wasn't in her rooms; he found her steady pulse northeast. She could only be in the war room or the library, and she'd warded the library closed after the accident. The library had been Agatha's domain. Most of the Abbey's documents and files were in the war room, but the histories and spell books were in the library.

Gonna have to talk to her about that. Agatha had been the Abbey's researcher, looking for prophecies related to the Midnight Sun, and he knew Nico was itching to get back to the books. Caretaker's mirror table showed its user what they wanted to look at, but without direction she would keep casting him out at random, hoping to hit on something important. She was at the table now, pushing herself to make up for Agatha's absence. He mourned Agatha, too, they all did, but Caretaker's grief was making the decisions, and he wasn't comfortable with that.

On the other hand, he wasn't comfortable trying to direct Caretaker, either. Caretaker had been slaying demons since before the Renaissance. She knew her own mind and had survived a thousand bloody battles. And just a month ago she had lost someone she'd been close to for actual centuries. The Midnight Sun was still six months away, and the Suns themselves were backup, anyway. There were plenty of powerful people monitoring the evolving dimensional shifts; another week or two for Caretaker to pull herself together wouldn't kill anyone. Team dynamics weren't his strong suit, either, but he'd keep doing what he could until she came around.

The kitchen was a modern remodel at the northwest corner of the barracks. Once upon a time there'd been a separate building housing the Abbey's kitchen east of the common room, set up to feed a small army, but all that was left were a few foundation stones. A series of spells kept the Abbey's pantries stocked, but Agatha had often cooked for the team. There was a table for eight, and regular kitchen appliances next to regular counters. Of all the Abbey's features—the towering forge at the north end, the drop-ceiling common room, the elaborate training yard—the kitchen was the coziest.

Nico was cooing over Charlie; the beast's spiny tail was tapping the tiled floor, a tiny echo in the hall. Blade turned through the wide-open archway, taking in the rich smell of coffee, the battered wood of the countertops, a glimpse of sunny trees through the small window. Nico was alone at the kitchen table, leaning out of her chair to rub Charlie's taut red gut. The hellhound was on her back, right leg twitching.

"Belly scratchin' and it feels so good," Nico sang, and Charlie's tail whapped. Physically, Charlie looked like several kinds of dog put together. Sort of a Doberman face and body shape, with cropped ears, but the heavily muscled chest and shoulders of a pit bull or Staffordshire. Her haunches and belly were lean, like a greyhound or a whippet. Past that, she was clearly not related to any of them; she was fleshy, hairless, and dark brick-red. Small, short horns were set over her glowing white eyes and her tail was a tapering cord with an arrow tip. Hellhounds were terrifying creatures, generally, even without being in attack mode, but Charlie melted for Nico. The only other pet at the Abbey—Ebony, Agatha's cat—was also a fan of the young witch. The feline familiar occasionally deigned to sleep in Nico's room, an honor not bestowed upon the other Suns.

"Pancakes?" Nico asked, looking up at him through her thick black 'do. She'd decided on an asymmetrical look and was growing out her mohawk, but the left side of her head was recently shaved.

"It's Saturday, right?" Blade walked to the fridge for the eggs and milk. Agatha had taught him how to make a few things so he could contribute to the care and feeding of their team, and he liked doing it. Robbie and Nico stayed up late and slept late, as a rule. Like him, Magik didn't exactly need to *sleep*-sleep, but they often rested on the same schedule. He expected the rest of the Suns would show by the time the first batch was done. Robbie would, anyway. Even without super senses, he always knew when pancakes were up.

"I'll get the plates and stuff," Nico said, and Blade nodded, lining up his ingredients on the counter. When Nico Minoru had first come to the Abbey he'd been annoyed by her lack of boundaries and filters, her endless energy, but she'd grown on him. Her infinite curiosity wasn't a front; she was genuinely interested in the people and things around her—an act of courage considering her childhood. Her parents had been murderous cultists, members of the Pride. Nico had gained her powers when the magical staff her own mother had tried to kill her with had bonded to her instead. The girl had used her new abilities to help other children of the cult run away, and she'd kept them safe. Her priorities were on straight.

Nico hummed to herself as she padded barefoot through the kitchen. She had been gutted by the dual loss of Agatha and Wanda, both of them her teachers and friends, but she had the right attitude to see her through, one she'd gained from lessons learned too young—nothing was solid, everything could change in a second, and somehow, you had to keep going.

We all know that tune.

"I was on the forums this morning, and Spidey posted an article about the alignment," she said. "It was just about Venus and the moon and a dust cloud, but the scientists are saying it could cause some disturbances to radio waves and the tides and stuff."

Blade smirked and dumped flour into a wooden bowl. "'And stuff,' huh?"

Nico grabbed silverware. "If they knew about the Midnight Sun, they'd poop their pants."

"Who pooped their pants?" Robbie asked, shuffling in. "Oh cool, pancakes."

The young Ghost Rider headed straight for the coffee. Charlie watched him hopefully, her tail ticking.

"Good morning, King," Nico said. Robbie's last name, Reyes, was *king* in Spanish, and Nico dropped it every now and again to needle him. "Tell me you'll do class after breakfast. Blade said he would."

"Can't, I've got Gabe," Robbie said. "Team Fortress for an hour, at least. We moved it to earlier. He's got a basketball game tonight."

"Oh, fun! I didn't know he played basketball."

Robbie nodded. "Wheelchair league. He's hoping to ride the bench. He only joined the team because he's got a crush on a cheerleader. My aunt's filming, though, just in case he shoots."

"Yeah, but what if he scores?"

"Gross," Robbie said. "Leave my baby brother out of your deviant fantasies."

He was smiling, but Blade could see a bit of tension around his disparate eyes. Robbie was devoted to Gabe and missed him terribly. They would video chat online but hadn't been together in person since Robbie had come to the Abbey, more than a year ago now.

Magik came in without announcement, nodding at the others. She poured herself a glass of orange juice and reached down to scratch Charlie behind the ears. Nico suggested a midnight movie party, and she and Robbie batted titles back and forth. Magik didn't offer anything but was relaxed, at ease, no tension in her slight frame as she watched them play-fight.

This is all good, Blade thought, as he poured batter and listened to the kids' banter, and then Caretaker walked in. The conversation immediately dried up.

"Good morning," she said. "Blade, I need to speak with you. In the war room."

"About what?" Nico asked. "Anything we can help with?"

Caretaker turned her cool gaze to the young witch. "Nothing you need concern yourself with."

Blade handed the spatula to Robbie, but it was too late. Nico had her chin in the air.

"It does concern me, though. It concerns all of us. We should all know what's going on. And it's not fair to Blade, to stick him with everything. The Midnight Sun is almost here, and—"

"Don't you think I know that?" Caretaker snapped, and then visibly took control of herself, lips pressing into a tight line.

Nico kept going. "—and we all want to help. I know you know that, and I know that you're hurting, we're all hurting, but you can't shut us out now. If we don't—"

"You're not ready," Caretaker said.

Nico stopped talking, her expression wounded.

Caretaker's tone softened, but not by much. "You've come so far, but we still have time to prepare. And I won't send you into danger unnecessarily."

Robbie piped up, flipping a pancake, "Isn't that kind of the whole hero gig, though? Running toward danger?"

Nico was starting to look pissed. "Most of my *life* has been danger unnecessarily. I'm ready, and I'm the weakest link. I joined the Suns because you said the world would need us when the dark came, but the dark is on our doorstep, and we still don't have a plan."

Blade half expected an explosion, but Caretaker looked calmer. She'd had her snap, was back under control. When she spoke, her voice had reverted to normal, crisp and slightly patronizing.

"There *is* no plan. There never has been, as I've explained to you more than once. Many protections will fail as the dimensions in play creep toward their occultations and transits; energies will fluctuate wildly for better and worse. Chaos agents will seek to exploit the shifts, and it's our job to watch and stand ready. You know this."

"My original point stands," Nico said. "We're supposed to be a team, and you're sending Blade out on secret missions without talking to us about it."

"I've asked him to follow a few leads that have proved false or unconnected to our mission," Caretaker said. "If sending the rest of you along would help and not hinder him, I would ask you to go."

Nico took the insult in stride and promptly changed tack.

"Why speak to him privately? Can't we at least know what kinds of dangers are starting to crop up? That's not, like, unreasonable."

Caretaker looked at Blade, who gazed back impassively. Caretaker wasn't used to justifying her decisions, but without Agatha to smooth everything over, it was incumbent upon her to make a few adjustments. Robbie and Magik were more comfortable with chain of command than Nico ever would be, and the young witch had a point—the whole team deserved to know what was happening, whether the information was useful or not.

"All right," Caretaker said. "Blade saw two soulless last night. They killed a man. I've just seen one of the killers meet with at least three other soulless, at a rest stop outside of White Plains, New York."

"Why are there soulless running around New York on a Saturday morning?" Nico asked. "What are they doing?"

Caretaker kept her face and voice perfectly neutral. "I thought it wise to ask Blade to investigate."

Blade nodded, and Magik stood up. Nico flopped into her chair with a scowl.

"You'll all have roles to play in the coming days," Caretaker added. "You will. And I promise, I won't keep anything from you that might compromise your safety, or our mission."

Nico's expression settled to disappointment as Robbie

slid the first stack of pancakes in front of her. Blade nodded at Magik.

"I'm going to change. I'll meet you out there."

He put his hand on Nico's shoulder on his way past the table. "Class when I get back."

He waited for her nod before he went to his room, the gloomy halls flashing by. He kicked off his trainers and started to dress, Caretaker's qualifier repeating in his mind. He was glad that she'd at least tried to mollify Nico; it was the most interaction they'd had since Wanda had left the Abbey... But the old warrior hadn't exactly promised to tell them everything, had she?

To be considered later. Blade armed himself and started for the east entrance off the foyer, slipping into his coat as he crossed the lawn, donning his shades as he stepped up to the dais. Shafts of tiny rainbows sparkled in the wind, mist from the thundering waves below refracting the overcast sun. Magik joined him a few seconds after he arrived, drawing her brilliant sword, a manifestation of her own life-force energy. Dark, glittering armor sprang up across her shoulders and down her arms, four slender silver bars sweeping up through her white-blond hair to protect her skull. Eldritch armor came with her role as Limbo's ruler.

"There is cover south of the group," she said. "Trees."

Blade nodded, and watched Magik cut a portal in the air, admiring her precise form. Magik's shining white blade didn't wobble a millimeter. The portal spun open, revealed the rough stone bridge formation she liked for traveling, bathed in the orange-red light of Limbo's ever-smoldering sky.

Time to find out what these bastards are up to. Together, he and Magik stepped out onto the bridge, the Abbey disappearing behind them.

○————————————○

ZARATHOS had slept for two whole days, sacked out like a big old slab of beef in the back bedroom of Fenn's stupid ugly house. Everything was so plain and utilitarian, and there was always that ugly green light, emitted by a dozen boxy machines all over the place; Fenn said it shielded them from observation, but the color was just *ugh*. Satana hated it. Like fluorescent mold, or some kind of American soft drink. Fenn came and went; when he was around, he mostly muttered to himself and was in his workshop or making new drawings. He had stacks of them, all covered with tubes and lines and math; he said he was currently working on a machine that would make Mephisto's skin burn off. To each his own, she supposed.

Satana stood in her dull room and admired her current body in the standing mirror, dressed in human casual—tight jeans, a snug, lacy pink cropped shirt that exposed her midriff and lower back, skin lightly tanned, crushed black leather boots with kicky heels. She'd glamoured her horns away, shrunk her chest a few sizes, and gone flat brunette, aiming for "approachable," but she'd been on Earth less than a week and already had more servants than she knew what to do with. A soul could be had for a single hungry kiss; she'd gathered a dozen on her first night out, and that was with her being picky.

Fenn cautioned her against drawing attention, but didn't turn down the help, sending the newly soulless out to "pave the Triumvirate's path to glory," whatever that meant. He never gave any details. Satana suspected he was settling old scores, but whatever. Gobbling fresh human souls again had boosted her power and charms a thousandfold and she was on fire; Fenn could do as he liked with the empty vessels, although she'd been thinking it might be fun to design some kind of matching uniform for them.

If the great Zarathos would just wake up, we could really get this party started.

She'd pressed Fenn for details about the Varkath Star— with Zarathos in a coma, it made sense that she should start looking on her own—but the mortal made a lot of noise about the power of three, and how only Zarathos could break the wards, anyway, and he was still fine-tuning the sensor they would need. Fenn's deferrals were irritating, but also boosted her confidence in his abilities; he knew better than to trust her, which implied some level of intelligence. Too bad his taste in clothes was so much better than his decorating skills.

At least I'm not teamed with a fool, she thought, and gave herself a birthmark, a tiny imperfection above the corner of her mouth. Yes, that was just—

There was the faintest tap at her door.

"Yes?"

The hot guy she'd picked up in front of the dance club spoke through the wood, his voice hushed. "Your Glory, the demon wakes."

Speaking of fools.

Satana fluffed her hair and went to the door, looking at the mirror over her shoulder to watch her departure. *Delicious.*

Out in the hall, the stud's gaze crawled over her shirt before he remembered to bow. Muscle memory, and she looked so good, she didn't blame him. She'd kept him because he was easy on the eyes, and Fenn didn't have any servants.

"If Fenn's around, let him know," she said, and walked down the hall to the upstairs back bedroom, her heels muffled by a carpet runner that was frayed along one edge. Fenn wasn't a wealthy man, and he seemed to be always in his head, inventing things, too fixated on his mechanisms of vengeance to notice or care about his environment.

She opened the door and stepped into the dimly lit room, where Zarathos was a ragged shadow on the bed. The candles on the dumpy dresser across the room flickered. The smell was better, less infection-y than yesterday, and the demon shifted at the sound of the door's hinges.

"How are you feeling?" Satana asked, mimicking someone who cared.

"The pain subsides," Zarathos rumbled, and sat up. The plain sheet covering him pooled in his lap, thankfully; she'd seen enough of his hideous junk when he'd been hanging naked in his cell. "I gain strength from the misery that soaks this realm."

No kidding, wow. Fenn had wanted her to feed the mangled demon souls, but Zarathos could recharge by simply existing on Earth, where humans exuded fathomless pain, despair, selfishness; arch-demons ate it right up. *Like I wouldn't know that.*

She could see that he was physically in much better shape. The being she'd dragged from Mephisto's prison had been a roughly humanoid mass of wounds and scars, broken bones and wasted muscle. In the last day his limbs had filled out, biceps and thighs going broad, and his chest had inflated to superhero size. The pits in Zarathos's crimson skull-face were filling in. Likewise, the deep scars slashing his torso were fading. His eyes glowed sulfur-tinted white, and most of his many small, sharp teeth had grown back. He wasn't dripping Hellfire yet—that had been kind of his "thing," along with breathing locusts—but it wouldn't be long.

No more wisecracks. From here in, she'd be singing *go team Zarathos.* At full strength, he could crush her like an insect.

"You will be rewarded for freeing me," Zarathos said.

Satana bowed her head and was still trying to think of something suitably humble to say when Fenn stumbled in, all twitchy and excited.

"This is the guy I was telling you about, Fenn," Satana said, and Fenn immediately started in on his pitch, the secret collection, the amulet, going over the thing about his mother losing her soul to Mephisto again. Sad story, lots of abuse and whatnot; soulless could get up to all kinds of craziness if they weren't reined in. It was no wonder Fenn was so invested in Mephisto's ruin.

Also explains his lack of social skills. She'd discovered in her brief time on Earth that Fenn was something of a crackpot. Clever, perhaps even a genius in his field, but not entirely sane. His energy was erratic, his gaze unfocused unless it was on his work.

"…which is why I approached Mistress Satana, to free you from your unjust imprisonment. As the Triumvirate, we will collect the Varkath Star and take Mephisto's kingdom from him. I have designed a thousand tortures for Mephisto, and ask only that I'm given the opportunity to see them fulfilled, once he has fallen and you've taken your rightful place. With the amulet, the Hell dimensions will be yours to command."

Satana watched Zarathos, curious if he'd have any qualms about turning his arch-enemy over to a mortal. Funny, Fenn hadn't promised *her* a leading role in the aftermath of Mephisto's fall.

Color me surprised. In patriarchal dimensions, men liked to do men things for other men. On the other hand, the hunting was always fantastic.

"*I* will destroy Mephisto," Zarathos said. Firmly. "He will howl for mercy beneath my fists until the end of time."

Fenn's shoulders slumped, and Satana decided to test how much influence she had.

She nodded somberly at the half-naked, recovering

demon. "All will obey your wishes, Dark Lord... and perhaps after you've had your fill of Mephisto's humiliation, it would amuse you to resurrect him, powerless, and give him to Fenn. As a token of your greatness, to reward this man for his efforts on your behalf. You'll be too busy ruling to oversee every detail of Mephisto's eternal agony."

Satana grinned and knew her eyes were sparkling. "Imagine the degradation. Crushed by his superior and tossed aside like an afterthought. Tortured by a *mortal*."

Zarathos's eyes flared with pleasure. "I *will* have much to do. I feel a great shift in the Balance. It is a time now for a single ruler who can expand the dark realms to encompass all. I will consider this token, and other expressions of my appreciation for your service."

Zarathos addressed the last to both of them. Fenn looked relieved, and Satana bowed her head again, fighting the urge to chuckle. Like shooting fish in a barrel, as the saying went.

"I am honored, Dark Lord," Fenn said.

"Where is this collection you speak of?" Zarathos asked.

"In a small vault, in Transia, buried in the eastern foothills of the Carpathians," Fenn said. "I haven't been able to identify its exact location, but I'm certain of the area. The collection was heavily warded to stay hidden and locked, but the dimensional alignment—the shifting balance, as you say—will weaken its protections, and I've created a machine that can help us find it. A kind of detector, keyed to measure magic-directed particles. My research shows that the collection may have been placed there by members of the Blood, which is why I thought you'd be best suited to unwind its locks."

"I corrupted many Blood," Zarathos agreed. "Turned them against their purpose to feed my energies. The fallen Blood were my soldiers in the war for Hell."

That's *why Fenn picked him?!* What an inanely stupid reason. The Blood were a long-lived line of realm defenders, usually overseers of more powerful beings, but having associated with some of them once didn't make Zarathos any more qualified for *anything.* Satana's sorcery skills were top-notch, she could snap most wards without breaking a sweat, *and* she wasn't an underqualified egomaniac. Now that big Z was conscious, they'd be bowing and scraping for the duration of the search, and all because Fenn had dug up the very loosest of connections and leapt to conclusions.

"I must rest and feed longer," Zarathos continued. "When I am restored, the Triumvirate will go to this place, and I will destroy the shields that keep the amulet from our grasp. Succubus, you will hunt souls to speed my recovery. Two score will suffice."

Fenn cleared his throat. "We mustn't attract notice, Your Majesty. I've been able to hide those soulless we already have, but too many will alert Earth's protectors and—"

"Let them come," Zarathos said. "No one can defeat me."

"Yes, but you're not—that is, you have not recovered your full strength, Dark Lord." Fenn was blinking double-time. "Better that the Triumvirate does not waste its time defending against attack until we can find the vault, at least, so that you can focus all of your formidable power on breaking the seal. I'm working on several devices to bolster our defense, but they're untested and—"

"Two score," Zarathos repeated, and lay down. "Now leave me."

Satana followed Fenn out into the hall. The demon was out cold again before she closed the door—she sensed him go under. He *was* stronger; she could feel his essence drawing psychic pain from every direction. What had been a trickle was now a stream.

Also, what a butthead. He hadn't even remembered her *name.* She'd make him say it, once she had the Varkath Star. And she was definitely going to drop Fenn into a hole somewhere, for creating such trying circumstances.

She looked at Fenn. "Who will be after us, if we're detected?"

Fenn's jaw went tight. "There are many. Witches and sorcerers, demonic half-breeds, scientists, mutants. They are already watching for disruptions, changes."

"And they'll know Zarathos is on Earth, when he leaves your house." Satana could mask her own presence, but Zarathos was too full of himself to consider hiding.

"No, I have a portable shield generator," Fenn said. "It's not as effective as the larger prototypes, but it should obfuscate our presence in Transia."

"Uh-huh," Satana said. "And when big Z blows the seal apart with his *almighty* power, it's going to cover that up, too?"

Fenn smiled, a small, creepy smile. "Once the Triumvirate get into that vault, it won't matter. We'll have all we need to accomplish our aim."

"The Varkath Star controls *demons*," Satana said. "What use will that be against Earth-born enemies?"

"You never asked what else was in the collection," Fenn said. "A shield that deflects Hellfire... and a spell that summons Mephisto."

Satana got it. Mephisto could be called up and turned against whoever the amulet wearer wished. The collection was a regular do-it-yourself take-over-the-universe kit; why it had been gathered and hidden was anybody's guess, but who cared? As long as they were the only ones who knew about it, it was theirs for the taking. There were more realms controlled by demons than not, and some of their dimensions were vast, filled with resources and rowdy Hellspawn populations. The great Balance between light and dark could be history, a bedtime story for cowering slaves to tell in the new chaos.

No rules, no limits.

"We can use the spell to command an audience with Mephisto, and force him to destroy our enemies," Fenn said. "He will be at our mercy."

Satana let surprised delight dawn across her face. "Oh, I see! That's brilliant, Fenn!"

Fenn beamed. "I will not let you down, Your Majesty. I have planned everything."

"About feeding Zarathos, though, all those soulless..."

"Perhaps you should kill your victims from now on," Fenn said. "We could hide the bodies, you wouldn't need to use magic to get rid of them. I have keys to a place I used to work, a shop that's been shut down for years. No one would find them there."

Satana pouted. Extracting souls was like poetry: it was breathing in a whole life, a delicate, powerful bloom of light and power transferring to her essence. Murdering vessels without magic to tidy things up was just messy. "I thought the Triumvirate needed soldiers. I wanted to make uniforms."

"The Triumvirate needs to keep a target off our backs a little longer," Fenn said. "Until we find the vault, just for another day or so. And then you can make a million soldiers and dress them however you'd like. Such an army would be a sight to behold, a triumph of flawless design. Better than any of us deserve to gaze upon."

Well, that's true. Fenn was a flatterer and mentally unsound, but he really did have a clear eye.

Fenn lowered his voice and leaned in as close as he dared. "My *only* desire is to see Mephisto suffer, my queen. I have no interest in who holds the Varkath Star once it's found, or what happens to me or this universe, so long as he suffers for his crimes. I would gladly kneel before Satana Hellstrom's throne, if she chose to rule."

Satana leaned in, too, enjoying the sudden panic that flashed behind his eyes. "I could make you kneel now, if you like."

"I have work to do," Fenn said, backing away. "I'll, uh, get you the keys to that building. Perhaps your servant can take you there? I'll assist in any way, of course. You only have to ask!"

He turned tail when he hit the stairs and ran for his workroom. The door downstairs slammed a second later.

Okay, fun again. Kissing Zarathos's gristly butt was going to be a chore for sure, but Fenn was a laugh and getting forty souls without setting the vessels loose would be a logistical challenge, like a puzzle. She liked puzzles.

"Hey, hot guy," she called, and the dance-club man appeared at once at the end of the hall. She couldn't remember his name, but he had a stellar profile. "Let's you and me go for a ride. I've got some collecting to do."

3

WHEN they stepped onto the Limbo bridge, power surged through Magik, flushing her skin, sending electric tingles to every atom. The hazy orange-red sky was flecked with giant pieces of a shattered world, floating in the seemingly endless realm that had once been Mephisto's domain. City-size chunks of earth and stone hung against the fiery backdrop in every direction she looked. Many were inhabited by the various haunted creatures and demons that called Otherplace home. There were old castles and tiny hovels, villages and cities, scattered forests of blackened trees, boiling lakes and icy waterfalls that poured endlessly through the strange sky.

Magik took a breath, refreshed by an influx of pure energy, her Soulsword burning brighter. She'd grown up in Mephisto's Limbo, one of the demon lord's "favorites"—

stolen from her family, trained to fight his enemies and beaten when she wouldn't obey. She'd finally grown strong enough to rebel and the extra-dimensional demon had retreated to his Hell, abandoning the smaller dimension that he'd ruled for so long. Magik hadn't wanted to take Mephisto's place, but circumstance had forced the issue. She'd had to fight time and again to maintain a title that she didn't want but couldn't abandon; Limbo was as much a part of her as the color of her eyes or the sound of her voice, and there were few limits to her power here.

Magik walked a step ahead of Blade, feeling the weight of a thousand eyes watching them, the watchers themselves unseen. All creatures kept a respectful distance from Limbo's Mistress and those she escorted through.

Concentrating on the coordinates Caretaker had given her, Magik slashed at the empty air in front of her and revealed a stand of stunted pines, dappled with sun and shadow. Birdsong and the hum of insects filled the air. Blade stepped through but immediately held up his hand, a sign for her to hold the portal.

It was no strain, not with Limbo's steady forces pouring through her, although she was curious. Blade had never asked her to wait.

"They're gone," Blade said, and breathed deeply. "Or... not."

He glanced at Magik. "I can still smell them, but they're not there. Do you get anything?"

Magik nodded. Blade was thoroughly self-sufficient,

a half-vampire with exquisite senses, certainly better than hers. But in Limbo, she was exponentially more powerful than anywhere else.

She stabilized the small portal and lowered her sword, then relaxed and listened with her whole self to what was on the other side. Sunlight, warm pavement, thirsty grass, diesel fumes and the rank odor of chemically treated waste. Small animals foraging, a thousand insects creeping, worms turning in the soil. A lone man sleeping in the cab of a truck, dreaming. There were two other vehicles close by, empty. Cars with people in them flashed by on the nearby highway, but the sleeping man was the only being around, and he had a soul.

Except. There was a smell of tainted energy, dissipating slowly, and a soft mechanical hum that didn't belong anywhere. It was coming from the larger of the empty vehicles. Magik concentrated. There was an energy, but it was complex, an amalgam of light waves and elemental power. There was something familiar about the feel, but Magik couldn't place it.

"What is that?"

Blade shook his head. "The sound? I don't know. I'll check it out."

The Daywalker didn't need help, but Magik was uneasy about the atypical energy. Why was it familiar, but not?

"I would come with you."

Even as the request came out, Magik reconsidered asking. Caretaker had not tasked her to accompany Blade, and after Nico's speech, the Blood warrior might feel that the Suns were defying her, undermining her authority. Caretaker was in her grief, sensitive, irritable. She'd sent Wanda away after the accident that had killed Agatha. Magik had liked both women, very much, but knew better than to get attached to people or dynamics. Strong feelings were not conducive to keeping Darkchilde locked away.

However Caretaker might feel about it, Magik wanted to go and didn't believe her presence would hinder Blade. Caretaker was very old, she saw all of them as children, but Magik maintained the right to make her own choices. She trusted Blade would tell her if he didn't want her along.

Blade bobbed his head, and they both stepped out of Limbo and into the spiky trees.

They were at the south end of a small rest area, their stand of pines alone on a concrete island. The toilet building was fifty yards ahead of them, flanked on either side by empty parking spaces and more islands of dusty greenery. To the right, a small, unkempt park with two picnic tables. A pickup truck was parked there in the shade of larger conifers, where the lone man slept. Farther along and on the other side of the lot, a battered SUV and a shabby recreational vehicle were side by side, seemingly deserted. The bright sun evoked shimmering heat waves from the asphalt.

Magik put her sword away. Her powers cut to a quarter of their strength when Limbo closed behind them, but she could still sense the strange energy coming from the RV, a tan behemoth that had seen better days. There were spots of rust at the door hinges, and the back bumper was wired on.

"That's the one I saw last night," Blade said, nodding at the black SUV.

He spoke a few words of power, dimming their presence. Agatha had taught all of them the simple spell, although Robbie had yet to master it. They wouldn't be invisible, exactly, but hard to see unless someone was staring right at them. They started across the lot toward the two vehicles, Blade breathing deeply again as they got closer.

"They're in the RV," Blade said. "Six people, but they're not moving or talking. And I still can't tell if they're fully human."

"That sound," Magik said. "A shield? It hides their nature."

Blade nodded, frowning. Such a thing was cause for concern. Soulless didn't have the wherewithal to hide; they wandered in their corrupted form and caused trouble for everyone around them until they were killed or imprisoned, like any regular sociopath. They could be commanded but did not lead or organize.

A blue minivan pulled off the freeway and slowed to a crawl, turning into the shadier lot. A family, with children in the back. They parked not far from the sleeping man, and the parents got out to usher the three young ones to the toilets.

"Let's do this out of sight," Blade said. "Can you stun the people inside the RV without killing them, or causing structural damage? I'd like to go in without shooting."

Magik considered. Energy blasts weren't difficult, but they created radiant blue-white light, and would knock the vehicle over. Most of her training at the Abbey had been about fine-tuning her control, but she still struggled to pull punches.

Not an energy blast, then. "I will push their air away. They will still be awake, only startled, slow to react. It might break the windows but should not hurt the metal."

Blade smiled, his teeth beautifully white. "Perfect."

They moved to the caravan's door, and Blade gave a nod, resting one black boot lightly on the dented metal stair.

Magik took a deep breath and leaned back like she was going to throw a ball. She bent forward suddenly, focusing a small displacement through her right hand, and touched the scratched door with the very tips of her fingers.

The RV visibly rocked, air *whooshing* and whistling through every crack, and a window at the front imploded with a dull crunch. Blade tore open the door and flashed inside. Green light spilled out onto the ground and air rushed into the vacuum, pulling strands of Magik's hair across her face.

Ragged voices gasped and choked. Magik hopped up the metal step and watched Blade dart back and forth between the men still standing, a living shadow of exact strikes and whipping black leather. Two bodies were already on the floor and Blade whirled and kicked and punched, hopping off the backs of the fallen to drive his elbow into another's throat, and apply his boot to the chest of a fourth. He moved so fast that Magik was still pulling the door closed by the time it was over.

They were all down and still except for one, whom Blade had bent over a crooked fold-out table, arms hiked up behind his back. He was blond and strongly built, but didn't fight, too busy drawing in coughing breaths. He, like the others, lacked a soul. They weren't people anymore, they didn't have dreams, only hunger for gratification and the pain of others.

"You were the driver last night," Blade said. "Why did you kill Pendragon?"

The blond gasped. "I'm not telling you anything."

Blade thumped his face against the table and the soulless let out a gabbled, angry shout. "Why is Pendragon dead?"

The thing didn't answer, and Blade thumped him again, less gently.

Magik turned to look for the humming machine, which was also the source of the green light—an unpainted metal box behind the driver's seat, the size of a large toolbox. She stepped over a dead soulless to crouch next to it. It looked homemade, some of the rivets didn't match, and it had a single switch on the side. Tiny pencil beams of deep neon-green shot from the edges on the top, eight in all, flaring where they touched the ceiling.

Gamma radiation? The signature had reminded her of Hulk, she realized, but the wavelengths were different, the intensity much more diffuse. And there was some magical element laced in, obscured, a negative darkness that she associated with demons.

"You can talk or I'm going to hurt you," Blade said, and Magik shivered. He was very convincing.

"We should take this with us," Magik said. "We have friends who might be interested."

Blade nodded, still focused on the soulless. "I'm pretty sure I can make these things obey, but you'll have to hold him. It's a spell I need my hands for."

Magik stepped forward and grabbed the creature's arm, locking its joints the way Blade had taught all of them, at the wrist and shoulder, pressing it to the table. He wasn't very old, mid-twenties perhaps, and had the strong, even features of a lead actor, except for his nose, which was now broken and bleeding over his mouth. His sky-blue eyes were dazed and slow.

"I don't think you will need any spell," she said, and set him on his feet in front of her. There were many soulless in Limbo, and she could push the less sentient ones by force of will, usually to clear them from her path. It was a matter of stimulating the right impulses. She'd never tried to make one talk, but it might work.

"What is your name?" Magik asked and took his hands. She didn't squeeze, but he wouldn't be able to get away. She created a state of gratification in his mind and his simple nature immediately took over, an echo of the identity he'd held before his soul had been taken.

"Jaden," he burbled. He smiled a "pick-up" smile, his teeth limned in blood. "And you can't take the shield, cutie."

"We are taking it," Magik said. "And we'll free you before we go. Who can stop us?"

"The Triumvirate. We should just split. They'll kill you."

"Who?" Magik asked.

"Like that liar, last night." Jaden's shoulders went back,

his chest out. "Mess with the bull, you get the horns. I was one of the first, you know? To start paving the way."

"To where?"

Jaden looked smug. "To the Star. To victory. And, I'm the strongest. I bench two-fifty."

"You killed Pendragon because he lied about the Darkhold?" Blade asked.

Blade's interruption snapped the soulless out of his light trance. Magik could feel her tenuous hold break and curl away.

Jaden tried to lunge for Blade, but Magik tossed him back on the table and extended her energies through her arms to press him into it, flattening him. Jaden was pinned. He had room for his chest to inflate, no more. He cursed steadily.

"I'm sorry, I thought I had him," she said. "I wasn't sure it would work. I can try again."

"I should have kept my mouth shut," Blade said. He was crouched next to the box and studying it carefully. He flipped a switch on the side and the green beams of light died. Magik could feel the change, like a veil falling away.

"You should take this thing home," he said. "Jaden and I will finish our visit and I'll clean up. I shouldn't be long."

Magik nodded, and they traded places, Blade taking over the struggling creature. She looked at the other fallen men as she stepped over them, thinking of Jaden's claim that he was the strongest. All the soulless had been young, physically fit.

There didn't seem to be a handle on the box, so Magik bent her knees, grabbed the sides and lifted—

—and something inside went *click*, and there was a hiss like static.

"Drop it! Get out!" Blade shouted, and dove for her and the box.

Magik let go and flew into and through the RV's thin metal door, dropping into a shoulder roll as the door clattered and skidded across the asphalt. She came up and turned. *I can send it to Limbo—*

Blade leapt through the door after her and sprinted by, throwing his arm over her shoulders and speeding her back to their stand of pines in a single breath.

A thundering, echoing *boom* knocked the big tan box off its wheels, and blasted the car next to it sideways. Blood and bits of tissue sprayed out of the broken doorway, along with hunks of the kitchenette's counter and wisps of sour smoke.

The blue minivan had just been pulling out, and their brake lights flashed. The slumbering truck driver leapt out of his cab, phone already pressed to his ear. Even without Limbo open, Magik could feel their shock and distress focused on the smoking, slanted wreck. They were afraid of the unsafe world.

"I'll be right back," Blade said, and darted toward the RV. He disappeared through the gaping hole and was back out again immediately, then opened and closed the door to the SUV. He was at her side once more before she had time to wonder why, sliding a few papers into his coat.

"Nothing to salvage," he said. "It's time for a team meeting."

Magik nodded, drawing her sword, troubled by their experience. Soulless were being created and hidden; how many more, and why? Who were the Triumvirate, and what did they consider victory? They needed to use the library and the Avengers should be notified, at least Doctor Strange and Bruce Banner. And Nico was right, the Suns needed to practice out in the world. She and Blade had managed, but things would have been much smoother if they'd communicated more, and more clearly. The team training exercises had covered division of responsibilities depending on threat, but not what to do when the threat changed.

Caretaker was right, too. We're not ready.

She slashed the air and they stepped back into Limbo.

○━━━━━━━━━━━━━━○

CARETAKER went to the war room after Blade and Magik took off, leaving Robbie, Nico, and Charlie alone in the kitchen. Robbie kept making pancakes, silently, giving Nico some space. Nico fed her short stack to the hellhound in pieces, not hungry. She wasn't mad, exactly. Caretaker had finally acknowledged their right to information, which was progress, but Nico also felt like she'd been put in her place, and she hated that concept with every cell of her being. Caretaker's age and experience had left her convinced that no one around her was competent, and that wasn't true or fair.

And she said you *aren't ready, looking at* you. Nico didn't have anything to prove, she'd gotten along just fine without anyone telling her whether she was capable... But she was technically not very old, even counting the time displacements she'd gotten sucked into, and she knew that wisdom was a thing.

Yeah. Like Caretaker, in her wisdom, banished Scarlet Witch from the Suns. Nico didn't entirely buy that it was a safety issue. Caretaker had never really been at ease around Wanda, had even seemed to resent her presence at times, which was crazy anyway. Wanda was great, friendly, funny, always up for movies, and overpowered in a way that Nico openly envied. She'd been an awesome Sun, and had loved Agatha.

Maybe that's the real issue. Agatha had loved Wanda in turn. Caretaker's own adopted child, Hunter, had been dead for three-hundred-plus years, the body resting in a fine stone crypt next to the Abbey. Caretaker kept the gardens there immaculate.

Maybe Caretaker just hated that Agatha dared to love and invest in someone else. The thought felt blasphemous, but there it was, anyway. The women had bonded raising Hunter together; maybe Caretaker was unconsciously jealous of Scarlet Witch for being alive and an object of Agatha's affection. Wanda was powerful, too, up in Hunter's territory.

Charlie let out a burp, smoke puffing out of her nostrils.

"Neeks, stop feeding her pancakes," Robbie said. "They give her gas."

Charlie's head snapped around to look at him, and she growled, her chest immediately bulking up. She didn't go full demon but was clearly prepared.

Robbie snorted. "You got a whole chicken for breakfast and there's kibble in your bowl—you're not hungry. Save some for us."

Charlie turned back to look at her, the dog's expression pleading—her little horns gave her a perpetual raised-eyebrow look—and Nico held out the last piece of her pancake. Charlie wolfed it and then lay down by Nico's feet, glaring at Robbie.

"I thought Magik would be back by now," he said, and turned off the stove, wiping his hands on his jeans. He carried a towering stack of pancakes to the table and sat down, immediately dumping a third of them onto his plate.

"What do you think is up with soulless running hits on people?" Nico asked. "And meeting in groups?"

Robbie waterfalled syrup over his stack. "Got me. Could be a cult. Blade will figure it out."

"At least we might hear about it now."

"Thanks to you," Robbie said. "You're right, we should know more about what's coming, even if we're not the ones going out. If something happened to Blade and we needed to jump in, we'd be kinda screwed on the info front."

Nico nodded. "Also, we've *been* trained. Precision exercises, focus tests, attack scenarios. I get that we have to practice, but I don't know what else she thinks we're going to learn in the yard."

"She's just trying to caretake," Robbie said. "And she said we'd have more to do coming up, another month of training won't hurt us. Blade's just too good, that's the problem."

"No lie." Blade was an expert fighter. There wasn't a weapon invented that he didn't know how to use, and he had about a million black belts. He was eagle-eyed and super smart. Since coming to the Abbey, he'd even learned a couple of spells from Agatha—straight power-word stuff, nothing that required real magical ability, but he was better at it than Robbie. With his vampire strength and senses, he was a one-man demolition team.

Charlie huffed, then trotted out of the kitchen. Nico heard footsteps in the foyer a second later, and the front door opening.

"Maybe they're back from—" Nico started, but then Blade appeared in the archway.

"Team meeting in the common," he said, and disappeared again.

Robbie grabbed a last, giant bite of breakfast, and they headed out into the hall that fronted the barracks. They hurried across the grand foyer and into the main north–south corridor. Caretaker's chambers were to the left, the door closed as always. Hunter's sealed room was on the right, just past the Abbey's main entrances. Charlie sat outside her old master's door, watching them pass. Whenever there was any excitement around the Abbey, Charlie went to Hunter's room. Even after a three-century absence, the beast was loyal to a fault.

The common room opened off the corridor on the right. Past that and south were the war room, the library, and of course the forge, which took up the Abbey's whole north end. A Sumerian fire-demon lived in the forge itself, a sentient creature that had been bound to service back at the Abbey's creation.

Nico had tried talking to it a couple of times when she'd first arrived, but Agatha said the demon preferred to be left alone. It apparently considered itself a contract worker rather than a prisoner, and found mortal concerns uninteresting.

She and Robbie walked into the common, a heavily wood-paneled lounge with lots of couches and coffee tables and a full bar on the east wall. Blade and Magik were talking to Caretaker, who didn't look happy. The three of them stood under the main chandelier next to Nico's favorite spot, an overstuffed chair next to a bookcase.

"...agreed, that they could hear about this," Blade was saying.

"I didn't agree to any such thing," Caretaker said. "And I don't appreciate you calling for this discussion before talking to me."

She turned her cold gaze to Magik. "If something had happened to you, he would have been stranded there."

"Nothing happened to me," Magik said.

Caretaker glanced over at Nico and Robbie, then folded her arms and sat down abruptly. "Since we're all here."

Blade took off his sunglasses and hooked them on his shirt, backing up a step so they could all see him. His smooth, deep voice echoed against the vaulted ceilings.

"Last night I went to check out an artifact dealer who said he had a Darkhold page," Blade said. "It was a fake, but a couple of soulless showed up and shot a grenade at him. They took off before I got a good look. Soulless are usually loners, people who sold their soul for whatever reason. They're not rare but they're not common, either. They're too antisocial to pair up, and you never see them in groups unless they're being directed. Usually by whoever made them soulless."

Robbie sank into the nearest couch, and Nico leaned on the arm. Magik stood and listened, her arms folded, next to Caretaker. The old woman was still frowning but she was listening, too.

"Today, we found more of them hiding in an RV at a rest stop, including at least one of the guys I saw last night. There was a machine inside that was putting out an energy shield, something that threw off our ability to sense them."

Magik spoke up. "Gamma radiation, but in streams of density that I have not seen before. The energy was amalgamated with base magic."

"We asked a few questions, got that the soulless are serving a group called the Triumvirate," Blade continued. "The one we talked to said that he was paving their way to 'the star,' and to victory. And he said that he'd killed that dealer because the guy had crossed the Triumvirate, lied to them."

"About having a Darkhold page?" Nico asked.

"Seems likely, but he was a grifter. It could have been about something else," Blade said. "Unfortunately, the shield generator had a self-destruct mechanism inside, and our interview time ran out."

"It triggered when I tried to move it," Magik said.

"I should have been more thorough," Blade said. "I hadn't considered it."

"I should have sent it to Limbo," Magik said.

"You shouldn't have been there at all," Caretaker said. "Perhaps if you hadn't been distracting him—"

"Magik got what little information we have, and I was glad for her help," Blade interrupted. "We know there's a group making soulless and looking for a star. Could be a real destination, a plane of ascension, or maybe an artifact. We know they have technology that can hide soulless creatures, and that it's at least partly gamma powered. I think we should talk to Bruce Banner. And Doctor Strange should be told. He should be watching for passive energy draws."

"We should also look for information about the Triumvirate, and anything about a star, or *the* star," Magik said.

"I took some paperwork off the group. I'll figure out who they are, where they might have crossed paths with a soul-eater," Blade said. "We should focus on activity in New York and New Jersey, the IDs I got are all local."

He looked at Caretaker, and everyone waited. She sighed.

"I have nothing against speaking with Banner," she said. "He'd know what technologies are currently possible with gamma radiation. Since you saw the machine, Blade, you should speak to him. Doctor Strange is quite busy right now, but I can look for energy transference in the area, and more soulless. Magik, you might listen for word in the otherwheres of this Triumvirate. At least one of them is a soul-eater."

"Robbie and I can hit the books," Nico said, and Robbie nodded. "The Montesi Appendix lists a bunch of mythical nirvanas, I know there are some about stars. And there's like five shelves on artifacts in the library."

As the word left her lips, she wished she could take it back. Caretaker winced like it hurt, the corners of her mouth turning down, but the expression was there and gone in a flash. When she spoke, her voice was steady, totally reasonable.

"I'll move some books here, where you can look for references," she said. "I'll do that now. Blade, please tell me if you're leaving the Abbey for your investigation. We'll need to coordinate with Magik for portal access. All of our classes will resume on Monday morning. I'll be at the table, if anyone needs me."

Not looking at any of them, she walked out of the room.

"Crap," Nico mumbled, as soon as Caretaker's footsteps were out of range. "I didn't mean it like that. I mean, I wasn't trying to push her."

"No, you're the worst," Robbie said. "You should feel really bad about using a noun in a conversation."

Nico appreciated the support but couldn't smile. Caretaker had feelings. It was easy to forget since she never showed them, but Nico felt bad for her.

"Team exercise in the yard before dinner tonight," Blade said. "I'm so used to working alone, I fumbled today. I interrupted when I shouldn't have, and didn't let Magik take care of a threat she was better suited to handle."

Magik nodded. "I didn't communicate properly."

"Eighteen hundred, and bring ideas," Blade said. "I'll be running background checks for a bit. In my room if you need me."

"I'll be in Limbo," Magik said. "Caretaker can call me back if transport is required."

"Kids? You good?" Blade looked at Nico and Robbie.

"I'll start on the books, Robbie's got that thing with Gabe," Nico said.

"I can cancel," Robbie said, but with hope in his voice. Robbie was not a book guy, and it killed him to miss time with his brother.

"I think I can *read* for a couple of hours without you."

Robbie smiled. "You know it's gonna hurt, though, right?"

"Kids are good," Blade said, and disappeared in a flash of trench coat. Magik followed, walking like a person.

Robbie stood up. "Thank you, seriously. I'll keep it short."

"It's cool. Next time Charlie barfs up blackened squirrel, you're on duty."

He laughed and was gone, leaving Nico alone in the big room. She heard a soft *thump*, and saw a line of books appear on the bar, laid out like a fanned deck of cards, their ancient spines cracked and tattered. Two short stacks of three and four appeared behind them a few seconds later.

Nico started for the bar, psyched to finally be doing something that mattered. The smell of the books, of magic and history, washed over her as she reached for the title on the end, and Nico was hit with how much she missed Agatha. She remembered a rainy day last fall, parked between the shelves while Agatha brewed tea and talked about transmutation theory, Ebony curling around her ankles...

Nico saw that Ebony was perched on the barstool next to where she stood, watching her. The fluffy black cat hadn't been there a second before. Her wide-eyed look was a question.

"Hey, gorgeous," Nico said. "Did you come to keep me company, or to protect the books? I promise I'll be careful. No blood-magic for speed-reading." Some of the Abbey's books reacted badly to certain kinds of magic. A year ago, Nico had accidentally set one of the library rugs on fire trying to hurry through an assignment. Lesson learned.

Ebony flicked her tail, then settled to the stool, purring. The cat had disappeared for a week after the accident, but then had started showing up randomly again like nothing had changed. She always seemed to turn up when Nico was missing Agatha, and the feline's presence was so like the old witch's that Nico was always comforted.

Nico cracked the Montesi Appendix and started turning pages. She was going to find something, she could feel it.

o————————o

ROBBIE walked out into the training yard a few minutes before six, rubbing his eyes. They were tired, gritty. The late-day sun seemed obnoxiously bright. The Abbey had tons of windows, but they were all narrow and high, better for defense than lighting.

Staring at old books all afternoon might have something to do with it. Nico had put him on artifacts, and he'd found well over a hundred items that had *star* in the name in just the first hour—the Star of Ichini, Starstone, the Star Sword of Astromidus. He dutifully wrote them down while Nico read about mythologies and tapped notes on her laptop. She was happy and intent, researching, but he'd been less enthused by the time he hit his third single-spaced page of star names. They needed more to go on.

Magik was the second to arrive, walking around from the south. She nodded at Robbie.

"You hear anything about the Triumvirate?" Robbie asked.

"Nowhere I thought to look," Magik said. "Did you and Nico find the star?"

"We found loads of 'em," Robbie said. "Turns out every other magician and his kid brother liked the name. It's right up there with *of fire* and *all-seeing eye.*"

"We need more information," Magik said.

Robbie nodded. There was nothing to add, and Magik didn't really do small talk. He liked that about her. She was based.

Nico popped out of the Abbey and jogged down the steps, finger-combing her damp hair. She'd said she needed to grab a shower after digging through all those dusty books. "Yay, I'm not late."

Robbie looked at his watch. Blade was always on time, but he only had about thirty seconds before—

"Robbie, think fast," Blade called, from behind him.

Robbie turned, hands automatically coming up. Blade threw a baseball, and Robbie caught it.

"We're on a city street and a building is about to fall on us," Blade said. He was standing in the yard in full gear, strapped with weapons, his long coat gently flapping in the ever-present sea breeze. "Who takes lead? Say their name and throw them the ball."

"Magik," Robbie said, and tossed the ball at her. Magik made portals—she could get them all out. She snatched it out of the air like it was a threat.

"The building appears to turn into a million snakes," Blade said. "Who gets the ball?"

Magik threw the ball at Nico, who used both hands to catch. Good choice. If the snakes were an illusion, Nico could dispel it. If they were real, she could hit them with a telekinetic blast and scatter them.

"Next time, say her name," Blade said, and Magik nodded.

"A dozen men with guns run out of an alley," Blade said, and looked at Nico. Nico started to toss him the ball, then changed her mind.

"Robbie," she said, and threw. Robbie caught it.

"Why me and not Blade?"

"Your chains," she said, and he nodded. Blade would make short work of a dozen gunmen, but as Ghost Rider, Robbie could wrap up the whole group at once in metal, with or without flames.

Blade held up a second baseball. "A hole opens up under our feet and we fall into the sewers—"

"Blade," Robbie said, but Blade held up his hand before he could throw, then tossed the second ball to Magik.

"I'm busy wrestling an alligator and need help," Blade said. "A deranged lunatic wearing a suicide vest appears and says he's going to kill us in five seconds. Nico's leg is broken."

"Give me the second ball," Magik said.

"I can help Blade while you get rid of the bomber," Robbie said. "And then we all get Nico out."

"A broken leg won't affect my spells," Nico said. "I could turn the alligator into a purse and put the bomber to sleep."

"Nico," Robbie said, and threw his ball. Magik held on to hers.

"There's no time for discussion," Blade said. "If you think the ball belongs to you, ask for it. If you don't want to throw, declare that it's yours. Got it?"

They all nodded, and Blade started again. Masked killers, exploding cars, innocent bystanders appeared. The Suns quickly developed a rhythm, calling out names, *here* if you wanted the ball, *got it* or *mine* if you were keeping it. The scenarios changed and evolved rapid-fire, leading to a number of hesitations and fumbles, but they were all into it. Nico added new storylines so that Blade could play, too.

Caretaker came out at some point to watch but didn't join them. She had power, a lot of it; she'd been studying magic for most of her long life, enough to create her own dimension. To avoid blowing up the Abbey when the Suns practiced at full strength, Caretaker created specially warded spaces that could absorb even Magik's strongest attacks, openings to the mirror image. She said her warrior days were long past, but Robbie suspected she could take all of them down if she had a mind to.

There was a natural break in play, and Caretaker's strong, creaking voice floated over the yard.

"The Earth passes into an abyss. Magik becomes Darkchilde. Blade is feral. Nico loses her staff, and the Spirits of Vengeance won't come."

Blade and Robbie were holding the baseballs. Robbie looked at Blade, who kept his gaze on Caretaker.

"Caretaker," he said, and Robbie echoed it. They both tossed the balls toward the flagstones where she stood.

Game over, Robbie thought. Caretaker had been through hell lately, but he wished she could see what she was doing to the team. Magik and Blade had both gone blankfaced, and Nico looked rebellious. Robbie had tried talking to Caretaker a couple of times since the accident, but she declared that she was fine, there was nothing to talk about. Nico said she was an autocrat. Robbie thought she was probably just lonely, and there was nothing anyone could do for that; shutting people out was a choice, even when it didn't feel that way.

Caretaker had made her point about who was in charge and didn't rub it in. She was hard but never cruel. "What did Dr. Banner have to say?"

"He said that without looking at one of the machines, he couldn't hazard a guess," Blade said. "And that the Avengers are already watching for concentrations of gamma energy."

"Anything on the soulless guys?" Nico asked.

"Two of them had juvie rap sheets, nothing serious. Joyride stuff. Of the four I could track, nothing in common except they were all in their twenties and athletic. None of them have been reported missing yet. The car's VIN was filed off and it's registered to a guy who died in 1924. The RV was stolen from a trailer park in Connecticut a week ago."

"The Triumvirate is new, I think," Magik said. "Their name doesn't echo in the places I touched."

"We found four specific apocalypse myths that involve going into or through stars, and about a dozen offshoots," Nico said.

"There are way too many artifacts to check out," Robbie said. "I stopped counting in the two-hundreds, and at least half of them were powerful enough to cause trouble."

Caretaker cleared her throat. "I saw the tainted energy of the soulless come up all over New York today, a dozen times at least, and each disappeared before I could focus in. I've tracked a pair of them who keep returning to the same location, but they disappear intermittently."

"What's the location?" Blade asked.

"A machine shop in Yonkers. Seems to be out of business. I can't see whatever's inside—there's a kind of haze. I'd like you to investigate."

"Just Blade, or all of us?" Nico asked.

Caretaker looked at Blade. "Do you feel you need backup? For reconnaissance?"

Blade hesitated. "No, but I think—"

"I'll await your report, then," Caretaker said, and turned to go back inside. "The coordinates are on the table in the foyer."

Nico opened her mouth to protest, but Blade made a shushing gesture and then held up a finger—*wait*—and jogged up the stone steps to follow Caretaker.

When the door closed behind them, Robbie exchanged looks with Nico and Magik. Nico was excited, hopeful. Magik kept her expression perfectly neutral, which was a giveaway that she was up in her head. Magik was almost as hard to read as Blade, when she was processing. Nico and Robbie always got blasted on poker nights.

"Oh, field trip, please-please-please," Nico sang.

"Don't get your hopes up," Robbie said. Caretaker led the Suns, it was her decision, and he could count the number of times he'd seen her change her mind on one hand.

"I'm not sure that we're ready," Magik said. "Today is the first day we've thrown a ball."

"But that's exactly why we *should* go," Nico said. "We're not going to experience fighting bad guys as a team without actually fighting bad guys as a team."

Nico looked at him. "Don't you want to get out of here, see what's going on? Put a hurt on some soulless? Help Blade?"

"Yeah, but not if it's going to lead to civil war," Robbie said. "Caretaker's got enough on her plate. She's having a hard time. Agatha wanted us to support each other, and Caretaker's one of us, isn't she?"

"Agatha would have called her out already," Nico said. "You think she wanted her library to be sealed up, or for Wanda to leave?"

"Caretaker means to protect us," Magik said. "She's afraid of losing another."

"But that's *her*. It's not okay for her to make decisions for all of the Suns based on what *she* fears," Nico said. "You get that she can't keep doing that, right?"

Magik nodded. Robbie did, too, and sighed.

As if by agreement, they all fell silent and watched the door, already shaded by the wooded cliff west of them, the nameless forest that towered over the Whispering Woods. Part of Robbie really wanted to go—the Spirits of Vengeance were always looking for a ride, and Nico made a strong case—but he decided it would be cool either way. It was still movie night and he'd had time with Gabe. A good day. As a Ghost Rider, he'd found it worked best for him to keep his expectations low and roll with whatever came along.

Robbie's stomach rumbled. Whatever Caretaker decided, he hoped she'd do it quickly.

○———————○

CARETAKER heard Blade come in behind her, alone. She'd been headed for the war room, and stopped at the base of the wide steps that led up to the forge chamber. Caretaker turned to face him, ready to get it over with.

"It's a recon," he said. "They can hang back while I look."

"They don't need to go," she said. "There's no reason for it."

"There is," Blade said. "We need to get used to a dynamic in the field."

"Not for this, not when there's no point in—"

Blade interrupted her. "Respectfully, you're not hearing me. You've assembled and trained a fine team, but your reluctance to let them grow is starting to undermine their confidence."

"Keeping all of you alive is my primary concern," Caretaker said. "You've felt the changes. Yama's realm has just begun its transit—we're still in the early days and magic will continue to destabilize. What if Nico calls for her staff and it doesn't come? Magik's energy channels could become blocked. The Spirits of Vengeance may be fighting their own battles. It's not a safe time to experiment."

"So it will be a better time, as things destabilize further?"

"No," Caretaker said automatically, and felt for a second like her head was going to explode. She wanted to tell him to shut up and go look, that they'd discuss it later if at all. The Suns were independent, talented, skilled, but she'd seen *thousands* of dedicated fighters come and go, each a bright and beautiful light snuffed out and turned to ashes, memories only to someone like her.

Ironic, isn't it? her spiteful thoughts whispered. She'd readied the Suns for a catastrophe, the darkest of seasons… and now that it was here, she found she couldn't bear to let them go. To watch them flare out and be gone, even though she knew that was the way things had always been, and always would be. Good people fought the good fight and died. She'd sit in her own cold, isolated tomb and erect memorials to the people she'd loved, as she'd done for too many years to count. The thought of staying alive was a weight, a lead suit that she couldn't take off for even a moment.

"There's always a time when a good leader has to step back, or the team members start to doubt themselves," Blade said. "You know this. You are a good leader, and it's time. I'll be there, and Magik's portals are stable. She can always bring us home if anything goes wrong."

He was right—of course he was right, and it was a kindness that he didn't point out that she was failing. She had to pull herself together. The gentle expression on Blade's face made her feel worse. She *knew* she was being a fool, she didn't need his sympathy, his pity.

You don't deserve it.

Caretaker swallowed it all down. The Midnight Sun approached, regardless of what she wanted. "All right."

She thought she'd have more to say, some encouragement or advice, but nothing came.

"We'll be back soon," he said. He turned to the foyer and was gone.

Caretaker stiffened her spine and continued to the war room. The dark, heavy wood of the large chamber soothed her fevered eyes. A thousand campaigns had been planned beneath the timbered ceiling. The unobtrusive counters and shelves were littered with useful books and familiar items, crystals, stones, scrolls. She moved to the mirror table in the sunken circle at the room's north end, taking a few breaths.

She and Agatha and the Sorcerer Supreme had fashioned the mirror table for the use of the Midnight Suns, from enchanted soul glass, and a conduit to the eternal energies of the long-dead demigod Ereshkigal, Who Judges. In the large, shining dark rectangle, the Suns could see what they asked to see. Caretaker often sensed energies through the images— all the Suns could, to varying degrees—which made it an invaluable tool for finding agents of chaos, but it was not infallible. Ereshkigal's eye was always open, but its focus could be difficult to shift. Caretaker was best with the table, and even she couldn't always count on its clarity.

She placed her hands on the cool obsidian top and steadied her breath. The empty portal dais swam into view, the shimmering eye widening to a sphere that hung over the table. Pale stone and grass, the sheer tumbling cliffs behind. Blade and Magik arrived first. They spoke, Magik nodding. Nico and Robbie were racing to meet them there, both of them grinning. Robbie was ahead until Nico jumped off the ground and floated next to him, matching his speed.

Blade addressed the Suns and they each stood tall. There were serious nods all around. Magik cut a portal and they went through, the evening sun blending with Limbo's flame-colored abyss. The portal closed behind them.

Caretaker changed her intent to the place she'd seen before, where the soulless kept returning. A dull-grey warehouse, three stories high and padlocked. There was a brewery in the building across the street, and the table kept trying to show her the harmless swing-shift workers that moved crates back and forth at the platforms.

She murmured a few words and her control steadied. She'd missed the flash of Limbo's light, but she saw a shadow slink across the building's roof. A moment later, she watched the other Suns join Blade, keeping low. They had found a way in.

Caretaker tried to follow them through a rooftop door, but it was as though they were descending into a heavy particulate mist. There was the vaguest sense of magic, a ward perhaps, but she couldn't decipher or dispel it.

The seconds ticked past, impossibly long, and nothing moved. The sun continued to sink, the shadows to lengthen. If need be, she could contact Magik. Caretaker had a simple spell that could project her wishes to Limbo; Magik would know she was wanted at the Abbey and—

Don't even think it, Agatha said, crisply. *You'll stand there and wait like a grown woman.*

Caretaker blinked, lost the building's image as she turned her head.

"Agatha?"

There was no answer, but the thought had been so clear, so exactly what Agatha would tell her. A ghost in her mind, then. It would join a legion of them.

Caretaker used the table to find the building again and waited.

4

BLADE climbed to the roof and listened to the abandoned shop. The sun was low in the sky, and a soft wind blew from the north. There were rats inside, spiders and their prey, but no other life. He waved the Suns up and they entered through a maintenance stairwell, Blade leading the way. As soon as the door opened, he caught a bad smell. Dark magic gone sour, weak but consistent, like a vapor. Like a powerful spell that had stopped being effective long ago.

Nico pulled a face and Magik's nose wrinkled.

"Protection ward, way past expired," Nico said. "Just leftover residue."

Good to know, and it explained the mirror table's blind spot. They slipped down the stairs and came out on a catwalk that spanned the dusty space below, a mid-sized machine shop. There were only two floors, offices and a railed balcony up top overlooking a few dozen grinders and mills covered in webby tarps on the high-ceilinged ground floor. Beneath the sour magic smell was rust, grease, sweat—

Blood. Not a lot, but it was fresh. He turned his head, seeking the source. On the work floor, southwest corner. The area was blocked from view by the overhanging offices.

"Wait here," he said, and dropped to the floor fifteen feet down. He darted through the equipment, into a dark hall that led him past a locker room and a broken, empty vending machine.

He saw tracks in the dust by an exit, and the blood smell was stronger. The shuffling tracks led to a breakroom. Blade peered in through the door's glass window and saw a sprawl of corpses on the floor inside.

Blade opened the door, the air wafting out thick with death. He counted eleven dead men. The blood came from defensive wounds on a few of the bodies, compound fractures of forearms and fingers. From the way all their heads lolled, it looked like their necks had been broken.

Body dump. More enemies of the Triumvirate? The victims were all young, athletic, like the men at the rest stop. Maybe whoever was hiding soulless didn't have another gamma shield handy. Easier to kill them than cover their signature.

There was a faint, pleasing scent lingering on some of the bodies, on hands and clothes. Blade leaned over one of the dead men and inhaled, tried to place the smell. It was like the sweet taste of blood, and the color of rain, and the sound of Billie Holliday singing the blues...

Pheromones. Succubus? Blade backed out of the room and returned to where the kids waited on the catwalk, moving double-time. He vaulted up the stairs and landed lightly next to Robbie.

"Dead bodies," he said. "In the breakroom by the southwest exit, and they're doused in pick-me chemistry. I think it might be a succubus. Magik, can you confirm?"

Magik nodded and dropped off the catwalk, stopping her fall just before her boots touched the concrete. She disappeared into the hall and was back a beat later.

"If it's a succubus, it's one with power," she said. "There are enhancements. It could be a sorceress mimicking the chemistry. I wonder that we didn't sense it at the rest stop?"

Blade shrugged. "These are fresher. And succubae don't usually hang on to their victims. We weren't looking for it. Anyone from the otherwheres come to mind?"

"A few," Magik said. "I can see if they're where they're supposed to be, but I'll need to—"

Blade held up his hand. A car was parking near the southwest exit.

"We got a plan?" Nico whispered.

Caretaker had said there were only two soulless visiting the shop. It would be easiest for Blade to handle them himself, but of course, he would think that. That was the thing about teams. *If it's going to work, everyone gets a turn.*

They all heard car doors slamming.

"Robbie, why don't you and I bring our friends in for a chat," Blade said. "You take whoever's biggest. Magik, stand by to keep them in place. And we'll need a spell to make them cooperative."

"Here," Nico said, raising her hand, and Blade nodded.

The lockbar on the exit popped open, sent a rattling echo through the building.

"Let's take care of this," Blade said, as Robbie's face morphed to a fiery, grinning skull, the glinting metal armoring his head, his eyes glowing. Nico ran her thumb along the zipper of her short leather jacket, drawing blood on the sharpened tooth at the bottom. She put her hand to her chest and pulled the Staff of One out through her black V-neck, a dull throb of purple energy forming in its eye as she rubbed her thumb across the wood's grain.

They jumped from the catwalk, Nico and Magik levitating before they touched down, Blade and Robbie landing on the stained concrete. Robbie shoulder-rolled to his feet. Blade ran for the door, arriving just as the Ghost Rider teleported in next to him.

Two soulless men carried a dead blonde woman in an evening gown through the door. When they saw Robbie and Blade, they dropped the body and tried to scramble back out.

"Gotcha," Ghost Rider said, and went for the big guy on the left, clearly a bodybuilder who'd been heavy-handed with his steroids. His spray-tanned skin had a rough look, and his neck was lost in a stack of muscle. He tried to throw a punch, but Robbie picked him up and tossed him against the wall.

The second soulless had a surfer vibe and a glass jaw. Blade punched him once and he crumpled.

Blade scooped him up and threw him over his shoulder, and saw that the Ghost Rider was carrying the struggling juicer over his head, walking back toward the work floor. Blade followed with the moaning surfer.

Robbie tossed the soulless to Magik, who caught him, pulling him next to her by his arm.

"Who are you? How—*how*?" The bodybuilder gasped, his face going red as he fought to break free from a joint lock, his expression furious and dumbfounded at once. He towered over Magik, outweighed her by a hundred pounds, easy, and his struggling didn't budge her a millimeter.

Blade dropped the surfer onto the dusty cement. He was groggy but starting to come around, sitting up and rubbing his jaw.

"Horum servorum voluntas fiet…" Nico spoke a binding of will, circling her free hand elegantly at the two men, her intent filling the room. She didn't even need her staff. It was done in a few seconds, and Blade marveled at how easy it was for her to direct them. They'd be pliable, helpful, unafraid. The surfer looked up, blinking, his sun-bleached locks hanging in his eyes. Mr. Universe stopped trying to get free. Magik lowered her arm and stepped away.

"Who are the Triumvirate?" Blade asked.

The surfer stared at him. "Are you asking me? I don't know."

"The Triumva-*what*?" the bodybuilder chuckled.

Not privy to anything about the great cause, whatever it is. "Who sent you here to dump bodies?"

"Roxy," the bodybuilder said, smiling.

"Her name's Elise," the surfer said, and then he smiled, too. "She's a goddess. I met her last night. She asked us to get rid of them for her."

"I wanted to do it," the weightlifter bragged. "I met her first."

"Where is she?" Robbie asked, his voice a growling hiss.

The soulless exchanged a look of confusion.

"Like, right now?"

"She calls us, we come," the bigger man said. "I want to serve her. You'll serve her too, if you know what's good for you."

"Believe," said the surfer, nodding. His jaw was swelling. "You'll *want* to, when you meet her."

"How does she call you?" Magik asked.

"She just… does? I can feel where to go when she wants me."

They big man nodded. "That's what it's like."

"Have you met any of her friends?" Blade asked. The soulless shook their heads. "Do you know where she lives?"

Same shaking heads.

What else can we get? These two didn't know anything. The Suns would have to wait until they were summoned and follow them. Caretaker would expect him to send the kids back and continue alone, but he didn't like the idea of pitching his beginner's magic against a soul-eating sorceress of unknown capacity. Magik and Nico had the skills, and Ghost

Rider's short-distance portals were a game-changer. *We could get the Hell Charger and—*

Magik's head whipped around to stare across the room, just as Nico spoke.

"There's something—" Nico began, urgently, and a shadow exploded among the machines, a blast of darkness that swept over Blade, and then he was gone.

o——————o

SATANA was about to close the deal with a hunk of green-eyed yumminess she'd picked up just crossing the street. Men were so easy; a penetrating look, a giggle, an "I've never done this before," and they happily followed strangers into dark, smelly alleys. Well, if the stranger in question was her.

His hands groped wildly and he was nuzzling her throat when she felt her newest servants touched by a will-binding spell.

"Sorry, baby, gotta fly," Satana said, and grabbed his head and snapped his neck. Not even time to swallow a soul. Even as he was falling, she sat down next to him and left her body behind.

She swept through the gray silence of the astral mists and arrived as a shadow on the floor of an abandoned machine shop, the place she'd been storing dead vessels. She didn't materialize power, only observed, letting her awareness spread. Fenn's old workplace had once been warded against magical invasion, which was odd but, more importantly, helpful; the spell's residual energy would confuse the collection of beings that had gathered among the machines. They were talking about her, loosely grouped around her bespelled servants.

A well-built vampire stood next to a tall, lanky, skull-faced demon… A Ghost Rider? The Spirits of Vengeance were ridiculous, crusaders, but they were powerful. Next to them was a little emo girl with a staff; she was the witch—Satana could feel her controlling the servants, her aura crackling purple. The staff she held was living and a part of her, blood-magic informed, not a small-ticket item. And the last member of the party bothering her boys—

Illyana Rasputina. Magik, Mistress of Limbo. The dimensional energy was unmistakable. Not Limbo proper, but the piece Mephisto used to hold. Satana didn't know her, but everyone knew her story—one of Mephisto's mutant prodigies who'd outgrown his whip. She looked like nothing, like a blonde child with a few muscles, but she packed her own Soulsword, the powers of Limbo, *and* she'd booted Mephisto out of his own house. Magik could have been a real role model, but she hung out on Earth trying to do "good" for mortals, neglecting the realm she'd rightfully won. A traitor to power and the hierarchy of existence.

Cute bangs, though. They suited her face shape.

These must be some of the Triumvirate's enemies that Fenn had talked about, perhaps the ones who'd slain their first recruits. Satana didn't generally keep tabs on empty vessels, but Fenn had said some of her soldiers had been slain. Lucky for the Triumvirate that she'd needed to stay in touch with her body-disposal crew.

"How does she call you?" Magik asked, in a stilted, stupid accent. *Yuck*.

At least the vessels didn't have anything to confess. Satana had talked about the mission a few times early on, tried to get some team pride going, but hadn't bothered lately. She'd been kind of busy, grabbing up souls and sending them to the grumpy jerk recovering at Fenn's house.

With her body elsewhere, there was only so much Satana could do. A juicy spell, obviously, but she couldn't take all of them on as a projection, so who to target? She could kick Magik's butt if she were home, just as Magik could kick hers in Limbo; on Earth? Not a sure thing, and the Limbo queen had a Mephisto smackdown under her belt. The Ghost Rider was no good, either. Hellfire didn't bother Satana, but the Spirits of Vengeance had access to Hell portals and liked to beat on demons; she didn't want to be noticed by them before the Varkath Star was in hand. The trashy little witch didn't seem like much, but her staff said otherwise; if she could hold it, she wasn't an easy target.

The vampire. He was built like a fighter and loaded with weapons. He wasn't a full vampire, some kind of human hybrid, and he was fed, but she could take care of that. Making men hungry was what she did best.

Do it fast. Blast him and get out. She didn't want to be caught in a counterattack away from her physical self. Satana started to draw power from her body, slumped in the alley across town, concentrating into her shadow even as she increased the glamour to hide her growing presence.

She drew from her crackling essence, recently stuffed with souls, and the conduit that connected her to the energies of home. Without a voice, she drew the letters of the spell in her mind's eye, the ancient tongue of demons weighting the intention. Her shadow deepened, began to spread as she gathered strength.

Magik and the witch felt her just before she let loose, but they were too late. Satana blasted the vampire with *hunger*, insatiable, and withdrew.

○———————○

NICO felt it at the same time Magik turned her head, a rapidly rising power in the shadows of the big blocky machines, a whirling darkness that was gathering mass and purpose.

"There's something there!" Nico called, raising her staff toward the threat even as one of the shadows burst. A beam of darkness like a river torrent arrowed across the shop and into Blade. The attacker was gone before the last of the powerful blast had been absorbed.

Blade had been leaning over the soulless beach bum and immediately dove for him, flattening him to the dirty floor. He wrenched the guy's head to one side and chomped down hard.

Blood sprayed. The soulless screamed and beat uselessly at Blade's head as the Daywalker drank. The weightlifter stumbled backward, and Robbie grabbed him as Magik hit the now-empty darkness with a blast of blue-white light. Metal squealed as heavy machines tore out of their moorings and crashed into more.

"Blade!" Nico shouted, and his head came up and snapped around, his scruff dripping with blood. His eyes were boiling red and unfocused, ravenous. He dropped the dying soulless and flew at her.

Robbie let go of the weightlifter to throw a chain, and the beefy man stumbled forward. Blade immediately changed course to go for the soulless, now the closest blood supply, dancing over the Ghost Rider's whipping chain in a blur. Blade grabbed the bodybuilder by his arm and clamped onto his wrist, savaging the flesh and drinking deeply. The soulless shrieked and Blade lunged for his throat.

Robbie whipped out another chain, the shining links hissing through the air, and slashed them toward Blade in an arc, trying to wrap him up.

Blade was already in motion, ducking and darting away. Nico held out her staff to reverse whatever he'd been hit with. She didn't need to draw up strong feelings to create drive; she was swimming in shock and horror. Blade was coming for them, starving, out of control. The weightlifter had pitched to the floor and was bleeding out.

Blade was circling them at a run, looking for the best angle of attack. Magik drew her sword and lunged for the speeding Sun. She slashed the air in front of her when Blade spun and went for her throat. Nico saw his wild eyes, bloody teeth gnashing, and then he was gone, falling into the disc of fiery light.

"Come on!" Magik cried, and followed Blade through.

Nico flew to the shimmering disc, Robbie at her side.

They landed on the bridge, Blade twenty feet in front of Magik and held at bay by whatever force she was extending through her outstretched hands. He snarled and clawed at the invisible wall she'd put up. Magik's silky hair floated around her face, energy pouring through her in a steady stream.

"His serum—" Robbie began.

"Mine!" Nico yelled, finally remembering what they'd practiced less than an hour before. Her chest filled with shame that she hadn't stopped the attack and she raised her staff, the energy flowing into the eye of the Staff in glowing purple spirals. She rose into the air, fixed her intention to counter what affected him.

"*Sated*," she named, and released the build-up in a directed beam. The purple light shot out of the One's wooden eye and enveloped the ravening creature that was Blade, sinking into him.

He dropped into a defensive crouch, a knife in each hand. Nico floated down to the pitted stone, between Robbie and Magik. They all saw awareness flood back into him, reason returning to his eyes.

Blade took a knee and vomited over the side of the bridge. He stood up and wiped his mouth, his jaw set. He was *furious*.

"She withdrew after her attack," Magik said.

"Anyone get a look at her?" Blade asked. He spat.

"It was a projection," Nico said. It was the only explanation for how she'd gone unnoticed and then disappeared completely.

"She's a dominant sorceress with dimensional power,"

Magik said. "I must travel. We should return to the Abbey now."

Blade nodded. The Ghost Rider shook his arms out and became Robbie Reyes again, his skull-face melting away. Nico let go of her staff and it disappeared; she felt its reassuring presence settle into her. Magik slashed a hole in the orange sky. Through the portal, the Abbey's woods were thick with gathering darkness, and Caretaker was striding across the lawn toward the dais.

We're alive and in one piece. That's all that matters. Nico held her head high as she followed the others through, but she knew she should have done better. She'd sensed something before she spoke up and had assumed it was the busted ward. She should have been more present, she could have warded the space herself when they got there, and she'd been too busy trying to think of questions for the soulless to consider that their maker might drop in.

It was all so fast. And they'd totally forgotten to communicate after Blade got hit. Nico had been in plenty of tight situations before, but she was shook, anyway. The legendary elite Midnight Suns, part shadow themselves, trained by Blood. The legacy mattered, the approaching Midnight Sun mattered, and they'd been blindsided on their first day out.

Because you were still thinking of it as a field trip, a group exercise, and not the life-or-death situation that it actually was.

None of her teammates looked happy, but they had nothing on Caretaker. The old woman had arrived at the dais and had her arms crossed, her silver-white hair tousled by the wind that swept up off the water. Her frown created a thousand wrinkles around her narrowed eyes.

"Soulless body dump," Blade reported, and wiped his mouth again. It didn't really help; the whole lower half of his face was bloody-wet. He spoke tersely, snapping the words out.

"I was attacked by a demonic spell from a projection. I slaughtered two soulless."

Caretaker had stopped frowning, at least. She had to know how much Blade would hate losing control.

"The team handled it," Blade continued. "If the Suns hadn't been there, I'd be running through the city right now, starving. Magik's going to find out who's making them. We can talk more over dinner. I'll take a moment—I need to clean up."

Caretaker nodded. Blade flashed himself to the Abbey's door and was gone.

"The demoness is using pheromone magic and can access her realm's energies," Magik said. She was still holding her sword. "There aren't many with the control to attack without form. I will go see."

"One of the Furies, perhaps," Caretaker offered.

Magik nodded. "I'll go now."

She waited for Caretaker to give her leave, turning back to the dais only after the old woman bobbed her head.

There was a brief, awkward moment after Magik disappeared with just Nico and Robbie and Caretaker, standing on the lawn and staring at each other. Blade was right, they'd taken care of things, so why did Nico feel like she should be apologizing?

Because that's what she expects. Caretaker rode all of them about their mistakes, she always had, and—

"Good work," Caretaker said, making eye contact with Robbie and then Nico. Her gaze was direct and somehow neutral. Not warm, but not disapproving for the first time in forever.

She immediately turned and started back inside.

Nico looked at Robbie, aware that her mouth was hanging open.

"Good work," he said, and held up his fist. Nico tapped it and realized that she suddenly felt a thousand times better about everything.

"Must… have… carbs," Robbie gasped, and clutched his chest. "Can we eat now, please?"

"Lead the way, King."

They followed Caretaker's retreating form into the shadows of the Abbey. Nico was amazed at how much easier it was to hold her head up. Magik was going to find out who'd been messing around, ruining and murdering people, and then the Midnight Suns were going to kick some butt.

5

MAGIK didn't go to her bridge or to the court's castle but to a deserted tower in Otherplace's winter lands, a crumbling vertical stack of frozen stone surrounded by barren fields and ruins. The tower had once overlooked a labor camp, but not in her time. There was a small chamber at the very top that she'd stumbled across as a child, looking for a place to hide from the demon who beat her; it was one of the very few places S'ym had never looked. The small room was cold and empty, rubble-strewn, only a few slit windows providing weak light, but she still associated it with safety, and it was an ideal place from which to travel unobserved. She wasn't afraid of interference or attack, but there was no point in giving her subjects any ideas. Limbo was relatively stable since she'd rebuilt it—the demons had their own hierarchies and ecosystems and appreciated her lack of ambition—but the Midnight Sun would inspire the power-hungry and restless everywhere to take action; sitting on the bridge in plain sight while she searched for the errant demoness was a needless risk.

She sat on the floor and crossed her legs, clearing her mind. Magik's role as Limbo's Mistress granted her access to all that occurred there. Every thought, every word spoken left an echo in the thin ether, and every Limbo-born demon living elsewhere could be tapped for information. Before, looking for the Triumvirate, she'd used the ability to comb through a hundred dimensions, and had come up empty... Only whispers of rebellion in places where there are always whispers. There was a sense of anticipation, of mad dreams in a rising wind, but nothing formed that she could catch. Knowing that they were looking for a possible succubus with dimensional powers similar to her own narrowed things down quite a bit.

Magik reached for access to the realms with female and female-presenting leaders, sifting through the thoughts of Limbo's spawn and filtering the data by intuition. She was looking for changes in leadership, sex magic, noticeable energy shifts... and she also listened for the names that had occurred to her since she'd first scented pheromones. *Hela, the Furies, Satana Hellstrom, Diantha of Torus, Nightshade, Anaconda...* None of them was a perfect fit, but the being that had killed those people and attacked Blade had been distinctly, deliberately female, as defined by patriarchal standards.

She heard about Belasco's new right hand, a witch with many lovers, and that the leader of Nhim had recently changed gender, and that Diantha of Torus was with child; the Furies had gone into security work, and Satana Hellstrom was missing her own party again. Nobody had seen her for a week—

Her attention caught on the last. Satana Hellstrom was a succubus and ruled her own small Hell dimension. She wasn't known for her ambition, but she had the right credentials.

Magik focused on her contacts in Satana's realm and found one she could use, a demon gangster milling around a cocktail party with a drink in his hand. He was in the demoness's throne room.

Satana's realm was private, well shielded, but Magik had her way in. She closed her eyes and slid into the demon's snarly black tangle of thoughts. The demon was E'yeth. He was not strong enough to stop her from dropping him into his subconscious and taking over. Satana's wards would block Magik from attacking, but she was only looking for information.

From E'yeth's hulking male body, she looked around the party, setting the demon's drink on a passing tray. There were at least a hundred beings standing around, talking, laughing, drinking, dressed in outlandish clothes that complemented the giant room's pink and purple décor. Pulsing, bland techno beats provided a background din. High on the stone walls, preserved bodies were set into dancing, leaping poses and dressed to match the design palette. The empty throne was on a platform at the chamber's far end, carved black stone that glistened in the moody lighting. A trio of robed officials stood in front of the platform, talking to partygoers.

Magik walked to the platform, bumping into a few people on the way as she learned E'yeth's dimensions. Thankfully, the demon was large and toothy, and no one complained. She pushed past a cluster of laughing women to stand by one of the officials, a single-horned demon with webbed fingers who was pontificating on whether some unnamed party had the nerve to challenge him for a promotion. He was quite full of himself, his pompous, nasal voice competing with the thumping music. One of his listeners referred to the demon as Lassel.

When Lassel took a breath, Magik extended her hand, interrupting. She smiled widely with big sharp teeth. "Great to see you. May we speak?"

She grabbed the demon's webbed, slightly damp hand and pulled him away from his small audience. She threw her free arm over his shoulders and let her essence flow through the contact, a steady, gentle pressure. She wouldn't be able to overpower or control him, but he should be influenced; he was Satana's charge, but lower-level demons always bowed before power. They walked slowly away from the platform, wending through the scattered, chatting groups of partiers. She murmured a few weighted words to further establish her authority.

"Lassel," she said, and looked into his glistening black eyes, pulling at his mind. "What's all this about the Triumvirate? What can you tell me?"

Lassel's voice was weak, distant. He didn't blink. "Her Glory's new venture. She'll return when they triumph."

"What is their goal?"

"I don't know. Veren said a mortal came to see her. No one witnessed the meeting. We only know what she told us before she left." Lassel's whine intensified. "You'd think she'd tell her *most* trusted advisor when we might expect her back, but of course, Her Glory blazes her own path. Ours is not to question but to serve in awe."

Magik noticed that a dark gray wall not far from Satana's throne shifted, and realized she was looking at a pair of rock demons. She didn't recognize the species, but they were vast. One of them nodded its giant block of a head at her and Lassel. Maybe the advisors weren't supposed to be wandering off with random guests.

"What about the star?" she asked.

"The Varkath Star?"

Magik nodded. *Varkath.* "What is it?"

Lassel shrugged. "It is what they seek to achieve their goal."

One of the rock demons started toward them, partiers hurrying to get out of its way. "What else did she tell you?"

"To imprison anyone who complains," Lassel said. "To tell each of her lovers that she meant to let them know, but she was in a hurry. That we will each be rewarded for our service, if we can remember not to trip over our own fat feet."

The rock demon thundered to a stop in front of them. E'yeth was a bulky demon but the stone monster was three feet taller, and nearly twice as wide.

Magik let go of Lassel, physically and mentally, and stepped back.

"Let her know that I miss her," Magik said, in E'yeth's deep voice, and the advisor finally blinked.

"Yes, I'll do that," Lassel said. "She meant to tell you she was leaving, but…"

He trailed off, confused, and Magik nodded. "She was in a hurry, I understand. Thank you for letting me know."

She turned and walked in a random direction, pulling out of E'yeth and the chaotic party and opening her eyes to the cold rock of the abandoned tower.

Magik stood and pulled her sword, thinking of the Abbey, finding the steady beam of the portal dais in her mind's eye. She slashed the air and stepped out of the tower and onto the broad, pale stone overlooking the ocean, the first stars appearing in the purpling sky overhead. She'd only been gone for a short time. The Suns might still be in the kitchen.

Putting her sword away, she hurried along the path that led to the east entrance. The torches flanking the door were burning, the light reflecting off the round, stained-glass window set above the entryway—the crimson dagger of the Midnight Suns, surrounded by gold. In the mornings, the foyer was lit up by the glowing symbol. Tiny moths fluttered around the torches, and there was a breeze from the east, carrying the sweet, faint scent of sleep magic through the woods. The Abbey was surrounded by curious, magic-rich places, gardens and woods and valleys that weren't safe to travel alone.

She hurried through the dimly lit foyer and heard voices

from the kitchen as she turned into the barracks.

"...then when the big day comes, the faithful will rise to Canopus and be reborn as immortals," Nico was saying. "No details on how, exactly. There's another one about Arcturus, where—"

"She's back," Blade interrupted, just before Magik stepped into the room.

Robbie and Nico both looked up from their half-full plates of pasta and salad. It had been conjured, as most meals were since Agatha's death. Blade's chair was pushed back from the table and he had his broad arms folded, his hair still damp. Caretaker had both her hands around a mug of tea.

"Satana Hellstrom is gone from her realm to join the Triumvirate," Magik reported. "She was apparently visited by a mortal a week ago and disappeared after. They are looking for something called the Varkath Star."

"To what purpose?" Caretaker asked.

Magik shook her head, walking to the table. Her place was set, a glass of ice water standing by, and she sat down and took a drink.

"I spoke to one of her advisors, and he didn't know," Magik said.

"Varkath," Nico said. "I know that name."

"He was one of the most powerful sorcerers this world has known," Caretaker said. "But well before even I was born. There are only legends..."

She stood up and held out her hands, and a leather-bound book appeared in them. She started turning pages.

"Who's Satana Hellstrom?" Robbie asked.

"Daimon Hellstrom's sister," Magik said. "She's a succubus who commands her own sliver of Hell. She is..."

Magik frowned, looking for the right word. She didn't know Satana personally but knew about her "party" dimension, and that she adorned her walls with the dead, and treated her servile advisors with disdain.

"...selfish," Magik decided. "She lacks morality. I know she has fought both for and against Earth's interests, as it suited her."

"What about this mortal?" Blade asked. "Any description? Gender, race?"

Magik shook her head. "I did not hear more, I'm sorry."

Nico smiled at her. "You got her name and what she's looking for. That's awesome."

"Good work," Robbie said, and leaned across the table with his fist out.

Magik touched it with her own. Robbie grinned and looked satisfied. It was odd, that such a minor gesture would create happiness, but Magik appreciated the acknowledgement.

"What does it say?" Nico asked Caretaker.

"'Nos qui verum dicimus dicere...'" Caretaker scanned the ancient handwritten page, frowning. "According to this, the Varkath Star is a myth. An amulet that can control Hell Lords. Said to be forged from the bones of angels and..."

She trailed off, pacing across the kitchen, then closed the book.

"I'll be back in a moment," she said, and hurried out.

"A triumvirate is a group of three power players," Nico said. "And we've got a mortal and Satana. Who's the third?"

"The human could be a messenger," Blade said. "We shouldn't assume anything at this point."

"Who are Satana's enemies?" Robbie asked. "Like, somebody she might want to control?"

Magik spooned noodles onto her plate. "I don't know her history well, but she holds no loyalty. It would be nothing to her, to attack another ruler for what she wants. But only if she thought she would win. Her domain is small. She would need more power to challenge anyone."

"So, she's making soulless for the Triumvirate, and they're after the Varkath Star," Nico said. "Which would give her the backing."

"A charm to control demons. Think bigger," Blade said. "Is it just a territorial dispute, or a power play to tip the Balance?"

"Just." Magik stabbed at her lettuce. Creatures of Earth didn't understand what a territorial dispute could look like for the billions of sentient beings that existed outside of their dimension. For all the soulless and evil that dwelt in the demon-ruled otherwheres, there were also slaves and innocents, worlds of delicate biodiversity and blameless animals. Sudden power shifts could cause untold suffering, as she knew too well.

"Sorry, Magik," Blade said, reading something in her face or body language that she hadn't been aware of expressing. "I didn't mean to imply that one is worse than the other.

Whatever they want, we need to stop them. Stealing souls and murder are good enough reasons."

"That Star would be a pretty handy item to have around, though, especially right now," Robbie said, and they all nodded.

An understatement. The only things more powerful than Hell Lords were the Elder Gods themselves. No one knew what the Midnight Sun would bring, but all feared one of the arch-demons might seek to exploit the chaos on Earth. The realm's guardians could use an amulet that would stop Baphomet, Asmodeus, Dormammu, Satan...

Or Mephisto. Magik swallowed her mouthful of food, barely tasting it. She was ambivalent about her former custodian. He was a brutal, terrible being, craven, cruel... But she'd spent so many years seeking his approval, emotionally starved except for his crumbs of approval. She could remember the look of pride he'd worn when she'd created her first portal. The smile he'd given her, the first time she'd slain one of his enemies. She remembered his strange, electric wit. She hated what he was, but he had defined her experience for so long it was hard to categorize her feelings, and so she did not.

Charlie trotted into the kitchen, panting smoke—she'd been out harassing the wildlife again—and Nico scraped leftovers into her bowl. Robbie and Magik ate and Blade tapped a gentle rhythm on his arm, his gaze distant. They waited, but Caretaker didn't return.

○———————○

CARETAKER had used a spell earlier to transport books to the common room, and decided to do the same to look for the Varkath Star. Better that than break the library seal.

Easier this way, she told herself, fully aware that there was more to it than that, but tired of her own whining. She closed the door to her study and sat at her desk, closing her eyes.

Quaerimus libros de stella Varkath, vel Varkath's Astro...

There were only three books that mentioned stars and Varkath in direct conjunction, not including the artifact reference she'd already found, and they appeared in a stack on her desk. Two of them were astronomy related. The third was a manuscript written by a monk in the 1700s, regarding collections of "godless" artifacts.

Caretaker scanned the faded, careful writing, and her eyebrows rose. The Varkath Star had been part of a small collection suspected to be in Transia, the Abbey's home for centuries, hidden in the eastern hills. A Mephisto cult was thought to have gathered the items—a summoning spell particular to the arch-demon, the amulet, and a shield that could deflect the fires of Hell. A powerful magician had sealed the collection in a vault with no marker and placed it under "eternity's binding, beneath the stone." It wasn't clear if the magician had been one of the cultists, or how the monk had learned about any of it.

She summoned a few more books, trying to find a cross-reference—something specific about the cult, or magical beings active in Eastern Europe at the time—but beyond a few misdirects and things she already knew, all she came up with was a nineteenth-century book of Transian myths, mostly fairy stories. There was a tale about the hills east of the township Mastara, where climbers regularly disappeared. Concealment spells *did* sometimes confuse people who accidentally happened across them; obfuscation magic could cloud perception, a person's sense of direction. On the other hand, the stony, desolate rocks in eastern Transia would make for treacherous climbing.

Caretaker flipped through the old book. The haunted village of Vanda-Gor was recounted, and the Bog-Witch of the Borderlands, as well as the mysterious warriors who lurked in the shadow of Mount Wundagore and led lost travelers to safety. The writer called the warriors *paladins*, which was pretty close. The Knights of Wundagore had been around since the last Midnight Sun, allies to the Balance and those who protected it. They had been dedicated to keeping the magical, haunted peaks of Wundagore from being exploited for ill. It was no easy task: the mountain was a place of great potential, an intersection of ley lines and natural portals, and its shadows were deeper than anyone knew. The Knights had been targeted by chaos agents since their inception. Hydra had finally found and destroyed their main compound around a century ago, torching their library and slaughtering an entire generation of fighters. Since then, the Sorcerer Supreme kept an eye on Wundagore. If the Knights still existed, they'd gone deep underground.

The last story in the small book was about a magical Abbey run by warrior nuns, near Transia's border with

Serbia, that had completely disappeared in the late 1600s. Travelers reported that the geography had changed, and there was a forest where the building once stood with no sign that it had ever been. How strange, to read about their home in a book of fairy stories.

Caretaker smiled a little. *Agatha will*—

Her smile collapsed. She no longer needed to file away anecdotes to share with Agatha Harkness. It was an insidious trick grief played, letting you forget what you'd lost for moments at a time, so that you got to relearn it again and again.

She was procrastinating. The Suns were waiting for her, and she needed to decide what to do. Satana Hellstrom and presumably two others sought the Varkath Star. To overthrow Mephisto, or did they have bigger plans? If the Suns could find out who else made up the Triumvirate, that might give them an idea. The gamma shield that Blade and Magik had described was man-made, although Magik had mentioned a magical element... How many of these devices were in play, hiding trouble?

The Avengers might be better suited to handle this. The Sorcerer Supreme had been traveling to the dimensions that would align during the Midnight Sun, to warn, to assess threats and defenses, but he would make time if she asked. Doctor Strange had history with the Hellstroms, and would understand the incredible potential for such an item, as well as the importance of keeping it from enemy hands. Dr. Banner and Tony Stark might use their science to track the gamma machines; their technology was quite advanced. The Midnight Suns could continue training, preparing for the greater threats that would arise as the alignment neared...

And it would really drive home that you don't have any faith in them at all, that you don't think they're capable, Agatha said. *On the eve of the Midnight Sun, with all that's at stake. You may as well disband them now.*

"It's my decision. You're not even *here*," Caretaker whispered, and heard how petulant, how childish she sounded, complaining to the dead about her burden.

Her gaze fell on the shovel leaning next to her desk, her weapon of choice when she'd been young and strong and full of bravado. It had been centuries since she'd used it for anything but gardening. No one had denied her the chance to fight, ever. And if someone had tried, she would have laughed in their face, because a single life was nothing in the battle to hold the line, even a very long life such as her own.

The Midnight Suns just proved that they're ready. You're the only one struggling here.

Satana Hellstrom was not even close to the worst the Suns might face. Caretaker wasn't convinced that the Varkath Star was any more than a myth, but the Triumvirate clearly believed in its existence. They had to be stopped, and the Suns wanted the job. Agatha was right. If she wasn't going to let them into the game, she should disband them, free them to make their own decisions.

Or keep doing what you're doing, and they'll just leave. Nico already has one foot out the door. They'll still fight whatever's coming, and all you'll have accomplished is making them doubt themselves.

There was a compromise. As soon as it crossed her mind, Caretaker picked up the monk's transcript and willed herself back to the kitchen doorway.

The Suns looked up from their places at the table. Robbie and Magik only seemed curious about what she'd found. Nico was ready to argue no matter what she said, her brow furrowed, her mouth pinched. Blade was willing Caretaker to make the right choice, his red gaze fixed on her own.

"The amulet is said to be in east Transia," she said. "Hidden in a magically sealed vault, somewhere in the hills. We need to find out if it even exists."

"More research?" Nico asked.

Caretaker held up the transcript. "The Abbey only has a single reference to the Varkath Star's location, and it's possible that this Triumvirate don't even have that much. We need to start searching. I'll go with you. We'll need to be looking for very specific signatures. If the rumor is true, the vault is concealed, possibly with an aversion spell, and mystically sealed."

She wasn't sure how the Suns would feel about her coming along, but Nico's eyes shone with excitement, Robbie smiled, and Blade looked reasonably satisfied. Magik nodded.

"When do we go?" Robbie asked.

"Now," Caretaker said. "If the Triumvirate hasn't found it, they're looking. Dress for cool weather—we're leaving in ten minutes. I'll see if the mirror table can give us anything and meet you at the dais."

The Suns rose as one, their young faces set, determined. Caretaker nodded at them and transported herself to the war room, not wanting to waste time walking. It felt good to take action; it was the right decision… and if anything went wrong, she'd be there to help. When they got back, she'd work on a spell to track Satana, to unravel whatever glamour the demoness was using to hide.

Caretaker placed her hands on the lip of the mirror table, waiting for Agatha to say something about micromanaging, but the dead witch wisely held her tongue.

○————————○

THE succubus had not satisfied his order by half, but Zarathos would wait no longer. He was well enough to break a Blood seal; his mind worked, and his sorcery was advanced. Waiting to achieve his full strength was a waste of time.

I will eat a million souls at once, when the powers of Hell surge to my essence. Mephisto's throne would complete his recovery, restore him at once.

Zarathos rose from the mortal bed and dressed, admiring his heavily muscled limbs as he painted them with clothing. Not as powerful as he'd once been, but getting stronger every second he existed among humans. Mortal suffering was at a peak, the lands ravaged by fear and disease; the "good" of mortal existence had always been a factor in the cursed

Balance, but on its current path, humanity was slipping toward failure.

So much easier to tip everything over. Hell's rulers clung to the Balance, satisfied themselves with foolish incursions instead of *using* their power. Mephisto was the worst of all, content with his kingdom of demons. When Zarathos ruled, he'd breed the ensouled, colonize whole dimensions of them, enslave and torture them. His subjects would grow fat on human suffering.

Zarathos left the tiny cell and walked the cramped corridor into an open space.

"Appear before me," he commanded, pleased at the strength of his voice; the walls trembled.

The man Fenn came from behind a door.

"I am your servant," he said, and bowed.

"Where's the succubus?"

"Satana is collecting souls for you—"

"No matter, I will find the amulet now," Zarathos said. "Take me to it."

Fenn bowed again. "Satana can transport us when she returns, Your Excellency. I haven't yet acquired portal magic."

Zarathos hissed. A succubus who could barely hunt and a man with weak magic. *Triumvirate* was a bad name; it implied an equality that did not exist. They had freed him, and he would not forget, but there were none who could stand at his side. The dimensions were aligning—he could taste the changes in the air. Soon, he would be strong enough to challenge Mephisto directly, without a human trinket...

But soon was not now. Now, he wasn't confident in his ability to travel the thick ether of Earth without depleting his energy. He'd been too long in Mephisto's prison.

Fenn tapped at a tiny machine. "I've asked for her immediate return, Your Majesty. Please be patient with your humble servants for our efforts. I have dedicated my life to Mephisto's ruin and am honored to walk in your magnificent shadow as you seek to punish him for his crimes."

Zarathos nodded, and Fenn continued.

"Satana Hellstrom lives to serve you, and wishes only for a realm larger than her own; she admires you deeply, adoringly. I have researched the amulet and created machines that will help us attain it, if the seal proves resistant." The man smiled, exposing his tiny square teeth. "And machines that will make Mephisto beg for death, powered by radiation and magic to run forever. He will suffer agonies untold."

Zarathos laughed. Nothing Fenn could make would compare to Zarathos's vengeance, but they had this thing in common. Zarathos appreciated the sentiment, even from a mortal.

Satana Hellstrom came into the small chamber, dogged by a soulless servant whom she dismissed with a wave. When she laid gaze upon his magnificence, her eyes widened, and she bowed her head.

"I have attacked the Triumvirate's enemies, Dark Lord," she said.

"Who?" Fenn asked.

"I didn't know all of them," the succubus said. "A half-vampire, a girl with a blood-magic staff. But the Mistress of Limbo and a Ghost Rider were with them. They were questioning our servants."

A Ghost Rider. Zarathos had history with the breed, forced to the acquaintance by Mephisto. The Spirits of Vengeance would be the among the first he would cull from the ranks of his court.

"How did you— What did you do to them?" Fenn's tone betrayed anxiety.

Satana smiled. "I made the vampire hungry. I didn't stick around to see the damage, but he was a big hunk of muscle, lots of weapons."

Fenn started to nod. "Yes, that might... That is, you may have—"

"It matters not," Zarathos said. "We will find the amulet now and vanquish our enemies."

"I'll gather what we need," Fenn said, and ran back through the door he'd emerged from.

Satana took a few steps closer to Zarathos, her gaze wandering to his chest. "You certainly look all better. Like you might knock down the house if you take a deep breath."

"I'll continue to grow," Zarathos said. Succubae were simple creatures, vain, drawn to physicality. Satana Hellstrom had achieved her own realm, which meant she was a cut above her kind, but it seemed she was still compelled by the draw of a powerful form.

"I know you will, my lord," she breathed.

Zarathos turned his head, letting her admire him. He had abandoned lust long ago—diversions of the flesh were a weakness—but he accepted his due and felt that the succubus deserved the sight. A billion gold statues would be made in his image, a billion altars painted with his likeness; blood sacrifices would be offered to the vision before her appreciative gaze. He'd once believed it his destiny to rule Hell, but a superior fate awaited.

Fenn returned with a heavy shoulder pack, and a mechanical cloak on a bracelet that shimmered green with radiation. He wore several blinking bracelets, but the cloak only drew Zarathos's attention. The magic supporting it was ancient, and unknown to him. The human had coordinates for the succubus, and she whispered and waved her hands.

Zarathos experienced her portal as a pulse of fleshy light, pink underlaid with necrotic black threads, and then they were standing on a mountain trail. The moon had set but the sun had yet to rise, the slate cliffs surrounding them dull and icy-bleak in dawn's deep blue pre-light.

Fenn started unloading his pack, his breath showing in misty puffs. "I know the vault is somewhere in this area, but there's a magic that upsets perception. My sensor will pick up the edges of the effect, but I'll need help to uncover the vault. It's said to be under stone."

Zarathos expanded his senses. The stones themselves had history, the soil surrounding them rich with blood and bone. He didn't feel any concentration of magic where they were, but there were a thousand tints and flavors, ancient, light and dark strains of expended energy staining the crevices and cracks of the hills.

The mortal pushed buttons on his machine and hung it from a strap so that the bulky box lay across his chest. Satana changed her apparel to a full, tight bodysuit of fur and dark leather and turned in a circle, her hands outstretched. Zarathos spread his arms and breathed deeply, but there were too many mystical layers to sort through, none of them potent.

Fenn started walking east, staring at a screen on the box. Satana and then Zarathos followed. The demon was pleased to be outside. How long since he'd last glimpsed any sky as a free being? The liminal light was clear, untainted by Mephisto's oppressive essence. In a matter of minutes, he would hold the key to Mephisto's ruin and his own ascendence.

Fenn halted abruptly. "It starts here."

Zarathos stepped ahead of him and realized the environment had suddenly lost its flavor. The ancient residue of the land's magical ruins had turned bland, odorless. Had he not been alerted by Fenn, he wouldn't have noticed the change, not immediately.

Satana stepped in front of Fenn and then backed up, an eyebrow lifting. "Now you feel it, now you don't."

The cloaking spell hid its treasure and itself, but it also masked the residue of the stones. To disguise such power so completely was a feat.

"I'll try to define the area," Fenn said, and started walking again. Satana transported herself onto the high rocks to the west, then to the east, a curvy silhouette against the fading stars. Zarathos concentrated, looking for some whisper of Blood or a magical thread hidden beneath the stones, but sensed nothing. Of course, his senses were not as strong as they soon would be, but he hadn't expected to get *nothing*.

Fenn and Satana returned to him, comparing notes. The area of the shield was roughly sixty feet square.

"How big is the vault supposed to be?" Satana asked.

"I'm not certain," Fenn said. "The description was vague, a small vault beneath the stone. It didn't specify how deep, either, but if we walk the entire area, step by step, one of us may be able to pick up a trace."

"Easier to do a location spell," Satana said.

"Spells have been attempted," Fenn said. "Though by none so powerful as you, Your Glory."

Zarathos had a simpler solution. He stalked back to well before the shield's beginning, the other two following.

He stopped and turned, picking out the boundaries of the shield by landmark—divots of shadow, outcroppings, a stand of weeds.

"Lend me your realm's power," he told Satana, and extended his hand.

"What do you seek to do, my Lord? You should conserve your strength to break the seal. I will be—"

"*Now.*"

Satana ducked her head and put her slender fingers against his palm.

Zarathos felt her sparkling essence atop a steady draw of

energies from her domain. Her conduits were narrow, and he suspected that she had constricted them purposefully, to avoid letting him take too much... or to know how much was there.

He used her power to wrench the connections wider. Satana gasped, and he held her wrist tightly. Flames leapt up from his skin, lapping at the base of his skull.

Zarathos raised his free hand and lifted the top ten feet of ground—the sections of cliff, the rocks and clay that were encompassed by the shield. The mountains would not move so he broke them where they were shielded. The world trembled and the sound was mighty, a thunderstorm of fractures and falling stones.

Fenn fell to his knees and covered his head with his arms as dirt rained down and the air became dust. Zarathos raised the displaced stuff high, scanning it for inorganic material. Nothing. He searched the open wound in the ground before them, saw bleeding roots and volcanic rock—

—and the darkness of a small open shaft in the rough center of the shield's boundaries. Barely six feet square and clearly unnatural.

Zarathos drew on Satana's strength and tossed the floating debris away, reveling in the destructive roar as tons of dirt and rock crashed together and thundered down into the chasm east of their position. More dust billowed over them, and Zarathos waved it off, his gaze fixed on the hole in the ground.

He let the succubus wrench her hand away, and she stumbled. He had replenished himself from her stores, was more powerful than he'd been before flinging the stone away. Fenn was still crouched and cowering. The Triumvirate had served their purpose, the vault of the Varkath Star was revealed. He would—

A handful of beings appeared on the other side of the pit he'd created. Zarathos recognized the Ghost Rider first, drawn to the flame of his eyes, the slim line of his shielded, grinning skull.

Zarathos projected himself into the Rider at once, left his body dumbly muttering a spell of projection and force where it stood. He molded his essence to the Spirit that inhabited the boy, found the intricate, woven power that could hold enemies in chaotic stasis, and grabbed hold. Mephisto had forced him to serve the Spirits of Vengeance, once; now they would serve him.

The Ghost Rider flew up into the chill dusty air, beams of fire-white energy bursting around his sleek skull, blasting into the four others of his group. Two witches, one old and Blood, one not fully grown, Magik of Limbo, and the half-vampire that Satana had spoken of. They were all stricken, frozen, suffering by means of the Ghost Rider's penance stare.

Zarathos stoked the Spirit of Vengeance's self-righteous morality to hysterical glee, further severing its thinking connection to the Ghost Rider. The beings that called themselves Spirits were most satisfied when punishing the "wicked," and this one was no exception; without its bond, it forgot its human host and threw itself into forcing atonement upon its victims. The trance would hold them for a few moments—all the Triumvirate needed to gain the Varkath Star.

"Kill them," Fenn said. "My Lord, if you see fit."

Zarathos ignored the mortal, ignored the urge to linger and feed off the psychic abuse. He willed himself to the square of darkness in the pit. Satana was at his side in a second, holding Fenn's arm. Zarathos glanced at the Ghost Rider and his shuddering victims, shrouded in the dull gray light of early morning, and then dropped down into the darkness. He'd be a god before they woke up.

6

AFTER Magik brought them to Transia, the Suns searched the cold, rocky dark for a cloaking ward, for signatures of power, but the area was apparently clogged with old magic. Blade and Caretaker kept shaking their heads, and Nico and Magik were both on edge, in perma-frown territory as they moved through the isolated rocks and stands of spindly trees. The mirror table hadn't had a clue for them, and Caretaker reiterated a few times that the amulet could be a myth, but they were all hoping to pick something up.

Robbie opened himself to the Spirits and was transformed, but Ghost Rider's senses weren't as sharp as the others' when it came to general magic. Soulless and evil, definitely, and he could smell black magic's corruption in a crowded room, but technical fancy stuff was subtle, not really his wavelength.

Nico finally asked her staff to *find*, and it dragged her northward a dozen feet. Just a direction, but they all started walking, Blade flitting through the wooded slopes ahead of them, Caretaker whispering and taking deep breaths, doing her magical searching, Magik and Nico wandering randomly to either side of the uncertain path. Everything was gray rock and spruce trees, nothing to fight or—

Ghost Rider stopped in his tracks, even as the other Suns froze, all looking north. Demonic power was surging somewhere ahead of them, a wave of ugly darkness.

"Fall in! Be ready!" Caretaker's command was backed by an echoing roar, a rumbling crack that sounded like a glacier exploding.

The Suns converged and Caretaker opened her arms, lips moving silently—

—and they were at the foot of a pit, higher in the rocky hills, the stench of demonic power mixing with the sharp scent of fresh clay and shattered rock, and—

Ghost Rider was hit by a barreling shadow, and Robbie Reyes was split from the Spirit.

He watched helplessly as he was lifted off the ground, demonic energy blocking his connection to the powerful entity that rode his mortal body, that existed to punish the guilty. The Spirit's penance abilities ignited, flowed through Robbie's limbs and outward, fixing on the other Suns.

Robbie clawed for some hold, but the Spirit had already found each of the Suns' private hells and opened them up, reflecting back at them the suffering of the innocents they'd harmed. The Spirit exulted in the service of forced atonement, and was delighted to have its powers extend to so many at once. It was blind to their identities, blind to Robbie, not interested in how it came to be attacking its allies; it was caught in the joy of dealing out punishment, and Robbie was a hostage, hanging in the cold air, gaze fixed on the horizon where the sun's glow was just creeping into the sky. At his feet, his friends suffered.

○————————○

BLADE had a knife in his hand ready to throw when Caretaker transported the Suns. He saw a demon across a freshly excavated pit, its massive, fanged red skull backlit by flames of Hellfire. A dark-haired succubus was at his side, a human hiding on the ground behind them.

He side-stepped to target the villain's heart—

—and wasn't in the mountains anymore. He was in the service corridor under a subway station, starving, reaching out to snatch the arm of a passing stranger. The stranger was a young man, black. He wore a hardhat and a reflective vest, carried a flashlight and a clipboard.

It wasn't me. The attack was more than a decade ago. Blade had been corrupted, poisoned, but what he felt now was the shock of the young man as he was snatched out of his life. His name had been Michael Wilson, Blade had learned later, but at the time he'd just been food. He'd tried to fight but Blade was too strong, too fast. Blade could feel Michael's panic and confusion and his absolute terror, his heart pounding, sinking into his guts as the truth of his world changed. He was going to die, a stranger was going kill him in the dark, and he would never see his mama again.

Blade's fangs sunk into the man's sweating throat and Michael's terror was completed by overwhelming pain, hot and barbaric as teeth settled into muscle, blood pulsing into the monster's throat. The horror of helpless violation, the primal abhorrence of being fed upon. Fervent prayers flitted through Michael's racing panic, promises to be better if he survived. A surge of survival instinct lent him a burst of last-second strength and he bucked and punched, kicked, fighting to live, but the monster had him pinned easily, and Michael was losing strength. What swept through him as his thoughts grew sparse and dim was a great sadness, that he would never accomplish any of the things he'd dreamed about, and that his family would be broken by his loss. He'd meant to do so much more.

Blade, Eric Brooks, cried out in self-loathing. He'd robbed the universe of a bright young man and everything he could have been, he'd dropped him on the cold cement like garbage and gone to find another victim. Blade had been stopped by friends, but too late for Michael Wilson. Blade had selfishly mourned the young man for years, visited his grave, sent money to his family… and finally come to a kind of peace with himself over things he couldn't change, never understanding what he'd actually *done*.

Michael wasn't the only one. Eric felt a dozen horrible memories rising, fear and pain he'd caused to people he'd never known. He saw chests hitching, heard dying gasps through throats raw from screaming, sensed muscles gone loose and weak in terror. They had suffered and died badly. He saw the ripples of devastation that radiated out from the lives of his victims, loneliness, despair, self-destruction, ripples that he'd created, families that had fallen apart. He was a monster.

○———————————○

MAGIK held her flaming sword in her right hand, her left extended to blast the demon off his feet—

—and she was in Limbo, Dormammu was going to kill her teammates, kill her, and she had no other choice. She opened herself to all that Otherplace was, absorbing the lives and essences of every creature that existed therein, sentient or growing, absorbing the atoms and the spaces between them that created the dimension's material reality. She channeled all of it into herself, expanding her capacity to hold it. She would send the X-Men to safety, travel back in time and learn better how to—

Magik *was* Limbo, shredding, withering, losing coherence, she was every blade of grass and every slinking beast, she was thousands of individual minds turning to realization, understanding, naked fear, she was the air catching fire and collapsing. She was genocide, ecocide, the matter of all, transforming the dimension into tornados of spinning power that she would apply to her own purpose. She was an abused mutant child collapsing the reality of everything to have her own way.

Magik was blasted by the mute agony of dissolution, a tidal wave of sentient horror and dumb, hopeless acceptance. As Darkchilde she had hurt many, but the mass scale of Limbo's unraveling was a force, an oppression, and she cowered beneath it, helpless. There could be no forgiveness.

o————————o

NICO had already been holding her staff, and she had a shield spell ready when Caretaker moved the Suns to the source of the dark magic and the thundering crash. She would throw up a barrier immediately and—

She saw herself clearly, a ridiculous little cartoon girl standing among heroes. All she had, all that mattered to her in life, were the connections she felt to the people she cared about, her chosen family. And yet when she'd been with the Runaways, she'd betrayed her closest friend on a whim, and Gert had died carrying that betrayal in her heart. Nico had tortured Karolina with indecision, she'd undermined Chase and left Xavin to die and introduced sociopaths to her *family*, she had made a hundred stupid, selfish decisions, fundamentally damaging those she claimed to love. And then she'd flitted away from the chaos she created to whine to whoever would listen, suck them into her drama, demand comfort she didn't deserve. She saw herself the way she looked outside of her own experience, through the connections she had willfully broken or neglected; she saw her own face, pierced and painted, her quacking mouth, her dumb hair, her desperate need to be seen and loved...

But she was damaged, unstable, an incompetent witch projecting a confidence she would never feel. She careened and crashed through the lives of everyone she touched and made proclamations about what she wanted, blind to the needs of her friends. She'd never seen it because she'd never been brave enough to look, but now she couldn't escape the awareness of her bloated, fragile ego, couldn't block the pain she'd inflicted without thinking twice, without thinking of anything but what served her best.

The Staff of One had retreated, left her to the shame of her frantic, hurtful existence. Nico wished her mother had killed her. She wished she'd never been born.

CARETAKER saw the demon Zarathos and drew her hand back. She would blast him with her own dimensional power—

—and then she was dying, her flesh clawed open by the demonic hands of Lilin, a useless sword dropping from her spasming fingers. She was young and brave, she'd trained at the Abbey with a hundred others and had believed, deep in her heart, that the monsters could be stopped. She had faith that enough of them together would slay the demons and bring peace to the land, it was what she'd been told every day from childhood... but she was bleeding out on the burning ground, ears ringing with the screams of nightmare creatures and the cries of her dying friends, the stench of brimstone and burning blood searing her senses. She was the pain of every soldier Caretaker had sent to their doom, too young to understand that they were fodder in a forever war; she was the realization of their mortality, their eyes finally opening as death came. The hopes and promises were nothing, words, lies.

You lied to them knowing they would fall. You lie and deceive.

Caretaker's heart ached with the truth. She saw Agatha's sympathetic gaze, her kindness when Caretaker told her about the orphaned Hunter; Agatha had helped her, committed to a partnership to raise the child, stayed to grieve with Caretaker for many years after Hunter's death and been her closest friend… and yet she had died without knowing very much of the truth. Caretaker saw Hunter's sweet young gaze turn black, reacting to the terrible stories she told about Lilith's murderous exploits. Which were true, all of them, but Caretaker had carefully omitted facts that might have changed things later. The child had trusted her, like Agatha, like the Midnight Suns, like thousands of young men and women who'd died to serve her agenda.

Not my agenda.

The thought rose from the awful morass of loss and sorrow. The Balance had always been at risk, and always would be. Perpetrators of chaos, agents of the dark, would never stop trying to take over, and there had to be forces for good and order just as committed to stopping them. That was the most important truth. Nothing else mattered, not who she was or what she'd done. She would lie to God to hold the line, and find a way to live with the shame because her personal misery meant nothing. It never had.

There were more dying soldiers crowding into her mind's eye, but Caretaker had found her center, and the visions were fading like images on old film. She could again feel the cold mountain air on her skin, glimpse the soft light of dawn against the sky behind the faces of the dying. The Suns were around her, and she focused on them, found the will to see them.

Blade was in a crouch, clutching the sides of his head. Nico lay on the shattered rocks, curled into a fetal position. Magik stood in a trance, trembling, weeping. Ghost Rider floated ten feet off the ground in front of them, grinning, eyes blazing, Robbie lost somewhere inside. Their attackers were nowhere to be seen, but only a few minutes had passed.

Penance stare. Caretaker found the words to shield herself, and felt the weight of her past slip back to where it belonged. The Suns were trapped in existential agony and enemies were close by, inside a hole in the ruined ground. A faint greenish light spilled from the open shaft, muting their presence, but the shield wasn't strong enough to hide what they were doing. A powerful spell was being chanted in demonic tongue, a spell of destruction that rattled the loose stones around the pit.

Take the Suns home, now. She probably could, her own magic still seemed stable enough, but her vision had reinvigorated her purpose, shut away her doubts. The Triumvirate could not be suffered to stay on Earth.

Caretaker raised her hands toward Ghost Rider and closed her eyes, found the Spirit inside Robbie. It had been spelled and rode without awareness or logic, its conscious connection to the boy lost; she could feel the streams of its energies pouring into the stricken Suns, their distress staining the air around them.

She spread her fingers, went for the simplest, strongest invocation she knew that would stop what was happening, a spell that she'd learned as a young woman. She imbued it with the force of her convictions.

"Den eíste efprósdektoi edó, sto ónoma ton progónon sas sas dióchno! I cast you *out!*"

The Ghost Rider's energies disappeared suddenly, and Robbie Reyes dropped to the ground, the blind Spirit vanquished. He just managed to land with his knees bent. He shook but immediately took a fighting stance, brought his hands up.

Released, the other Suns came to life. Blade whipped out a large-bore pistol, aimed it at the narrow, open hole in the ground. Nico cut her hand and manifested the Staff of One, used it to lift her to her feet. Her eye makeup had run and tears still trickled down her pierced cheeks, but her gaze was fierce and focused. Magik swung her sword and rose a few feet off the ground, high color rising to her pale face, her damp eyes narrowed. Caretaker could feel they'd been psychically battered, but each had immediately compartmentalized, refocused.

"It's Zarathos," Caretaker said. The Ghost Rider Johnny Blaze had tangled with Zarathos more than once; she recognized his hideous fanged red skull. "He's a powerful demon. Robbie, you can call the Spirits back. The spell was tailored."

Robbie wasted no time, flames of rage flaring from his streamlined skull. He hissed, the Spirit incensed by the trespass.

That makes all of us. Caretaker started drawing energy to hit the Triumvirate, to blast them out of Earth's dimension. Satana Hellstrom and a human man were with Zarathos, picking away at a signature that was unknown to her, too faint beneath the strange gamma light to understand.

The vault of the Varkath Star collection. It was no legend.

"I will send them away," Caretaker said, and stopped talking so that she could concentrate. She would slap them off the skin of the Earth and into the void.

"Nico, put up a shield for us in case there's debris," Blade said. "Magik, connect to backup power. If they manage to stay put, we'll need it. Robbie, we're going to attack anything that comes out of that hole."

The Suns broke into action. Caretaker could feel their shifting energies, Nico's blood-magic, Limbo's light breaking on the stones, the Ghost Rider's vengeance lust, but she kept her gaze unfocused, her attention fixed on drawing from the Abbey's haunted grounds. There were energies she didn't dare breach, but her control was excellent; she sifted what was safe, felt her essence extend past her mortal form. A blast might send the Triumvirate anywhere, but they'd be gone, lost, far from their goal, and the Suns would have the Varkath Star to prevent their return.

There was an explosion of demonic power from the narrow shaft, radiating in all directions. The ground rumbled and shook, but Caretaker raised her hands, silver light arcing between her fingers, the fine, strong power lifting her into the air.

7

ZARATHOS tried to ditch them after winding up the Ghost Rider, but Satana grabbed the quaking Fenn and followed. No way she'd gone through all this trouble to miss her first and best chance at the amulet, and she was going to make Zarathos suffer for his disgusting behavior. He'd *taken* from her, blown past her restrictions and stolen from her essence.

"We should kill our enemies," Fenn warbled again, and he was absolutely right, but Zarathos dropped into the mineshaft, intent on his goal, and Satana stuck to his tail, still holding Fenn's arm. She heard the big Z's boots crash into rock below, echoing up the tunnel. She floated herself and the human to a landing. They had gone deep, a hundred feet at least, and the shaft had opened up wide, Zarathos's heavy steps rebounding off widely spaced walls. The air was stale and clammy and there was no light except for the glimmer of Fenn's gamma toys. His specs had been knocked awry, green reflecting from his smudged lenses.

Satana snapped her fingers. "*Light.*"

Pale orbs of cotton-candy light bloomed in the air, revealing a cavernous chamber, practically the length of her throne room, though not quite as tall. The big hollow was tumbled with rocks and boulders but otherwise empty... except Satana could finally feel the energy of the concealing spell.

Damn. It was *still* hard to discern, an absence rather than a presence. She experienced it like an overloud silence—the instant of time before an alarm went off, the millisecond before a cough. There was nothing there, but it was a nothing that had purpose.

Zarathos had already found it, a place on the chamber's east wall. There was no marking, it was the same chunky rock that made up the whole room, but the absence there was thicker.

Zarathos pulled one arm back and let fly, slamming into the rock. Cracks rippled from under his fist, dust clouding, and he drew back and hit again, and again. Chips of rock flew, clattering and echoing. In a few seconds, he'd hammered out a rough square in the gray stone, about three feet across. It looked like an old iron box, but Zarathos's blows bounced off the dark metal, carved out its shape in a thousand splintering shards of stone.

Elder Gods. There were powerful meddlers frozen outside, perhaps seconds from recovery, and Zarathos had the magic to just clear the darned thing, but *no*, he needed to flex those meaty biceps.

Must be pumped up off that power he stole. Satana was drained. She felt similar to the rare occasions she had managed to get a hangover, achy and fragile. Zarathos was a pig.

It finally occurred to the muscular demon to clear the space magically, after he'd gone a foot deep. A cave the size and shape of a decent walk-in closet opened around the vault he'd uncovered, the transmuted rock sifting down like powder. The vault itself was bigger than she'd initially thought, longer across the top than at the ends. It looked like a big steamer trunk of seamless, discolored iron. The container rested on a pounded trestle of gray stone. There were no handles or openings, no hinges.

Zarathos smashed it with his mighty, bleeding fists, and the rock beneath it cracked, but the vault didn't wobble. He tried to lift it, grunting heroically, really putting his back into it, but it was hammered down tight, fixed in space by intersecting magics. Fenn scrambled closer to the vault, fiddling with his machine.

Zarathos stood tall and put his fist in the air, breathing deep. He started to invoke the energies of the chaotic air, the incantation rumbling out of his lipless mouth in a deep monotone. The flames that crawled up his skull burned high, forming a crown of fire.

The demon got specific, inviting destruction of his desire's prison, winding in his intention to hold what was inside. He was pulling up some heavy, dissonant power, but it wasn't the tornado she'd expected, more of a tropical storm. Energy crackled in the air.

Tick tock. Magik could toss them into Limbo and beat on them, and the Spirits of Vengeance were going to want blood. *Who even knows what the rest of them do?*

Satana probed at the web of spectral mist that protected the vault as Zarathos's spell echoed through the chamber, the smell of ozone filling the space. There were countless delicate threads of intention woven into the metal and the air around it. The vault still shielded itself, its energy evasive, off-putting, but there was a sort of curiosity buried in the mass of overlapping intentions.

Satana followed the strange trait, looking for its purpose. The vault wasn't sentient, but its magic was aware of conditions in the ether. She could feel its recycling intention, still fresh after untold centuries, but what did it measure, and why?

She couldn't think anymore. The chamber was awash with darkness and power, the big Z amped up to take his shot. Fenn stumbled behind a boulder and ducked down, still punching buttons on his device, fumbling in his pockets at more tiny gadgets.

Satana watched the arch-demon bring up his bulging arms, his incantation echoing into a round, a dark song, the words thickening the electric, brimstone air. All the energies he'd called forth coalesced, gathered into a ball of white-orange lightning that flashed between his powerful hands.

This might actually work. And the demon wasn't half as strong as he would be in another few days. As much as she hated to admit it, she'd be hard pressed to match his will. Satana edged closer, ready to snatch up the amulet.

Zarathos hurled the brilliant orb at the vault, shouting the final words in a victorious cry.

"...malus ad esium!"

The gathered power splashed across the vault like a broken water balloon and instantly dissipated, shaking the walls. There was no effect on the box. At all.

Zarathos sagged, spent, and in the bland, drained air Satana felt what was going on outside. The Triumvirate was about to be hit by a freight train.

Satana stepped to the shaking demon's side and dragged Fenn to them by will. The mortal squawked and stumbled backward, tripping on rocks, cradling his machine. As soon as he was close enough, she made a hole and pushed all of them through.

They landed in Fenn's living room, almost too late. As her tunnel snapped closed behind them, the faintest echo of the psychic blast that pounded the cavern whispered through. The echo knocked all of them off their feet. Zarathos crashed onto the coffee table, snapping off two of its legs. Fenn yelped and tumbled into the sofa.

Satana had landed on knees and elbows, and lowered herself flat to the fake wood floor, exhausted, fuming. Zarathos was out cold—he'd blown a fuse—she was hungry and weak, and they'd led their enemies to the vault. *And* left them alive, because Zarathos and his big fat ego had been so sure that he'd succeed.

Maybe they won't be able to open it, either. The hope was faint but not entirely unrealistic. Even in his weakened state, Zarathos should have at least put a dent in it. The spell he'd used would have cracked open a diamond.

All we have to do now is completely recover, figure out how to break the seal, fend off attacking realm protectors packing big magic, and keep Zarathos from triumphantly leading us to failure, as is his nature.

Satana pressed her cheek to the cool floor and closed her eyes.

o——————o

GHOST Rider and Blade dropped into the dirt pit and took positions on either side of the tunnel going down, keeping a healthy distance. Caretaker floated over them within an invisibility stream of crackling power, her lips moving silently, her gaze distant. Purple mist floated all around the Suns, glittering through the first rays of sunlight, more of it pluming out of Nico's raised staff; the color faded to invisible as it radiated outward. Magik had opened a portal and stood in the glimmering orange disc on the ground behind Caretaker, holding her flaming sword.

Ghost Rider felt energy changes deep underground, the Spirit sensing them like Robbie might notice a faraway sound: a car door slamming a block away, traffic in the city. The input was muffled, unclear, but the Spirit caught the black scent of demon, felt a shift in pressure as the ground rumbled. The Spirit of Vengeance was snarling to get after

Zarathos for what he'd done and Robbie was right there with it, horrified, angry, but Caretaker was about to lay down the law and it wouldn't do to get in her way.

The leader of the Midnight Suns had her hands raised, energy snapping up and down her arms in branching veins of strobing white. Her short silvery hair floated and twisted around her face. She'd worn black since Agatha's passing and the brilliant glow of her magic stood out like lightning against her dark clothes.

She brought her hands down suddenly, aiming at the hole, and a white river of light slammed into the narrow shaft, pouring up through her body and out of her, a raging torrent of power and intention.

It was over in a few seconds. Caretaker floated down and landed, scowling. Ghost Rider caught the reason as the energy blast dissipated.

"They got out before it hit," Caretaker confirmed. "But the cloaking spell is still intact. Can you feel it?"

Robbie couldn't feel anything, the air seemed strangely blank except for Nico's protective mist, but the other Suns nodded as they fell in, gathering around the hole. All around them, the hills were waking up to a new day, birds singing, woodland creatures stirring. There was no evil nearby.

"An emptiness," Magik said.

"An absence," Nico agreed, and Blade nodded again.

Robbie shifted his perspective, looking for a negative rather than a positive, and found what they were talking about. The magic was elusive, clever. He would have missed it without a clue.

"We'll all go see," Caretaker said. "Nico, keep our shield going. Blade, you're rear guard. Robbie, help him down, it's deep."

Caretaker waved a hand and disappeared into the shaft. Magik and then Nico followed, levitating after her. Blade was still scanning the rocky hills and stunted trees when Robbie touched his arm and opened a door into the hollow beneath them.

They stepped into a rock-strewn cavern just as it lit up, Nico making her protective mist glow. It was like standing in a snow globe of neon glitter that had just been shaken, motes of glowing light spinning lazily throughout the vast room. Robbie could smell demon on the tainted air, but the scent was fading fast.

The vault was in a small chamber off the east wall, surrounded by rubble. Robbie portaled to it just as Caretaker got there, the other Suns right behind. It looked like a big packing crate, or a trunk made out of old iron. The metal was smooth; there weren't any openings.

Caretaker put her hand on the vault and closed her eyes. A frown formed.

"Tempus cincinno," she murmured, still frowning. Her strong fingers traced lines and circles across the flat top.

"Time lock?" Nico reached out to touch the metal. Her makeup was smeared from crying, and Robbie had to force his guilt to a back burner. The Spirit in him howled anew for retribution.

"Explains why they couldn't get in," Blade said. He and Magik had also reached in to touch the vault.

"Why?" Robbie asked. He'd mostly been an ass-kicker before joining the Suns. His magical education was preschool level.

"Time locks are set to expire based on variations in ethereal energies," Nico said. "Kind of like carbon dating, but in a time capsule, and it measures atomic vibration. When the spells are done properly, they're pretty much impossible to break by brute force. The magic either has to be unwound, which can take forever, or you just have to wait."

Magik cleared her throat. "You can also mimic the conditions the seal requires, but that only works for poorly made spells. Which this is not."

Caretaker shook her head, her eyes still closed. "The signature is centuries old. Magic of the Blood."

"Any idea when it's going to open?" Blade asked.

"It is fraying now," Caretaker said. "There are hollows open within the weave. Recent."

The Midnight Sun?

Blade gave it voice. "Could be coordinating with the alignment."

Caretaker finally opened her eyes, kept the frown. "Perhaps."

"I can take it forward," Magik said. "Travel until it opens, bring back what's inside."

"No," Caretaker said. "No time traveling until after the alignment. It's not safe and you'll expend too much energy."

"Let me try," Nico said. "Just an opening spell. The Staff might automatically adjust the environment to make it happen."

"Or it might send all of us six months into the future," Caretaker said. "No. We'll return to the Abbey and fashion an unspelling. We should at least be able to speed its decay."

"But they could come back with their own unspelling," Nico said.

"We're leaving it here?" Robbie asked. He felt like he'd missed something.

Caretaker smiled faintly. "Try to take it."

Ghost Rider took a stride closer, eager to burn off some energy, then fell into a squat, looking at the pile of rocks underneath. The vault was fixed in the air, floating a handspan above the rubble. It wasn't going anywhere. He stood up.

"Nico's got a point," Blade said. "The Triumvirate got away, and it could be set to open off of anything—magical attack, interaction... We should at least guard it."

"The rate of dissolution is gradual and they're not strong enough to take it," Caretaker said. "And while I'm working, the rest of you are going to track the Triumvirate on the mirror table and stop them from returning. Zarathos was depleted or he would have blown up half the mountain, but he'll gain strength the longer he's on Earth. We already know Satana is collecting souls, but transport has a cost. The best time to attack is now."

The Spirit in Robbie roared with approval, and the other Suns straightened up, shaking off their nightmares. Robbie hadn't been privy to what the Spirit had witnessed through the penance stare, but something in Caretaker had changed, for the better. Her shoulders were back, and her blue eyes snapped. She was engaged, present, ready to fight.

Ready to let us fight. The Spirit of Vengeance gloried in Robbie's thirst for payback and Robbie rolled with it, feeding the Spirit his own self-righteous anger. Zarathos had used him as a tool to hurt his friends, and that bastard was going to be sorry. The Triumvirate was toast.

Magik sliced a portal and they all ran through, Ghost Rider at the head of the pack.

o———————o

AT the Abbey, Blade sent the kids to change into stealth gear and headed for the war room. Magik always dressed light, usually a tank and shorts because her armor got hot, but it was full dark—nearly 2300—and she was showing too much pale skin to sneak around. Nico needed to take the flashy pins off her coat, and Robbie was in a soccer jersey. They had the magic to deflect attention, but Blade also thought they all might need a personal moment after what had happened.

Blade took a minute himself, "walking like a person," as Nico liked to say, through the Abbey's cool corridors. When he passed Hunter's room, Charlie fell in at his side, bumping Blade's thigh with her head.

"Good girl," he said, and crouched down to pat her neck, resting his cold fingers on her hot, velvety skin. He could still feel echoes of Michael Wilson's terror and sorrow, and didn't try to dodge the feelings. He petted Charlie and breathed through the sadness, comforted by the hellhound's friendly company, the faint sounds of the other Suns getting ready drifting through the still air. What he wouldn't do was hate himself. There was no way to make up for a lost innocent, ever, but taking action to make things better was the way through, the only way that he'd found; even monsters could be useful. He knew it, and the truth kept him sane. That hadn't changed.

Something changed Caretaker. He looked up at the forge's heavy door, in shadow at the Abbey's north end. She'd gone straight to it, saying she'd meet them in the war room shortly. The forge chamber was a cavern hewn from giant blocks of quarried stone, the oldest part of the Abbey. The air inside was always warm and thick with magic. It was a good place to meditate, if the fire-demon was sleeping. Blade wondered what she'd seen that had flipped her switch.

"Hey, Charlie!" Nico hurried across the foyer. Black hoodie, black jeans, black combat boots.

The hellhound thumped her tail, whapping dust out of the Berber rug in the corridor, and Nico knelt to pet her. She looked up at Blade, stroking the dog's sleek back.

"You doing okay?"

He nodded. "I'll live. You?"

Nico stood up, still rubbing behind Charlie's ears. "Yeah, I just… I know I'm a selfish jerk sometimes, I don't always think before I act, but I just want you to know—"

"You're good," Blade said, fully aware that she wouldn't be deterred.

"—that I'm not trying to be such a weirdo, and I'm way better than I used to be, and if I'm ever bothering you or being too whatever, please just tell me to stop."

"That never works," Blade said, and won a smirk from Nico, and a flash of relief. She dropped it and they continued to the war room.

They were the first to arrive and walked straight to the table of shining black glass. After Caretaker, Nico was best at running the table. Robbie and then Magik came in a minute later, both in black, just as Nico called up a wide overview of the Hudson River. The image played on a sphere the shape and size of an exercise ball, hovering over the shining black table. A million lights sparkled to either side of the Hudson's dark water. Cars and cabs crawled the streets between the glowing buildings.

"Where was the machine shop?" Nico asked, and Blade pointed to the Ludlow area, then followed the river south, stopping around Riverdale.

"And that's the warehouse of the dead artifact dealer," he said. He studied the image, finding Mount Vernon, east. "Two of the soulless came from around here. Seems like everything is happening just north of the city. I wouldn't include the RV; it had been traveling."

Nico nodded. She took a breath, and the Eye zoomed in to cover the rough triangle north of the city proper. Woodlawn was at its center, four hundred acres of bones and monuments, adjoining Van Cortlandt Park to the west. Thousands, hundreds of thousands of tiny white dots and lines appeared overlaying the sprawl, far fewer of them in the uninhabited areas. They blinked and jumped, joining the millions of city lights.

"Oops," Nico said, and the new tracings changed to red.

Robbie leaned in, watching the tiny specks glitter, the minuscule lines winking in and out of place. "Souls?"

"Some, but mostly exchanges of power. Like, intense interactions and feelings. I was thinking we could look for energy transfers that end in dead spots. We're assuming Zarathos is hiding under one of those shields, right?"

Blade studied the vast sea of sparkles. "We have to narrow it down some. Did anyone get a look at the man who was with them?"

A round of negatives. They'd all noticed the faint gamma glow, the shield that had muted the demons, but the Triumvirate's third had been crouched and covering his head.

"Zarathos will draw psychic pain only from humans," Magik said, speaking up for the first time. Her voice was subdued. "He has been Mephisto's slave. Very recently freed, I think. His power was not even at half strength."

"So we're looking for blank spots, right?" Robbie asked. "There are about a million."

Nico shook out her shoulders and blew out a breath slowly. "Negative energy only…"

Nearly half of the red glitter disappeared. Blade was surprised there'd been that many positive interactions happening in the state at this hour, even on a Saturday night.

Caretaker walked into the room, striding with purpose. She stepped to the table's other side and put her hands on the glass.

The picture sharpened, and the lines stopped jumping, blinking out. There was a sense of direction added, each tiny line flaring at one end before snapping away. Like little flashing pointers.

They all looked for patterns, but it was Nico's picture, so she felt it first.

"There, right over the park," she said. "In that spread-out area."

"I see it," Robbie said.

The Eye of Ereshkigal blinked, and the new image was a neighborhood where the apartments and shops had given way to individual homes, tightly packed. There were hundreds of sparkling red dots and lines, just like everywhere else... but in one spot, all the lines were arrowing in a single direction, disappearing into a small blank space.

Nico tilted her head, eyelids fluttering. The table's eye closed in, the angle changed. The red tracings disappeared, became the faintest smudge of pinkish light. There was a cluster of dark one- and two-story houses, a few lights on, television screens flickering. Not a lot of cover, but there was some shrubbery, a line of thick hedges, and there were cars parked on the tree-lined streets.

"That's Park Hill, I think," Blade said. He couldn't get any sense off the buildings, the light was too diffuse, but at least one of them was eating energy and blocking the fact. The lots were too close together; the blank spot covered at least four houses.

"There's a street name… Addison? Edison. It looks like a dead end. A cul-de-sac." Nico tried to get another angle, but the table wouldn't focus any closer.

Blade didn't know the area, but Robbie was already tapping on his phone, thumbs flying.

"Got it," he said, seconds later, and handed his phone to Blade. There was a satellite image of what was on the table, one pair of homes on the north side of a cul-de-sac, backed up to a pair facing a different street. A line of hedges ran between them. Blade tapped one and the address popped up; it was for rent. Technology was its own kind of magic.

Caretaker took her palms off the table, looking at Blade. "I expect you'll be extremely circumspect in your approach."

Blade nodded. The Suns had been caught off guard, twice, but that was before they'd known what they were up against. They needed to get in close without being noticed, surprise the Triumvirate… and then let Magik toss them into Limbo, where she'd have the power to manage them, at least to some extent. The Suns could attack with a territorial advantage. "Nico, can you cloak our magic going in?"

The witch nodded, chewing at her lower lip. "I should've done it before. And put up a defense against spells. I wasn't thinking."

Magik and Robbie were throwing off the same kind of low-grade guilt as Nico. The penance stare had unsettled all of them. Blade understood how Robbie felt, losing control, and while he had an idea of Nico's experience based on her apology, he couldn't imagine what Magik had gone through. Of all the younger Suns, Illyana had the most baggage, and undoubtedly the biggest body count. Blade was still trying to come up with something appropriately reassuring when Caretaker spoke again.

"Our mistakes inform us, if we survive them. You are each powerful, talented, brave, and the Triumvirate will fall at your hands. And if we can collect the Varkath Star, we'll be able to protect Earth from demonic attack throughout the alignment, and beyond. The Midnight Suns' success will be assured."

Caretaker didn't smile, but her calm confidence was like a balm, and Blade responded to it as much as anybody, restored somewhat by her simple approval. She was right. The Suns were going to put an end to whatever self-serving bullshit the Triumvirate were up to, stop them from doing any more damage.

"Let's go," Robbie said. "And if we wrap it up fast, it's still movie night. Fast and Furious marathon in the common when we get back."

Nico rolled her eyes. "We did that last week."

"We *started* it last week."

She punched him in the arm and Robbie pulled a stern face, pointing at her dramatically.

"Violence isn't always the answer, young lady," he said, and just managed to block a second punch. Both of them were grinning, eyes shining. Magik even smiled a little at the performance.

Blade nodded at Caretaker. "We'll be back soon."

"I'll be here," Caretaker said. No reticence, no hesitation.

Good. Whatever she'd seen, it had reminded her of why she'd formed the Suns in the first place.

Blade led the team out of the war room, remembering why *he'd* joined. They were going to handle the hell out of this.

8

MAGIK'S portal opened onto a dark alley between two of the houses, next to a clump of garbage and recycling bins. To their right was a line of tall, browning hedges. Nico spoke protection for the Suns as they stepped out, careful to glamour the spell's power draw. She didn't call for the Staff of One—it was loud and proud, and right now they needed sneaky.

Spell accomplished and holding—it would deflect demonic energy, as well as hide them from notice—Nico looked around, searching for the house that was collecting soul energy. She could feel darkness swirling in the air, like the very faintest of breezes...

"It's one of those," Blade whispered, and nodded to the houses behind the hedge. The one on the left was a two-story, pale-yellow cracker box facing the tree-lined street. It was slightly bigger than its neighbor, a tan ranch-style home on a heavily landscaped lot.

Nico observed for herself. The energies she sensed seemed to be going to the larger house, but it was hard to say. The entire block was humming with shifting power.

"I'll take a closer look," Blade whispered. "Wait here."

He flashed away, silently. A dog barked a block over, a car started up, someone was taking out the trash. It was weird to be in a regular neighborhood after so long at the Abbey, surrounded by normal people doing normal people things. The air was cool but unpleasant, heavy with darkness; the feel was mildly oppressive, like the mugginess before a thunderstorm.

The smell doesn't help. The garbage cans weren't new, and the summer had been hot.

Blade flashed back to them. "It's the yellow one. Windows are all blocked, there's one person downstairs. I can't get anything except that his heart is beating, but there are a lot of machines running inside."

Nico frowned. The steady flow of psychic energy seemed to be stuttering, like something had interrupted it.

"I think they might be moving," Nico said. "Something's different, the draw is losing coherence."

"Best time to kick in the door, then," Blade said. "A third of the Triumvirate is better than none, and we can get one of those shields for Banner to look at. I'm going to grab whoever's in there and then we'll reassess. Robbie, Magik, come in through the front when you hear us. Nico and I will go in through the back. Let's be cool—there are a lot of civilians around and we already know this guy's a bomb-maker."

Nico nodded along with the rest of them, maintaining their protection as they cut through the hedge. She was glad for all the practice Caretaker and Agatha had pushed, teaching her to divide a part of her focus to maintain a spell while turning her attention elsewhere. It wasn't exactly second nature yet, but she was getting better all the time.

Blade and Nico split off from Robbie and Magik, who circled around to the front. Blade flashed to the low back steps next to a tattered rose bush and waited for everyone else to get into place. He held up a hand to Nico, reaching toward the back door's knob with the other.

"On five," he breathed, and held up a finger, then two, then three. Nico reinforced the strength of her cloak deflector, ready to manifest the Staff at the first sign of trouble.

Blade pulled the door open. It had been dead-locked, but the wood splintered around the metal bar with a splintering crunch, and they were inside, moving through a bare kitchen that smelled like disinfectant and was daubed in eerie green light. The light gave off a magical flavor, faint but palpable.

Through a hall and into a living room, where a lone man sat on a couch in front of a broken coffee table. Blade was on him in an instant, picking him up and pushing him against one of the bare white walls, faintly lit by one of the green-light machines. The guy didn't resist at all. He was hot, looked like James Dean with better hair, but his eyes were vacant and somehow flat and his energy...

Soulless. His energy was as blank as his gaze, flat and threaded with darkness. Like an empty room full of squirmy shadows. Nico instinctively put her right hand in her hoodie's pocket, touching the taped bit of razor she had brought along.

Blade held the soulless up easily. "Check the other rooms, and watch out for—"

BOOM!

o———————————o

FENN had commissioned a detection web for a block in every direction of the rental house. He hadn't been certain the spell would work—the mystic who'd made it was still learning—but it was triggered less than an hour after their return from Transia. The breach was less than a second long, and he only knew because his sensor bracelet flashed red; he had no magical power of his own, but he more than made up for the lack with technical prowess.

Fenn quickly gathered his important papers, sorry to let go of the workshop, but the bulk of his designs were safe; he'd planned all along for unexpected visitors, although he'd hoped to avoid them until farther along. No matter, his resources were in place. He had rented three other houses and had lines on a dozen empty ones suitable to their purposes. There were alarms and escape plans for all of them; he'd placed a mechanical sensor in the Transian vault chamber, jammed into a crack in the floor, so that the Triumvirate would be aware of intruders. He'd financed the entire Triumvirate plan himself, his not inconsiderable life's savings were invested, and while Zarathos's first attempt to open the vault had been unsuccessful, Fenn knew it was going to pay off. The vault was sealed by a degrading spell. He'd taken measurements; with a bit of consultation, he'd be able to work out exactly when it was due to expire, certainly well before the alignment... and he had two powerful, committed teammates to help hurry the process along.

Zarathos was still on the floor in the remains of the coffee table, but seemed to be asleep now rather than unconscious. Satana had refused to move him to his room. She was in a terrifying mood, but she acted promptly enough when Fenn told her the enemy had arrived. For all her faults, Satana Hellstrom had quality survival instincts. She transported them to the rental van parked a block away, along with a hefty box of equipment. At Fenn's request, she left her servant behind, the better to lure their attackers in.

Fenn plucked his detonator out of the box of toys and crawled into the driver's seat, leaving the succubus and the groggy demon in back. His portable shield bathed the stuffy space in warm green, hiding them from the invaders. He put his key in the van's ignition and waited until his phone alerted him that the rental property's doors had been breached. It didn't take long.

Satana appeared in the passenger seat, her arms folded across her ample bosom, her succulent lower lip pushed out. "Now what?"

Fenn smiled and flipped the switch on the side of the detonator. "Now, this."

He pushed the small red button on top of the box, and the earth trembled. A beat later, the roar of a massive explosion cut through the night. It was actually six separate explosions, including four of his marvelous hybrid gamma shields, but the blast was a perfect harmony, a sustained note of deadly destruction.

Still smiling, Fenn started the van to drive them into the city, to their next sanctuary. The Triumvirate would prevail. Fenn had dreamed it. He'd been called crazy and worse through the years by those who'd dismissed his righteous ambition as unattainable, who'd dismissed *him,* his pain, his loss, his visions of vengeance and chaos. He'd been cheated and lied to, underestimated, laughed at, but he had persevered, never lost sight of his purpose. Fenn would have his vengeance, and the last laugh. And he would laugh loudest and longest.

In his rearview mirror, Fenn could see the glow of new fire, and was satisfied.

o———————————o

THE explosion was thunderous, a deafening crash of destruction. Magik was standing next to Ghost Rider when the house around them became a tornado. Metal, wood, concrete, plaster, pulverized and splintering debris flew, igniting, a hurricane of pressure and sound blasting Magik's senses.

The Suns were slammed off their feet. Magik spun through the air, blind and lost, slashing at a giant piece of burning couch that tried to take her head—

"Usporiti!" Nico's voice cut through the chaos of disaster, purple light flashing like a strobe—

—and the spray of smoking debris seemed to freeze all around them.

Not quite frozen. Magik hit the floor, looking up wide-eyed at a thousand broken bits and pieces hanging in the air. The house was still coming apart, but at a crawl. Billows of dust and smoke inched larger, and chunks of wall and flooring sprayed in extremely slow motion from the blast sites, radiating outward. Flames painted what was left of the walls.

Magik rose, saw Nico holding her staff, scratched and bleeding from a dozen small wounds, surrounded by the suspended rain of smoking, flaming matter. Blade had been launched headfirst into the wall and came up holding the dead soulless, the creature's flesh slashed by shrapnel; its blood ran freely—Nico's spell had not affected flesh. The Daywalker was also bleeding, but his wounds were already healing closed. He dropped the corpse and ducked a tangle of flaming wire a handspan from his face. Ghost Rider lurched to his feet and spun through the destructive rain, knocking bigger debris out of the air with his chains.

The night sky was visible through the gaps of the expanding house. Flames had erupted all around them, but like the rest of the chaotic destruction, the fires crept ever so slowly, lighting the collapse with strange shadows and banked heat.

"Here!" Magik called, and cut a portal through the morass, the familiar light of Limbo like fresh air in the choking ruin.

"It'll go back to normal if I leave!" The Staff of One seemed to float in Nico's bleeding fingers. "It'll blow up the other houses!"

"I've got it!" Magik called. She put her right foot in Limbo and let its power flow into her. In her mind's eye she extended a heavy umbrella over the exploding house, a wet blanket of gravity. All around them, the arcs of ascent and descent halted, every particle weighted to fall. It wouldn't stop the fires but should keep the blast radius confined.

"Go, go!" Blade pointed at Magik's portal and Robbie ran through, his Spirit's face grinning. Nico sidestepped for the disc, concentrating, and Blade was at her side in an instant, lifting and carrying her to the portal. Blackening splinters and ragged, flaming drywall gently descended all around them, floating like the lightest snow. Blade weaved them through it in a flash, small pieces pattering against his whipping coat.

As soon as they were on the bridge, Magik stepped into Limbo after them. She narrowed the disc but kept its visual window open.

"We're clear," Blade said, and Nico let go.

The Suns watched the explosion return to speed. A house's worth of fiery, floating debris slammed into the ground, flames and smoke billowing upward, sparks soaring. The homes surrounding it didn't seem to be damaged.

"What was the spell?" Magik asked Nico.

"Slow down," Nico said. "In Croatian."

The Staff of One didn't like to repeat spells, often

redirecting Nico's energies. The witch was continually looking up new ways to ask for useful things. She could say *open* in hundreds of languages.

"They went somewhere," Blade said. "We'll find them."

"Damn straight," Robbie agreed.

They sounded far more confident than Magik was feeling. So far, the Triumvirate had stayed ahead of them and the Suns had yet to land a blow, besides denying them a few resources. She wondered if Mephisto knew that one of his most unwilling servants was on Earth, seeking an amulet that could control him. She had not faced Zarathos before, but Mephisto had delighted in relaying stories of the rebellions he'd quelled; the inter-dimensional demon had been a favorite, as Zarathos had been so easily tricked.

For a fleeting instant, she considered letting Mephisto know. The Hell Lord would fetch Zarathos back to his prison, the Triumvirate would be dissolved... but of course, Mephisto was never an answer to any problem. He was petrol to flame, always, and might take such a message as proof that she felt anything about him, which she did not.

Magik cut a portal back to the Abbey, suddenly tired in spite of the power flooding her system, the resuscitation of physical contact with Limbo. She vaguely hoped that the Triumvirate would lay low for a few hours. In Transia she'd been brutally reminded of the horror of her existence, of the apocalypse she could become, and she very much wanted to walk the Abbey grounds, clear her mind of everything but the salted wind and the cool darkness. She was proud to fight alongside the Suns, she trusted and respected them, but solitude was what she craved most when she felt this way. The blackness that lived in Magik's soul was always looking for weakness, a way to get out, and for the first time since she'd come to the Abbey she could feel the Darkchilde clawing the walls of her prison, eager talons gouging at the tiny cracks in the stones. Emotional pain created those cracks. The evil would never get out again, ever, but the Ghost Rider's penance stare had stirred Darkchilde all the same and Magik needed her mind to be clear and steady. She needed some peace.

Perhaps the others felt the same. They walked to the Abbey without speaking. When Ghost Rider became Robbie Reyes again, he had lost some of his earlier enthusiasm, his shoulders slumped. Nico reabsorbed her staff and held her hand over a deep scratch on her arm, her eyes red from smoke. Blade's expression was unreadable, as it so often was, but Magik thought he might be tired, too.

Caretaker opened the front door. She looked them over, assessing their condition at a glance.

"They got away and tried to blow us up," Nico announced.

Caretaker nodded, stepping back so they could file inside. "I'll need more time to research the vault's mechanism and prepare our spell. You should all rest. You've done enough for today."

"But the Triumvirate's on the run," Robbie said. "We should hit them before they have time to get settled."

"And track them how, if they're moving?" Caretaker asked.

"The Midnight Sun is just beginning. It's a marathon, not a sprint, and you'll be no use at all if you don't take care of yourselves. We won't always have the time, but we have it now. Take it."

She turned and walked away, back toward the war room.

"She's not wrong," Blade said. "I want to do some more digging, see if I can find anything on whoever owns or rented that house. Unwind, eat, get some sleep. We'll be back at this bright and early."

Magik didn't wait for Robbie or Nico to protest, or argue again about which movie to watch. She nodded at the other Suns and turned, the cool night welcoming her with open arms, soothing, uninterested in who she was or the things she'd done. When she was a thousand years in her grave, the ocean would still beat against the lonely cliffs, the moon would still shine on the whispering trees. Magik embraced her insignificance and was comforted.

9

THE moon rose and set, and the Abbey was finally still, as silent as a tomb. Caretaker sat at her desk, making notes and calculations, calling up books that she needed to consult. She'd taken the vault's measure in its underground chamber and believed it was meant to open prior to the Midnight Sun, but only by a few weeks. By her rough estimation, the lock would fail when the Nowhere's outer rim reached the path of the alignment, four months from now. The seal was strong, she doubted she could break it outright, but she was confident that she could at least unthread its perception of time, speeding up its dissolution.

And what does it mean, that the vault was set to open now, in the shadow of the alignment? She sat back in her chair, pinched the bridge of her nose. The collection had a spell to summon Mephisto, a charm that could control him, and a shield that could defend against his favorite method of attack, a blast of Hellfire. Somebody had sealed the items away to call forth Hell's ruler at a chaotic time of shifting possibilities. *To empower him, hand him Earth's realm? Or to make him a pet to an ascending ruler?*

In a way it didn't matter, but she was frustrated by how much she didn't know, and curious as to how the Triumvirate had learned about the collection. No one had stumbled across it accidentally; the mirror table still couldn't find the exact spot, the concealment spell diverting all attention, and the villains were well prepared for their effort—gamma shields to hide behind, booby-trapped lairs, self-destruct mechanisms. The human member of the Triumvirate had to be responsible; neither Satana Hellstrom nor Zarathos were engineers. But what was *his* goal, and how had he known about the vault?

A descendant of the Mephisto cult, perhaps. There was no Zarathos cult that she was aware of, but humanity believed in all manner of madness; it was possible. Zarathos had reason to hate Mephisto—if he got the Varkath Star he'd presumably dethrone Hell's ruler… But why would a human care about the reordering of Hell's power structure?

Theorizing is fine when you've got free time, but keep focus on what matters most. They can't have the Varkath Star. We need it.

Caretaker would fight the Triumvirate no matter the circumstances, but having the Varkath Star, now… She could lay to rest a fear she'd carried for centuries. There were prophecies about the Midnight Sun that could not be allowed to bloom, and an amulet of such power would prevent the worst of them.

She summoned a pot of black tea and went back to work, only marginally aware of the hours slipping by. She already had pieces of more than a dozen strong spells, phrases and intentions that should resolve different parts of the seal, but she wasn't confident about bringing them all together. Agatha would have known how to take the disparate parts and weave them into a seamless assault, but of course that was another thing that didn't really matter.

Nico might be able to do it. The girl's potential was vast. She was barely trained, her work with the finicky Staff of One still inconsistent, but she already had access to energies that had taken Caretaker decades to cultivate. The girl could assist, when it was time.

The time is now. Today. You can't wait. The Triumvirate would go back to Transia soon. Perhaps they were there now, chipping away at the magic that kept them from the Varkath Star. Satana and Zarathos were both sorcerers, although Caretaker suspected neither was particularly adept; their forceful attack on the vault hadn't indicated a measured or discerning approach, or that they knew how the seal operated. She hoped she was right. Caretaker went back to her work, forcing herself to focus.

She was researching the possibilities of adding a corruption incantation when there was a light tap on her door. Caretaker looked up, realized the sun had risen.

Nestled between cliffs, the Abbey was almost always in shade, but looking through the trio of windows behind her desk, she could clearly see the trees surrounding the grotto. The dawn was well past.

"Yes?"

Blade stepped in. "I got a name connected to that house."

"Oh?"

The dhampir nodded. "John Doe. He signed a one-year rental agreement about six weeks ago."

Caretaker wasn't sure why he looked pleased. "Not a name that will advance our search."

"No, but it gave me an idea," Blade said. "I found a storage unit less than an hour north, rented on the same day, under the name Max Mustermann. John Doe in German."

Caretaker nodded. "That's something."

"I'd like to take the Suns with me to check it out," Blade said. "It won't take long."

"Now?"

"Why not? They're awake, eating breakfast."

"Take Robbie and Magik," Caretaker said. "I'd like Nico with me. Ask her to meet me at the forge when she's finished."

Blade nodded. "When are we going back to Transia?"

Caretaker stood, picking up her pages of notes. "Later today, I expect. Don't linger in the city."

Blade nodded again and was gone.

Caretaker started for the forge, stretching her back as she walked, feeling her age. She climbed the wide stone steps and entered the cavernous chamber, the giant round window into the demon's lair alight, as always. The Sumerian demon slept most of the time but was always burning, lending warmth and light to the wide, shadowy room where the Suns sometimes practiced. The chamber had been formed by elemental magic and still echoed with vibrations of the force used to create it; the bonds that held its demon in place were vital and strong. Both imbued the chamber with a magic-friendly signature of possibility, an excellent environment for creation; the Abbey had produced some of the finest metalwork currently in use by Earth's greatest fighters. The Sorcerer Supreme was overdue to visit, in fact. He'd promised to help her forge new armor for the team. She'd meant to call him weeks ago...

Why did I think I had more time? The twenty-first century's alignment had been mapped out since the last Midnight Sun, written and prophesied about for a thousand years... and yet here it was, and she hadn't gotten around to a hundred vital tasks she'd meant to complete before the rise. Time was the greatest magician, hiding its own passing, casting the illusion that there would always be more.

Caretaker walked to the center of the chamber and sat cross-legged on the bare floor facing the forge's great window. The flames were low, banked to the bottom half of the glass, the inscriptions circling the round chamber glowing only faintly. When in use, the flames filled the chamber and heated the entire Abbey to an uncomfortable degree.

She took a few breaths, relaxing, and had just retrieved the necessary books from her office when Nico came in. The young witch sat on the floor next to her, reading the titles that Caretaker had assembled, stacked in front of them. She had a small cut under one eye and a bruise on her collarbone but looked much better for her rest, her eyes bright and alert. Caretaker handed her the papers, gave her time to read through them. Transmutation of atomic energy, a spell to induce natural decay, oxidation magic, lines of negation, will of ownership.

"We must create an intention that includes all of these elements," Caretaker said.

Nico nodded. "What about a thread picker? Like the Virottio?"

The Virottio was an ancient song, sometimes used to create space within established spells. It culled incidental power created by overlapping intentions.

"Yes, good," Caretaker said. She'd only been thinking of the seal, not the whole. The chant would make an excellent framework. She summoned *Songs of Transfiguration* from the library and handed it to Nico, adding a line to her notes.

Together, they opened the books and spread them out in a semi-circle, turned to the useful spells. The forge's firelight splashed across the faded pages, the dusty scent of ink and paper rising into the magic-rich air. Nico retrieved her laptop and made her own notes while they talked over the correct order, the girl both thoughtful and thorough. Agatha had taught her well, guided the bold young witch to the layers of nuance that complex magic required.

If she'd spent more time with Nico and less with Scarlet Witch...

Caretaker pushed the thought from her mind, refusing to follow it. She and Nico would break the seal, the Midnight Suns would vanquish the Triumvirate, and the Varkath Star would ensure that the alignment passed without upsetting the Balance. There could be no other outcome.

ZARATHOS woke up to confusion and shouting panic.

"Come on, baby, you don't have to push, I'm totally—ahhh! What the hell is that? What are you doing? Hey! Hey, *stop!*"

Zarathos opened his eyes and saw the succubus pushing a mortal at him. The man was fighting her, his face a mask of panic, but the succubus easily dragged him to where Zarathos lay, covered by a blanket on a cot in a small room.

"You should eat, my lord," Satana said, bowing her head while the frightened human flailed in her grasp.

Zarathos grabbed the man and brought him in close, slapping his hand across the vessel's chest, finding the light there. He cracked his own essence open, exposing his fathomless need, an emptiness inside of him that clawed hungrily for soul energy, eagerly pulling at the distressed human. The mortal shrieked as his soul spilled out of him, an ethereal vapor extruding from his pores, leaking out of his face holes. Zarathos accepted the drift of light, pulling it into himself.

The mortal kept squawking for help, so he twisted its head around and killed it, sucking up the last dregs of its energy before dropping it onto the floor.

Zarathos sat up on the rickety cot, trying to remember everything. Green light came from a box in the dusty corner of the little room. *The seal, our enemies...* Had they traveled in an automobile?

"Bring me more," he rumbled, and Satana bowed her head again.

"Of course, my lord." She pulled a slim device from her tight pocket and tapped at it. "They deliver themselves now. Isn't that amazing? I only had to put up my picture and they come here. Well, Fenn has me meet them on the corner, but that's no hardship. It's a great time saver."

"What of the vault? Our enemies?"

"Vault's still sealed—Fenn says it's on a timer—and our enemies have retreated for now." Satana turned toward the corridor, raised her voice. "Hey boys, a little help in here?"

A pair of fresh soulless entered the room, turned their servile eyes to the succubus. She motioned at the dead man.

"Take this away. Put it the room with all the boxes."

Her servants nodded, promptly set to work. As they carried the body out, Fenn sidled around them and walked in.

He bowed deeply. "Your Excellency."

"What timer do you speak of? The vault is sealed by time?"

"Yes, master. That is why your brilliant show of incredible might was unsuccessful. I have researched the seal's magic. It will open very soon, before the alignment." The red-headed mortal smiled, a sly smile. "And I believe our enemies will assist us. They have sorcerers of their own and will try to open the lock themselves. We won't have to wait long."

"We will go now to secure the vault," Zarathos said. A time lock. He had sensed some complexity to the vault's seal and ignored it, certain that his power would blow it apart.

"You and Satana must regain your strength first," Fenn said. "I'll know if the chamber is breached. We need not hurry, only be ready to move in and claim the amulet when the seal is broken."

"Who are these enemies?" Zarathos asked. "I saw the Ghost Rider, and the Mistress of Limbo. The old woman was Blood."

"Another was Blade, a vampire slayer," Fenn said. "He is half vampire himself, a fighter of some renown. The staff-bearer is a witch, Nico Minoru. They came for us last night, but we easily escaped. I believe I may have injured some of them; there were no bodies discovered, but they wouldn't have walked away unscathed. These Midnight Suns are no match against my machines. They cannot compete with your strength, Your Highness, or Satana's clever guile."

The Midnight Suns. Demon fighters. Zarathos had fought against the Midnight Suns long ago, but the members were not the same.

Zarathos stretched his arms. He was tired but so much better than when he'd escaped Mephisto's prison, his body strong. He had produced his breaking spell using power taken from the succubus, who was weak; the vault only remained sealed because of this, and because the nature of the enchantment was unusual. It was no reflection on him that he had overextended himself on borrowed power. If anything, it proved he could dominate his limitations by force of will.

A light flashed on one of Fenn's arm decorations. He frowned.

"Someone has found one of my storage units."

Satana brightened. "Right now? Where? I'll go."

"Unnecessary, Your Glory. It is only old equipment, nothing we can't afford to lose—"

"I will go," Satana said, clearly, and Fenn's head bobbed.

"Of course, mistress. I'll get the address. Only you mustn't lead anyone here, or reveal your presence to them."

"Do you think I was born yesterday?" Satana asked. "Come on, chop chop!"

Fenn hurried out. Satana walked to the side of Zarathos's cot and gifted him a smile.

"You will have your fill of souls when I return, Dark Lord," she said. "You will bathe in mortal essence and stand ready for your rule."

"And you will have your realm doubled, when I hold the Varkath Star," Zarathos allowed. She was weak, Fenn was weak, but Zarathos could not be fastidious in his condition. He should have waited before. The Varkath Star would have been his by now if he'd been able to rely on his own power to attain it.

"I care only that you will be my master," Satana breathed, the warmth and admiration in her gaze unmistakable. "I care only to be at your side when the vault opens, to witness your ascension."

Zarathos lifted his chin. His subjects were loyal, as was his due.

Fenn returned with instructions, and Satana disappeared in a pulse of pink light. Fenn backed out of the room, bowing, apologizing for the coarse environment, re-pledging his fealty.

Alone once more, Zarathos leaned back on the creaking cot and drifted into a healing sleep.

○————————○

THE storage unit was at one of those sprawling, empty complexes of tiny orange and white garages outside of Kingston, manned by a bored clerk in a small front office. Robbie went to find out the unit's number while Blade and Magik waited in the shade outside, between two rows of garages. There was a lone security guard sitting in a golf cart next to the office, reading a paperback and eating a breakfast sandwich out of a bag.

Robbie joined them a minute later. "337D," he said, and pointed northwest.

They started walking, keeping to the shade. The morning sun was bright, the air redolent of exhaust fumes from the nearby expressway. "How'd you get the number?" Blade asked.

"I told him Uncle Max had a stroke and couldn't remember whether or not he'd rented a unit."

Blade nodded. Clever. "Did the clerk remember Mustermann?"

"He never saw him. It was an online thing. He said he mailed the key out to a post-office box in Long Island a month and a half ago."

They walked to the end of the row and turned left, past a couple of dumpsters crammed with broken-down boxes. There were a few people visiting their stuff or unloading more, but only a smattering.

Unit 337D was in the last row of units near the back corner, lifeless except for a few flies buzzing around an empty soda can on the ground. Blade glanced around—no cameras—and grabbed the handle to the sliding garage door. He felt the lock snap when he lifted it, a brief squeal of metal that was hidden by the rattle of movement.

Machines and pieces of machines sticking out of boxes. Blade took a deep breath, hunting for chemical smells, hints of explosive materials, but there was nothing. No magic, either.

Old metal. Broken things.

"What is all this stuff?" Robbie asked. He touched what looked like a photo enlarger on an umbrella stand.

Blade shook his head. The unit was stacked with bizarre-looking equipment—boxes of switches with panels hanging open, mismatched metals soldered together and decorated with wires. Some of the pieces looked like expensive stereo equipment, sleek and well designed; more of it looked like science-fair robotics, homemade and unrecognizable.

The three of them started looking through the unit. Besides the unknown machinery, there were some unopened boxes of parts—small lights and circuit boards, mostly. Robbie came up with an engine block from a V-8 in a box of scrap metal and Magik found a hologram projector with a busted lens, but Blade couldn't even guess at what most of the junk was. Nothing appeared to be in working order. There were no personal items at all, no papers or photos or receipts.

Blade turned around, hands on his hips, frustrated. It was corroboration that their John Doe had built the gamma shields, but he'd already assumed as much. Demons weren't generally big on mechanics.

"Oh, hey," Robbie said, and lifted a moth-eaten canvas duffel bag out of box. The side was emblazoned with a faded red symbol, so dirty it was barely visible, but Blade recognized it instantly. A red skull atop six curling tentacles, bleached to a murky pink.

"That's Hydra," he said, and reached for the bag. Was the Triumvirate's human member associated with Hydra? The organization had been laying low since the Avengers blew up their command a few years back, but the fascist group had deep, ugly roots. Hydra had existed in some form or another since the rise of *Homo sapiens*.

Blade dumped the bag's contents on the cement floor, and a thousand assorted screws rattled out. Nothing. They dug around for a few more minutes, but the duffel was the only Hydra-related item they could find.

"You think Hydra's backing the Triumvirate?" Robbie asked.

Blade shook his head. "Not really their style anymore, is it? They're nation-building and buying politicians, making bank. Plus, the gamma generators are partly magical, and Hydra hasn't used mystics in decades. If John Doe has a connection, I don't think it's current."

"It's a place to look, perhaps," Magik said. "Inventors or engineers once associated with Hydra?"

That's a long list. "Maybe," Blade agreed, but he thought it was a dead end. Every other villain on Earth had a connection to Hydra; they were like a boot camp for egomaniacal lunatics. *Not much of a lead, but we could reach out to Captain America, see if he—*

Blade cut himself off. A burst of mystical energy had flared close by, there and gone before he could analyze it. *Gone or hidden?*

"We should go," he said, backing up a step from the open door. He hadn't seen any kind of alarm or sensor, but that didn't mean there wasn't one. He turned to look at Magik—

—and Zarathos stood in her place, towering over the boxes of junk, his giant red skull wreathed in flame. His piggy white eyes glowed with malice. Sour brimstone filled the air.

Blade snatched a pair of knives off his chest harness, but Robbie was already Ghost Rider, already whipping a chain at the giant.

Zarathos bellowed as the burning links wrapped around him and he whipped out a glittering longsword, smashing the chain to the ground. He stumbled backward, knocking over a stack of boxes.

"Emam ane es ianquin!" The demon shrieked, his baritone shaking the walls.

Blade flipped his knives at the demon's gut, one-two, but Zarathos was fast, striking them down with his sword, still gabbling furiously. Blade launched two more with the same result. The demon was an expert swordsman, as good as—

"Wait!" Blade shouted, but Robbie had already launched to tackle the demon, howling, and they crashed into more boxes, metal clanging to the ground.

Blade lunged forward and grabbed Ghost Rider's shoulders, jerking him back, but not before Robbie got a few punches in, hammering the demon's crimson skull. Robbie and his Spirit fought against the restraint, hard, and Blade struggled to hang on. Ghost Rider was violently strong. Zarathos backed against the metal wall of the unit and held his sword defensively, more nonsense thundering out of his lipless fanged jaws.

Ghost Rider broke Blade's hold but didn't attack again; Zarathos stayed in his defensive position.

"Magik?" Blade asked. He put up his hands, palms out.

"Es tu uru an!" Zarathos said. He sounded angry, threatening, but he lowered his sword slightly.

"We see Zarathos," Blade said, hoping she could understand, that the illusion was only one way. Agatha had taught him a spell that could melt glamour, but it took time and they needed to get gone, now. They'd been attacked by someone he couldn't sense at all. "Make a portal."

Blade mimed holding a sword and cutting a portal, not daring to draw his own katana. Zarathos glared at them, then sliced the air in front of him. Blade saw nothing, but felt the opening's magic, could smell Limbo's light air breeze into the stuffy little garage.

The giant demon put a foot forward, and the portal snapped into view. His massive, muscular frame wavered and then melted like cotton candy in water, dissolving, revealing Magik's slight form underneath. The smell of brimstone disappeared, replaced by the smell of burnt flesh; there were a dozen red weals across Magik's upper arms and the tops of her thighs from Robbie's chain, several blistering. Purple swellings rose along her jaw and her lower lip was split. Her gaze flicked back and forth between Blade and Ghost Rider, her teeth tightly clenched. She looked fully prepared to kill them both.

"We couldn't see you," Blade said. "Or smell you, or hear you. I'm so sorry, but we have to go right now."

Magik nodded but gestured for them to step through the portal first. Blade didn't blame her; if he'd been jumped like that, he wouldn't feel great about turning his back on his teammates right away, either.

As soon as they were all on the stone bridge, Robbie let go of the Spirit of Vengeance and started apologizing profusely. Blade felt bad, too. The glamour had been note-perfect. He'd only recognized Magik by her sword work.

If I hadn't... It didn't bear considering. They'd been seconds from tragedy.

Magik kept them on the bridge for a moment before cutting a door back to the Abbey, her wounds fading to bruises and pink burn spots by Limbo's thin orange light as Robbie continued to apologize. She stood with her eyes closed, her shoulders relaxing as the swellings and cuts healed.

"I'm just really so, so sorry," Robbie repeated, and finally stopped to take a breath. Magik hadn't said a word.

"If I had seen Zarathos, I would have attacked him," she said, finally, and Blade felt his chest loosen up.

"Your sword work was impeccable," Blade said, and Magik opened her eyes to look at him.

"Better than my knife throwing," he added. "If you'd gone on offense, you probably could have taken both of us."

Magik made direct eye contact. "Probably?"

Robbie and Blade both grinned and she smiled very slightly, the cut on her lip only a thin scratch as she turned to open a portal. Blade fervently hoped that the trauma of being attacked suddenly by two of her friends would fade as quickly.

The Triumvirate was racking up quite the list of offenses. Blade wondered if they knew how much trouble they were in. They'd pissed off all the Midnight Suns, and Blade for one wouldn't rest until they were very, very sorry.

10

NICO and Caretaker worked on their unspell for several hours, writing and rewriting to get everything tight. Magic was a lot like coding, Nico imagined. Not that she knew much about computers, but she knew there wasn't room to mess around. It wasn't like art, where you could smudge a funky line and keep going. If you wanted your program to work, everything had to be where it was for a reason. Complex magic was way more science than art.

Or, it's like an essay, and regular magic is a poem, she mused, gazing at the forge's endless fire while Caretaker read their final version, squinting at Nico's laptop. Nico knew they had it, could feel how right it was. Forming the intention reflected its energies in the thick ether of the forge room and gave off a kind of tingly smell, like spices.

Their unspell would gut the vault's seal, drain its power, and confuse its measurement capacity.

Caretaker finally nodded and handed the device back to Nico. "We're ready."

"I should eat before we go," Nico said, sending the spell to the printer in her room. Her computer said it was 1:33 p.m. "You think anyone made lunch?"

Caretaker had mentioned when the other Suns had returned, hours prior. Nico hadn't heard them come in, but Caretaker had a connection to the portal dais. She always knew who came and went.

"Let's see," Caretaker said, and stood up, dusting at her legs.

They left behind the rich warmth of the forge chamber and walked toward the barracks, not speaking. Caretaker wasn't the kind of person who liked to chat, and on a personal level, they didn't have much in common. Caretaker didn't like to laugh or watch movies, Nico didn't care about gardening, and the generation gap was about as wide as it could get. They both fought evil with magic, but that wasn't really a conversation starter.

They walked through the grand foyer, Nico smiling to herself, trying to imagine. *So, you fight evil using magic? Me too! Well, we have that in common. Yep, evil sure is bad. Good thing we've got magic to fight it.*

Caretaker slowed before they entered the barracks, turned to fix Nico with her cool blue gaze.

"I'm impressed by your work, Nico. I hadn't realized that you had done so much with deconstruction."

Nico smiled. "Last New Year's, Agatha spelled a copy of *The Golden Bough* to stick to the library's ceiling and said we could only use negation to get it down. I kind of went off the deep end researching."

Caretaker smiled, too, but her eyes were sad. "She was a good teacher."

Nico nodded, ready to talk more, *hoping* to, but Caretaker turned and started toward the kitchen again. Discussion closed. Nico followed, working to be grateful that they'd talked about Agatha at all without Caretaker going off on Wanda's recklessness.

The other Suns were in the kitchen, sitting over a plate of untouched sandwiches. They looked up as Caretaker and Nico came in. Blade and Magik wore neutral expressions, but Robbie looked unhappy and the atmosphere was weird, like they'd just walked in on an awkward conversation.

"What happened at the storage unit?" Caretaker asked.

Blade answered. "An attack. A full-sense glamour, probably Satana Hellstrom's work."

"Magik turned into Zarathos," Robbie said. "And we tried to take her down."

"I am undamaged," Magik said, and then no one spoke for a few seconds, and Nico understood the tension. Going through Limbo healed Magik, of course she was undamaged, but that didn't mean she hadn't been hurt or freaked out.

Nico felt bad that she hadn't been there. The Staff of One could dispel any illusion. She had dozens of words for *reveal* memorized.

"Did you find anything useful?" Caretaker asked, totally ignoring the subtext.

"The Triumvirate's John Doe may have been connected with Hydra at some point," Blade said. "There was an insignia on an old duffel. But no, nothing useful. Broken equipment, spare parts."

Nico couldn't stand the look on Robbie's face, the way his shoulders were hunched. "In better news, we have a spell ready. You guys up for a trip to Transia? We can go now. Maybe Satana will show up and you can make her apologize."

Robbie perked up a tiny bit, and Magik's jaw tightened but she sat up straighter. Blade looked like Blade, cool and dangerous. Nico had known him for more than a year and still couldn't read him most of the time.

"After lunch, I thought," Caretaker said. "From now on, the Suns travel as a team. I won't always be with you, but the rest of you will stay together, at least until the Triumvirate has been dealt with."

There were nods all around, and though Nico had lost her appetite at the thought of her friends fighting, she went to the table and grabbed half a sandwich. She needed the protein. She sat down and ate fast, almost matching Robbie for speed. Magik and Caretaker ate little, Caretaker laying out their plan between bites. They would go to Transia and ward the area around the underground chamber to alert them to enemies and protect against demonic attack; Caretaker and Nico would perform the unspell while the others kept guard, Magik and Ghost Rider at ground level,

Blade down in the vault's chamber with them.

"The vault may not open immediately," Caretaker explained, "but we should be able to pinpoint exactly when the seal *will* break, based on its rate of decline. We'll simply make a point of being there when it does."

"Zarathos will keep getting stronger, though," Robbie said. "If you weaken the seal, what's to stop the Triumvirate from blasting through?"

Nico felt comfortable answering. "No way that thing's going to open before it says it will. It's, like, *the* most complex magic. Think of the seal like a metal cage, set to open right at midnight. We can fuss with the lock, weaken some of the bars, but it is *closed*. If we fuss correctly, however, the clock moves to quarter 'til."

"Yeah, but what if they use the same magic?"

"Satana and Zarathos are both sorcerers, but they're also demons," Caretaker said. "An unspell requires subtle light magic they can't access."

"The human might be able to," Robbie said.

Nico smiled. "Then he already would have, brainiac."

"Quit flirting with me, witch, I'm trying to eat."

"You ate three sandwiches, you're not *trying* anything."

Robbie took a big bite, spoke through a mouthful. "So you're saying I'm a winner."

Caretaker stood, a look of mild distaste on her old face. "If we're all ready."

They split up to dress, Nico grabbing her coat and the printed spell, reading it through again as she walked out to the portal. Limbo opened beneath Magik's blade, and they all stepped through, Nico mentally reciting the order of the intentions they'd be working with.

"Nico, you'll ward the area, please," Caretaker said, as Magik opened a hole onto the Transian hills. It was night in Transia, dark and cold, the moon just rising. It was a good seven or eight hours later than home. The deep pit of broken rock looked bleak and forbidding.

Nico cut her thumb and drew the Staff, stepping to the front of the group. As always, she pulled from her strongest emotions to propel her intention, finding a memory from her time at Murderworld. The Staff ate blood and pain but it also shaped her will into reality, a deal she knew she was lucky to have. Most people suffered with nothing to show for it.

She thrust the Staff of One through the portal. "Tiakina me te whakatupato!"

Maori for *protect and warn*. She felt the Staff draw from her and send out a wave of energy, the same purple mist she'd conjured a dozen times. The mist disappeared as it radiated outward, blending into the air. Magic like the silkiest webs domed over the shattered ground, created a bubble of energy that would deflect most magical attacks and alert those inside to attempted trespass.

The Suns followed her into the cold dark, stepped from the Limbo bridge into the empty pit. Blade literally ran a perimeter check, silent and super fast, circling the area as the rest of them moved to the blacker hole in the ground.

Robbie and Magik took up guard, backs to the hole. Caretaker motioned Blade close and touched his arm, touching Nico's shoulder with her other hand, and transported them to the bottom of the well.

"Oro lux," Caretaker said, and a brilliant orb of yellow light sprang to life near the chamber's roof, a good twenty feet overhead. The light was too bright to look at directly, but the dusty stones were well lit. The room was huge, as big as the forge chamber and then some. Everything looked the same as earlier, cold and empty. Off to the left, the vault just hovered over a pile of rubble in its tiny cave.

Blade stayed at the bottom of the shaft, while Nico and Caretaker approached the metal box. Nico let go of the Staff and it floated next to her, intent on maintaining its protection. They stood on either side of the vault, and Caretaker nodded at her.

Here we go. Caretaker opened her arms and started to sing the Virottio in her strong alto, Nico joining in on the third ancient word with harmony, creating their frame for the undoing. The air between them grew charged, molecules spinning and listening as their song opened lines of force into the chamber. There would be no blast, no lightshow; if they were successful, the seal would only become less than it was.

Nico closed her eyes to focus on the repeating sounds, becoming them, finding oneness with her purpose.

o———————o

SATANA was enjoying a full-body massage when there was a tap at her door.

"Yes?"

Fenn stuck his head in and immediately jerked it back out. His voice warbled from out in the dingy hall. "Your Glory, I apologize for the interruption, but I have reason to believe that our enemies are in Transia right now, at the vault."

Satana sat up, waving off the four shirtless, empty vessels who'd been rubbing her naked flesh.

"Go make a cake," she said, and they bowed and promptly filed out, their hands still dripping oil. They pushed past Fenn and two more soulless she'd left standing in the hall. There were a dozen living empties crammed into Fenn's new house, which was smaller and uglier than the last one. Most of the new soulless were Zarathos's leftovers; the spare room was already full of dead bodies. Fenn had put some of the vessels to work moving boxes around or assembling more of his devices.

Satana dressed herself in leather and sable, decorating her legs with matching dagger sheaths that strapped to her thighs; the silver blades were enchanted, and also complemented her jewelry. She was more than ready to watch Magik get beat up again by her teammates. The morning's fun at Fenn's storage unit had been cut stupidly short when the vampire had somehow caught on, but Satana had been too busy feeding since to stew about it. There hadn't been "dating" apps the last time she'd been on Earth.

Fenn was waiting outside her door, wearing a wool

overcoat and holding a box with lights on it. "It may be a false alarm, my queen. I only know that someone has entered the vault's chamber. I will fetch Zarathos—"

"The Dark Lord rests," Satana said. That, and he wasn't strong enough. He'd be an albatross. He'd steal from her again, too. "We'll take a look and wake him if he's needed."

Fenn looked uncertain but bowed his head. Maybe it had finally sunk in for him that Zarathos was more trouble than he was worth. All he did was eat and flex.

"How do you know someone's there but not who it is?" Satana asked, leading him down the stairs.

Fenn got that look in his eyes that he got when he was talking about one of his machines. He touched one of his bracelets. "A motion sensor smaller than a pebble, a most complex design that triggers off of..."

Blah blah. Satana tuned him out, glancing at her phone. Her next delivery was an hour out, a bartender called Eric. She would hit the Suns with a full glamour, turn all of them into monsters; she and Fenn would enjoy the show and be back before her date arrived.

They stepped into the small home's dining area, stacked with more boxes of Fenn's things. Machinery, mostly; Fenn was a packrat, she'd decided. His first house had been spotless compared to this one. Satana shooed a soulless out of the room and got ready to transport.

"We should go in close to the site, but not right on top of it," Fenn said.

No kidding. "Sure, that makes sense."

Satana breathed deeply and touched Fenn's arm, let her essence surround them, and then pushed them through the membranes of the Earth, a soul's worth of her energy spent and gone. They came out in the woods just south of the Transian pit, Satana cloaking them as soon as they hit. Through the dark trees, they could see the shadowy crater and at least two figures guarding the well into the ground. The Ghost Rider was one of them, his eyes glowing in the dark like tiny fires. The other wore Magik's signature.

Fenn took a step closer and Satana grabbed his arm. They stood just outside an invisible cloud of blood-magic power. Satana couldn't see the magic, but it smelled like sandalwood and she could feel it, like standing next to a powerful, humming machine. It was a controlled space.

"It's warded," she whispered. "They'll know if we approach."

Or attack. Satana scowled. Her glamours would die in the protected air.

Fenn promptly crouched where he was, started playing with his machine. This one had dials and a trio of tiny screens. Satana stretched her awareness and felt the forces working underground. A strong spell was being performed, threaded with magic she didn't recognize.

"They're affecting the vault's seal," Fenn said.

Crap. Satana couldn't attack or move any closer. She had a spell that might dissipate their shield, but they would know as soon as the energy was tampered with.

Is this how it's going to be? We stand here and just watch them take it? If the Varkath Star was as powerful as Fenn claimed, it could control her, too. Once the Suns had it, the Triumvirate's mission was dead in the water, her hard-earned shot at proper leadership lost.

Fenn looked up at her. "We should get Zarathos."

"And what's he going to do?"

"Surely he's strong enough to attack the Suns."

Satana shook her head. "He'd might knock out a couple but there's no way he can take all of them down, not yet." And he'd drain her to get that done, leaving them stranded in front of their enemies.

Fenn was fiddling with his dials. "The seal still holds, but it is changing. There's... less of it."

They needed a diversion. With no magic.

Satana picked up a palm-sized chunk of stone. "Stay here. I've got an idea."

She skirted the controlled space to the west, closer to where the rock well was located, stepping lightly. The Ghost Rider was closest to her, a lanky shadow with fiery eyes some forty feet away, scanning the hills to the east. The Spirits of Vengeance were sexless, but the Riders were almost always male; the Spirits dug the testosterone.

Satana cloaked herself in shadow and let her essential nature spark, turning up the attraction surrounding her. She pulled back her arm to throw.

○————————○

THE stony Transian hills were silent except for small night sounds: tiny creatures nestling in their hollows, bats flitting through the dark, a cold wind from the mountains to the north ruffling the tops of scattered trees. Ghost Rider studied the landscape, Nico and Caretaker's magic thrumming beneath his boots. At his back, Magik was quiet and watchful.

Ghost Rider hoped the Triumvirate would show. His whole body itched to fight, to send the demons back to Hell, to hurt them. Robbie still felt rotten for having attacked Magik, and the Spirit was determined to take Zarathos down for using it against the Suns. That the demon had once been among the Spirits' ranks, even unwillingly, seemed to make it especially furious. Its vengeance had been put off too long already.

A small piece of rock landed at the lip of the open pit and clattered down.

"I got it," Robbie said, and felt flames jet to life around his skull at the thought of smashing his fist into Zarathos's ugly face.

He teleported to the edge of the pit and scanned the shadowy trees, feeling for demons... and there was a smell, a delicious, fascinating smell. It pricked at Robbie's skin and tantalized the Spirit, promising gratification, a fulfillment of all desires, and it wasn't just a smell. There was a kind of excitement, too, an anticipation, like a sunset on a Friday night when you've got plans, like opening a Hell portal and stuffing a wicked soul inside, knowing that the world was better for it.

Ghost Rider hopped onto the lip of the pit and took a single step into the trees, ready to attack, Robbie's body amped up and sweaty with that mad-good smell thick in the shadows, every part of him aching to get closer—

Demon. The Spirit scented the rank undertone buried in the goodness a second too late.

A gorgeous woman flashed in front of his eyes, smiling, and drove a silver dagger into his guts.

Ghost Rider howled and threw himself at her, grabbed her, but she flashed out before he could get a good grip. He jumped to his feet, turned, shot a chain at moving shadows to the east. The knife-tipped links slashed across the dark, cutting through branches and leaves, and he could feel a demonic portal snap open and closed.

Ghost Rider shrieked again, furious, and then Magik was by his side, her Soulsword dripping fire... and Robbie realized that the dagger was still in his body, its slender handle jutting between his navel and his right hip. The metal was demonically forged, enchanted. It burned, and the Spirit yanked it out in fury and threw it to the ground.

Hot blood spilled from the wound. The Spirit stayed with Robbie, blocking the pain, lending his body strength, but the damage was deep. Robbie could feel his guts swimming, a loose, wet feeling. He took a step and more blood poured out, too much of it. He stumbled.

Magik put her arm across his shoulders and moved them back to the open hole in the ground in a single step, shouting down for help. Robbie tried to tell her that he was fine, not in pain, but his legs were shaking, he couldn't make them stop, and he...

The thought dwindled to a tiny black speck in a sea of them, and even the Spirit couldn't keep him awake.

THE unspell was a complicated litany that both Caretaker and Nico seemed to know by heart. Blade felt the energies gather and thread, felt the vault's strange seal reacting; the glowing chamber was heavy with shifting forces and intentions. The women sang and chanted, directing the invisible streams with gestures and words.

Blade leaned against the rock wall at the base of the deep, narrow shaft, arms folded, watching. What they were doing was remarkable, nuanced magic performed by experts. He could feel the seal's energy changing. Caretaker and Nico both had their eyes closed, their expressions supremely placid, neutral with concentration. The Staff of One floated by Nico's right hand.

The magical energies pouring silently through the cavern seemed to settle, drawn at once to the metal vault. There was a feeling of release, like the air had been holding its breath and had finally let go.

Caretaker opened her eyes, touched the blackened metal. Nico did the same.

"Very soon now," Caretaker said, and Nico nodded. They both looked like they'd just woken from a deep sleep. They listened to the seal, examining complexities that Blade still struggled to see; the concealing ward still held. He only heard a buzzing fly somewhere in the chamber. High above, a rock fell into the pit, and he directed his attention upward, tilting his head. Movement. Ghost Rider's boots crunched against shards of clay and stone.

"When will it break?" Nico asked. "It's on the verge now."

"The next shift of dimensional alignment," Caretaker said. "Two of the twelve are already beginning to cross. The next will be the Shalidas Collective. Its outer rim will touch the alignment in about thirty hours. After that, we'll have a full month before the next transit reaches us. When we get back to the Abbey, I'll—"

The Ghost Rider screamed in fury, the tang of blood sizzling down through the tunnel's cold air.

Blade flew upward, clawing and kicking off the rough stones as fast as he could toward the hole of night sky overhead. Ghost Rider shrieked again, enraged, and the smell of blood thickened.

Blade leapt out of the pit just as Magik shouted to them. He drew his sword and charged to where the blood had first spilled, south, outside of Nico's shield. Satana's pheromones still lingered but she was gone.

He scooped up a bloodstained dagger, its properties tingling against his fingertips, and flashed through the trees, following the succubus's smell along the needles and leaves. Satana and John Doe had been here, the smell of the man lingering, sweat and mild soap; Blade saw his knee prints in the dirt, a straight edge denting the ground in front of them. *One of his damned devices—*

"Blade!" Caretaker called, and he flew back to the pit, boots eating the distance, tucking the dagger into his coat, sliding his katana back into its scabbard. Magik was supporting Ghost Rider, its sleek head hanging. Robbie's belly was distended, pressing against the tight, narrow lines of his coat, and blood coursed down his right leg.

Blade picked up the semi-conscious Ghost Rider, felt the Spirit's rage rising through the leathers like a fever, and Magik slashed a portal to home.

11

CARETAKER didn't wait to act. As soon as they were on the Limbo bridge, she had Blade lay Robbie on the pitted red rock and put her hand over the boy's wound. The blade had to have been enchanted to pierce the Spirit's deflection magic so deeply, to make it bleed so. The Spirit couldn't heal where the knife had gone in.

"Here," Blade said, and held up a slender dagger, wet with Robbie's blood.

Caretaker touched the metal with one finger and took its measure, understanding its effect, setting her intent to counteract it. She kept her right hand on the wound and put her left on the Ghost Rider's gleaming forehead. The Spirit's presence was in the way.

"Begone, so that I may save him," she said, ready to cast it out, but the Spirit understood. The hot metal under her palm melted to clammy flesh. Robbie groaned.

"It's okay, you're okay," Nico breathed.

"Open a portal to the Abbey," Caretaker said. "And be quiet."

Caretaker felt the Abbey open to her, its carefully built energies spilling into Limbo, charging her with power. She hadn't needed to heal a demon-blade wound for many years, but the words fell from her lips like she'd never stopped.

"Caro sanat, ad Abana sanat, hic puer salvus erit…"

Limbo's thin ether sped the process of her spell. His liver and bowels had been punctured beneath the flesh, and she cleaned the blade's enchanted molecules from the injuries, flung them from Robbie's body and into the fiery air. The sliced tissues began to knit back together.

"…emundare vulnus ac prohibere infectio…"

Caretaker treated the healing organs and flesh with an anodyne intention. She massaged his marrow to speed the replacement of lost blood cells and finished with a few words to pull him into a deep sleep.

She sat back on her heels and sighed, then looked up at the Suns. "He'll be fine in an hour or so. And ravenous."

Nico sagged, blowing out a deep breath. Magik stood in the portal disc that opened to the Abbey's sunny day and nodded, her lips a pale line. Blade crouched and lifted the sleeping youth, cradled him to his broad chest.

"Satana stabbed him," Blade said. "She had John Doe

with her, outside the shield. They ran as soon as the deed was done."

"Why was Robbie outside the shield? Didn't I tell you not to separate?" The burst of anger came out of nowhere, but Caretaker couldn't seem to help it; she was tired and had a child's blood on her hands. She stood up, furious. "You could die. You could *die! Why won't you ever just do as I say?*"

Nobody answered but they all watched her, watched an old woman lash out. They couldn't understand. They didn't know what they stood to lose.

Agatha's whisper was a cool hand across the back of her neck. *Stop this now.*

Caretaker wasn't sure how, but she took a breath and found a way. For Agatha.

"I'm sorry," she said. "I was scared."

"Me too," Nico said. "That was awful."

"You healed him," Magik offered.

"Nice bit of magic," Blade said. "Let's get him home."

Caretaker would always be outside of them, outside of everyone; her heart was a vault of secrets that would keep sealed... but she felt their forgiveness, their offered connection, and accepted gratefully.

Caretaker led them through the portal and onto the dais. "Put him to bed. We'll meet in the war room. I need to change."

She removed herself to her rooms, relieved to be home and away from sight, ready to grind the Triumvirate into paste beneath her boot heel. The vault of the Varkath Star would open in just over a day. Plenty of time to track the demons and destroy them, drop the treacherous human into a jail. Or Hell. Hell was sounding pretty good.

○————————————○

ZARATHOS listened to the mortal and the succubus babble on, his rage growing. Fenn happily announced that, by his machine's calculations, the seal would now dissolve in twenty-nine hours. Satana gleefully recounted stabbing the Ghost Rider, and Zarathos could stand it no more.

"Why did you not wake me?" He rose to his feet, kicked the flimsy cot away. "I would have destroyed them!"

Fenn dropped his head, but Satana looked at him brashly.

"My lord, you still need to rest and—"

"I do not need to rest, I need to feed!" Zarathos felt his eyes ignite with rage. "I need more than your weak offerings, this slender trickle of sustenance! I will feed properly, now, and the Triumvirate will return to Transia to break the seal."

Fenn's eyes were wide. "Master, we must keep hidden or risk attack. We can—"

"You dare to question my command?" Zarathos took a step toward the puny mortal. He cowered but kept speaking.

"No, of course not, only let me—that is, the Triumvirate will attend to your needs at once. I know a place. Give me one minute."

Fenn scurried out and Zarathos looked at the succubus, who sparkled with soul energy. She'd been eating steadily, attending to herself. Weaker demons could sustain themselves on a handful of souls. He needed more and had been too patient with the Triumvirate's miserable efforts. They had dared to go to the vault without him, but not again.

Fenn returned with a gamma box, green light spilling out. Zarathos could again feel the pulse of low magic beneath the light, old and strange. He wondered where Fenn had found it; the human was no sorcerer.

"Ready," Fenn said, and gave Satana an address and a direction, somewhere far south.

Zarathos believed he was well enough to transport them, but let the succubus expend her energies, saving his own. The Triumvirate depended on his power to achieve their goal, to take the amulet and dethrone Mephisto; he would not waste it. And in fact, he had none to waste, the way Satana Hellstrom had been starving him. Transportation was the least she could do.

The Triumvirate flashed from the lowly room into the back of a building filled with soul energy. Men, women, and children sat in wooden pews, all turned to face a god-shouter on a platform at the front of the room, the crowd humming with life. Ritual crosses littered the walls, stained glass in the high, small windows.

A church. Zarathos grinned, just as the first mortals noticed Fenn's green light splashing through the room, the first shouts of alarm rising into the rich air. Zarathos barred the big room's doors with a wave and walked slowly toward the platform in front, enjoying the escalating fear and panic.

The psychic energy ignited his fire, flames running up his back to lick at his skull, and he took his time gaining the raised dais, the better to develop their terror.

The god-shouter begged the one god to save his flock from the devil, his eyes popping out of his head, his hand making crosses in the air. Zarathos laughed, and the dread of his audience grew.

Many of the humans had run to the doors, but there were more than a hundred souls watching as Zarathos grabbed the white-collared flock leader by his shouting face. Zarathos dug his fingers in, felt the man's features crush beneath his mighty palm, and the people screamed in horror. The combined distress of so many was what Zarathos had been missing, infinitely more satisfying than the dribs and drabs he'd been offered.

"I will feast on your souls!" Zarathos thundered, and the mortal anguish crested, pouring into him. Some of the churchgoers had dropped to their knees, which was appropriate. Zarathos absorbed the dying god-shouter's soul, a rush of power and light joining his essence, and dropped the empty vessel to the floor.

He raised his arms, calling to the bright sparks that the vessels carried. He felt their resistance, felt them cling desperately to the people they served, and heard Fenn scream from the back of the room.

"Not me, Master!"

Zarathos didn't care, Fenn would serve him anyway, but Satana grabbed Fenn and the two disappeared, leaving

Fenn's machine behind. No matter. When Zarathos had eaten properly, he'd have the power to go to Transia himself.

Zarathos opened his upraised hands and his own hungry core, an endless black vacuum of need that demanded feeding. The emptiness of his pith wrenched the human souls from their screaming holders.

Ahh. Zarathos breathed in, his chest expanding, his muscles bulking impossibly larger. Soul energy was the most powerful, the most satisfying. The screams fell away, the palpable fear dimming as the drained mortals turned into walking meat. They were afraid now only as dumb prey animals feared a predator near their water, nervous and watchful. Fenn's gamma light played across the stained-glass windows, reflected in the newly blank eyes of the disensouled.

Zarathos ate well, finally, and grew strong.

o———————o

CHARLIE trotted in while Blade was taking Robbie's boots off. Robbie was laid out and snoring on his bunk. Nico petted her, assured her that Robbie was going to be fine, fully aware that she was soothing herself. Robbie was tough and Caretaker had healed him, but Nico had been freaking, standing on the Limbo bridge. Robbie was the best guy, a sweetheart, and that trash had stabbed him like it was nothing.

Blade covered him with a blanket and nodded to her and Magik. Nico conjured a pitcher of water from the kitchen to put on Robbie's nightstand before she followed them out. The hellhound stayed behind, laying down at the foot of Robbie's bunk. *Good girl, Charlie.*

Blade walked with them toward the war room instead of flashing ahead. "They weren't around when we got to Transia. How did they know we were there?"

"Perhaps they have their own mirror table," Magik said. They walked through the foyer, their steps echoing faintly off the polished wood.

"They knew we were at the storage unit, too," Blade said.

"A spell to find us when we're not at the Abbey," Nico said. "Magik's portals create energy. Maybe they're watching for the signature."

"Maybe," Blade said. "Or it's one of John Doe's machines. If he can make shields that hide supernatural energy, he can probably work up a silent alarm with no trouble. I heard a buzzing in the vault's chamber, thought it was an insect, but it could have been something else."

Caretaker wasn't in the war room yet. Magik walked to the mirror table and touched the black glass. The rocky hills of Transia expanded over the table but the Eye still refused to show them the concealed vault, only the stony cliffs around it. There was a thick, dark fog where the ancient spell held sway.

"We need to go back and ward the area," Blade continued. "If there's a trip wire, I'd like to find it, but more importantly, we need to know if they show up to hurry the unsealing along."

"But if they're finding us through a portal signature, they'll hit us again," Nico said.

"They'll hit us anyway," Blade said. He paced the dark wood floor, his jaw set. "Better to handle it now than when the Varkath Star comes into play."

"I can spell the rocks or trees to be aware of trespass..." Nico trailed off, thinking. The Abbey's dimension was closed off. Caretaker had allowed for some radio frequencies to pass through but nothing magical, not without a portal. How would Nico know if the Triumvirate showed?

I'll stay in Earth's realm. Caretaker would object, but Blade was right about needing to know. Nico didn't think the Triumvirate would have any luck pushing the seal, she and Caretaker had stripped it to its bones, but she didn't know for certain.

"I will go to the vault and guard it," Magik said.

"We should all go," Nico said. "We can camp out, keep an eye on things."

"I think we should ward it and then track the Triumvirate," Blade said. "John Doe's resources can't be unlimited. We can keep digging. We might still stop them before they go for the amulet."

"Zarathos will be gaining strength," Magik said. "The mirror table might find him now, through the gamma shields."

Caretaker appeared in the doorway, holding a book open. "The Shalidas Collective's rim will reach the alignment path in twenty-nine and a half hours, approximately. The vault will not open before then. We need not return."

"John Doe's a bomber," Blade said. "He could be seeding the vault's chamber right now. And if I find his trip wire, maybe we can figure out who built it."

"The Triumvirate might also change the environment to block us from access," Magik said.

Nico hadn't even thought of that. Zarathos was an archdemon. He could transmute the whole mountain into dust, surround the vault with deep space or fire or something. "I could do a stasis spell, just for the area around the vault. We can at least prevent them from changing the geography. We can go now, be back before Robbie wakes up."

Caretaker's mouth was all pursed up. She didn't like it, but she wasn't saying no, either.

Because it's a good idea, and we can't just show up in twenty-nine hours hoping there aren't any more surprises. Nico held her tongue, aware that anything else from her might tip the old witch back into *no*, readying herself to argue. Thankfully, Blade spoke up.

"We have to throw everything at this," he said. "You know that."

"We should wait for Ghost Rider," Caretaker said. "I meant what I said, about the Suns staying together. You— *we* are stronger as a team."

"You're right, but the Triumvirate is going to know the seal is breaking," Blade said. "We can't let them make another move before we set up some boundaries."

"All right," she said. "But we'll not linger. Magik, you'll hold a portal open next to the vault's well. Nico, you'll protect us as before while Blade looks for this sensor. I will perform a spell to confirm the integrity of the grounds, and ward them with our own alarm."

Nico was impressed. Of course Caretaker could monitor her spells between dimensions. *I'll be able to do that, someday. Maybe.*

Caretaker raised her hands, and then they were all outside at the dais, the sun beating down. Magik cut a portal, and they saw a handful of dark, amorphic shapes flee the Limbo bridge, disappearing into the shadows of the air.

Nico wrinkled her nose as she stepped into Limbo. The bridge had been scoured of Robbie's blood. Otherplace was full of strange, hungry creatures.

Magik opened another disc, the Transian night blooming in front of them once more, and Nico cut her hand on her jacket, the flow of blood allowing her to draw the Staff of One out of her chest. She thrust it through the portal and remembered the look on Robbie's face when the Spirit of Vengeance had departed, how helpless she'd felt—

—and before she could speak, an invisible presence grabbed her arm and yanked her through, raising her high into the cold air. She saw the hideous Zarathos standing by the shaft in the ground, giant and absurdly muscular, his huge red skull grinning with its piranha teeth.

The Suns roared out of the portal behind her, Caretaker hitting the demon with a white blast of energy that knocked him backward. Blade and Magik both ran for him with their swords out. Zarathos dropped Nico and she hit the ground at an angle, crashing to the dirt.

The monster drew back one massive arm to pitch his counterattack, dark energies whirling around his flaming skull, racing to his raised fist—

"No magic!" Nico screamed, and the Staff's eye exploded in a silver-purple blast of power, outlining the demon's gesturing form in brilliant light.

The spinning blackness all around him disappeared.

"Es arium vareste!" he shouted, and gestured violently toward Caretaker—and nothing happened.

Caretaker gestured back at him. "Abite!"

Again nothing happened, and Nico realized that Magik's Soulsword and armor had snapped out of existence, too. She stopped ten feet in front of Zarathos, defenseless, without a weapon.

Crap! The staff still trembled beneath Nico's fingers, but the air had gone dead and flat all around them, empty. No access to dimensional power, no spells for anyone. No magic.

Blade darted in and slashed at the demon, distracting him from Magik. Magik danced backward.

Reverse, reverse! Nico fumbled for a word to undo her thoughtless defense just as Zarathos backhanded Blade away from him, knocking the Daywalker into the trees behind the pit. Blade was up in a flash and running back in.

"Sword!" Magik shouted, and Blade lobbed his katana at her, throwing the balanced blade so that the handle reached her first. Magik snatched it out of the air and went in low, striking at Zarathos's right leg, marked a line of writhing darkness along his thigh. Thick black ichor oozed out.

The demon kicked, catching Magik's shoulder with his boot as she tried to dodge past. Magik hit the rocks and rolled to her feet, came up and spun to attack again. Zarathos grabbed for her and the blade sliced through his hand, nearly taking his thumb off.

Zarathos roared and fell back just as Blade ran in and stuck a pair of knives into the demon's side, under his ribs. Zarathos turned, swinging his massive arms to slap Blade as he tried to retreat. Magik darted forward and landed another strike, cutting behind Zarathos's left knee as Blade launched more knives, faster than Nico could see. Two stuck in the demon's chest, another clattering off his skull, a fourth burying itself in his collarbone.

The last time Nico had tried to undo a bad spell, she'd reversed time, which caused more trouble than the original offense. *Not reverse, something like turn around or—*

Zarathos shouted more words of power in the demonic tongue, useless, striking blindly at Magik and Blade as they traded off attacks. Blade's left arm cracked audibly when the demon swung a roundhouse that landed on the Daywalker's shoulder, his arm suddenly hanging and limp.

"*Nico!*" Caretaker shouted, furious, demanding.

"Jihada dambe!" Nico cried, *reverse direction*, and the Staff of One's eye exploded again, drawing from her, the blood-slick wood vibrating in her hand.

The night air gained substance, thickening, energies flowing back into the blank air—and they surpassed what had already been and continued to grow, power crackling and gathering in the darkness of the pit, spitting through the cool night in sparks and flashes.

"Magik, get us out!" Blade shouted, just as Zarathos started to shout a dark spell, waving his bleeding hands. A spiral of anti-light appeared in the sky over the demon, the slivers of void whirling down to pour into his clutching fingers. Wind started to ripple outward from his muscular form.

"In nominee Hastur istas tenebras dispellimus!" Caretaker pointed at the spinning threads and crackles of white lightning spun through them, arced between them, breaking them into mist.

The light of Limbo spilled onto the scarred rocks. Magik tossed Blade's katana through the portal and then blasted Zarathos with her free hand, a strong pulse of blue-white energy knocking him a step backward. Blade hurtled for the disc.

"Go!" Caretaker cried, and invoked a glimmering shield in front of the portal, a thick, blurry shield of spidery white threads winding into a wall between Zarathos and the rest of them.

Nico stumbled into Limbo, Blade sweeping her through. Magik held the portal as Caretaker backed in, still holding the energy shield.

"Natura suam formam tenet," Caretaker said, a simple spell

for the immediate landscape to maintain its natural intention, the words weighted with power drawn from the storm of swelling energies, the very air packed with possibilities. The strong magic flowed into the dark pit, settled into the rock, curled into the branches of the surrounding trees.

Zarathos hurled something at the shield that ate through the holes in the magic's weave, collapsing the white web. Caretaker fell back and the portal snapped closed. The Staff of One went still in Nico's hand.

Nico held herself together for about two seconds, and then she saw Blade wincing, pushing his dead left arm up as the bones started to knit back together, saw Caretaker's terrible scowl and Magik's grim expression.

"I'm sorry," Nico said, and the tears just started coming. She'd messed up so bad—she'd panicked and nearly gotten all of them killed.

"You stopped him from blasting us into Transylvania," Blade said. "It beat the alternative by a mile."

Caretaker shook her head. "He shouldn't have gotten through that shield. Even with the rise of energies."

"The alignment," Blade said. Still scowling, Caretaker nodded.

"He's been feeding," Magik said. She'd retrieved Blade's sword and handed it to him.

Nico was slightly dumbfounded that no one was pointing out her bone-headed move, and remembered what Robbie was always saying, about working not to let his ego get in the way of reality. She was the only one blaming herself.

Maybe they aren't as interested in obsessing over your mistakes as you are.

"At least there's a stasis now," Blade said, and Nico was grateful for that much. Caretaker had managed to take care of some of their business. If the Suns had to fight the Triumvirate over the vault, they'd do it in the Transian foothills on solid ground.

Assuming Zarathos doesn't get a whole lot stronger in the next twenty-four hours, and John Doe doesn't blow everything up. Which there's no reason to assume.

"I need to communicate with the Sorcerer Supreme," Caretaker said. "It might take a little time. The rest of you will keep looking for traces. The Triumvirate are leaving bodies or soulless in their wake. They can be tracked again."

"And if we find them while you're traveling?" Blade asked.

"No one leaves the Abbey until I return, for any reason," Caretaker said. Firmly. "If I can't contact him by this evening, we'll re-evaluate. Magik?"

The Suns' leader gestured at the open bridge and Magik dutifully swung her sword, splitting the hazy air. Nico followed them back to the Abbey, wiping her eyes, not entirely unhappy that they were grounded for a few hours. She wanted to refresh her mental dictionary of commands and look up some new ones, have some solid intentions ready to go for the next time the Suns met with the Triumvirate. She also wanted to flop on her bed and scream into her pillow over her dumbass mistake.

And I want to see Robbie. She thought a big dopey smile

from Robbie Reyes was just what she needed. She'd tell him what had happened, and he'd make a joke about how much she sucked and they'd both laugh, and she'd be ready to let it go the way the other Suns already had. Caretaker was so right about being stronger together, and not just in a kick-butt kind of way. Agatha and Wanda were gone but the remaining Suns had formed a tight dynamic, every one of them with strengths to share, stuff like clarity, humor, compassion. When she was younger, Nico had felt strangled by the very idea of obligation, but she saw now what an asset it could be when you undertook it with people you could trust.

Caretaker blipped out on their walk across the lawn, the cliff west of the Abbey already throwing its shade across the grotto's whispering cottonwoods and aspens. The tops of the trees to the east were still in full sun, but it felt late. Nico understood the desire to hurry. They had just over a day and the mirror table couldn't see the vault of the Varkath Star, the demons were hiding, and they didn't know who John Doe was or what else his machines could do. Plus, they needed to sleep sometime, and the Triumvirate would keep making soulless as long as they were on Earth.

"You did right," Blade said, touching Nico's arm lightly. He used his left hand, and nodded at both her and Magik. "We got this."

He'd hung back to say as much. Nico nodded back because that was the deal, that was part of the obligation. No fear in the face of danger.

"The Suns will stop them," Magik said.

"We all know it," Nico agreed, projecting the same absolute confidence as the older Suns. It was the only acceptable attitude. Doubt and worry were mind-killers. And if they were wrong, if they *didn't* have it, they'd all be dead and could feel stupid later.

12

SATANA pulled Fenn out of the Zarathos all-you-can-eat because the Triumvirate needed him, and Zarathos was too thick to consider the ramifications of sucking up the human's soul. Soulless lost motivation, big time, their higher functions ruined; it cut their intelligence by a good half. Without his soul, Fenn would stop caring about getting back at Mephisto and his handy technical skills would be lost.

She popped them back to Fenn's house and was about to go back to the church—in Florida, of all places—when Fenn insisted that she wait and ran off to grab some big bomb thing. Satana was not feeling the appreciation she was due for shlepping His Royal Darkness off to fill up on souls or saving Fenn from destruction, and she resented the time lost. All the more so when they got back to the church and

Zarathos was already gone. The greasy bastard had ditched them once more, presumably heading off to Transia to throw himself at the time lock again.

Fenn had her wait again, surrounded by milling soulless in the doomed church. A bunch of them had been trampled and she killed the suffering ones, annoyed by their obnoxious moaning, while Fenn set up his bomb and retrieved his gamma shield. It took about forever for him to get the timer set—he wanted it to explode just after they left so that Zarathos's mass feeding would go undetected. He was worried about the Midnight Suns, and Satana couldn't say she blamed him. With Zarathos 'leading' the Triumvirate, the meddling super-friends had an easy target.

As if I needed confirmation, she thought, as she and Fenn arrived in Transia just in time to watch a portal to Limbo slam closed in Zarathos's screaming face.

The arch-demon raged in a great circle, pulling knives out of his body and throwing them, the fine blades whizzing through the air. The black tar of his blood stained his bodysuit in a dozen places.

"Your Highness!" Fenn shouted, ducking. Satana shushed him, stepped in front of him before Zarathos's rage turned to the only available outlets.

Dammit. She had to cool him out before he murdered their team.

She bowed deeply, aware that her cleavage had worked miracles many times in the past. "Dark Lord, let me heal you."

Zarathos shrieked and stamped his feet. "That witch,

that little witch! I'll impale her on that staff! They *cut* me! They'll die for this. I will grind them to meat and bone. I will *destroy* them!"

"They cheated and tricked you," Satana soothed, moving in closer. "The Midnight Suns are vexing but you will crush them. When you gain the Varkath Star, you will torture them for eternity, burn them, feed on their agony. Here, let me heal your wounds. You were one against many and they cheated …"

Zarathos inflated his chest and let her touch him, muttering nasty curses all the while, a few of them viscerally revolting. Satana turned up her calming pheromones and mentally recited a spell that sent topical anesthetic to the tips of her fingers. She couldn't heal anything, but the cuts were already closing thanks to his feast, and he wouldn't know the difference. She was careful not to let him grab her. By the time she stepped away, he was back to his regular angry self, and Fenn finally dared to speak.

"We only have to wait for the vault to open, Your Highness, and keep behind one of my shields until it does. We can visit other places with more souls, and—"

Zarathos disappeared, dropping into the shaft of the vault's chamber.

"Come *on*," Satana snapped, and grabbed Fenn's arm. Elder Gods, she deserved a medal, what she put up with.

They joined Zarathos in the chamber. He blasted the ceiling with Hellfire, the chamber lit up by a smokeless sheet of furious yellow-white flame that crawled across the rocks overhead.

Zarathos stepped to the vault. He put his giant hands across the top and tilted his head back, measuring what was there. It was the first time Satana had seen him stop to think or assess before immediately going all alpha, and she heartily approved. The Midnight Suns weren't a joke. They'd ducked real damage at every turn and somehow put a serious dent in a time lock. Taking the Varkath Star from the boys on her team wasn't the challenge for Satana; keeping the Suns from stealing it was.

Fenn was poking around in the rocks. Satana focused her attention on the seal. There was definitely a lot less of it, but the whole thing was still warded to hide, and she had no idea how the Suns' witches had managed to set the clock forward without traveling in time. Human magic was weird, mostly weak, but they could do a few things that demons couldn't. Reworking an intention from its roots was one of them.

"The realms touching this one take a breath to exhale darker air," Zarathos said. "The seal remains intact until they breathe again."

"Twenty-nine hours, Dark Lord," Fenn said, restating what they had already told him. Fenn's need for vengeance was a driving force like Satana couldn't imagine, the way he kissed up to Zarathos. The mortal had to know by now that the big Z was pretty much a walking liability.

"Where are the Midnight Suns?" Zarathos said. "I will smite them now. They won't live to challenge me for the Star."

Fenn cleared his throat. "I have searched for them, my lord, but I believe they hide in a dimensional pocket outside of Earth's realm. I think it's close, though."

That narrows it down. Fenn maybe didn't entirely grasp the concept of dimensions, or how they interacted. Most humans struggled with the concept, along with timeline awareness. *Close* was a measure of distance that didn't apply.

"So, if we can't get to them, we should maybe think about making it hard for them to get to the vault," Satana said, almost asking it as a question.

"The old Blood witch locked the ground," Zarathos rumbled. Satana had noticed, but Fenn looked surprised.

"Locked it how? Um, Your Highness?"

Satana answered. "Natural environments have intention. It's not strong magic, but they resist sudden change. If you've got enough power, you can reinforce their physical stability."

"I will kill her," Zarathos said.

"Yes, my lord," Satana said. "You are wise to think of how to stop them from reaching the vault. Fenn's bombs can be used—"

Fenn nodded eagerly. "We can mine this chamber. I have prototypes that—"

"—and there's nothing stopping us from setting a few traps of our own," Satana continued. "We both have friends who would delight in tearing apart self-proclaimed defenders of Earth."

"All of my friends are dead," Zarathos said. "They were slaughtered by Mephisto."

Satana bowed her head, hiding her clenched jaw. It was like working with a toddler that you weren't allowed to beat. "He will pay when you have the Varkath Star, my lord. I only meant beings of chaos in dimensions we can reach."

"I will call upon Nightmare's children from the Dream Dimension," Zarathos said. "The beast-warriors of Brimstone! The Reapers of the Elysian Fields!"

Satana nodded and smiled, screaming inwardly at his choices. Messing with the Dream Dimension was asking for trouble. Nightmare was called that for a reason. Collective-unconscious-type entities were too much like real Elder Gods for her taste; they had agendas that no one could fathom and were frankly upsetting to be around. Brimstone was chock-full of stupid warlord thugs who'd kill their own families to get to an amulet like the Varkath Star. And the Reapers worked for Hades—they didn't just galivant around doing their own thing. No wonder Zarathos didn't have any friends—he was terrible at picking them.

"Sumerian fire-demons," Satana said, pointing at Zarathos as though he'd suggested it. "They're unstoppable on Earth and always looking for something to burn. Or the hellhounds of Yama's dimension—they're as big as horses and easy to control. You are clever to consider which allies would best serve your ultimate goal without wanting the amulet for themselves."

Zarathos was nodding, impressed with himself, hands still pressed to the obstinate vault. "I will choose them as an artist chooses his medium, a craftsman his tools. We will stop the Suns from reaching this vessel, so that the Triumvirate only is here when it reveals its treasure."

"The look on Mephisto's face, when we force his attendance," Fenn said, his eyes gleaming. "I will read the spell while you don the Varkath Star, master. He will know that the Triumvirate are his undoing."

Finally, all rowing in the same direction. Satana turned and surveyed the big chamber with an eye to design, considering the pit overhead, the lay of the rocky hills around them. She could ward the area. It wouldn't hold, but it would force the Suns to come in from a different direction…

She visualized what they could do and where, organizing the possibilities, thinking of the gauntlet that two demonic powerhouses could create with the help of a tech wizard. She had servants to help them, and they could make a lot more when Zarathos fed again.

And we've barely got a full day! Satana was excited. This was a thousand times better than unveiling a new color scheme or fashion trend. Zarathos was strong and getting stronger, Fenn was already cackling and muttering to himself, and she had a thousand brilliant ideas sizzling away, ready to be culled for the brightest and best.

This is why the Star belongs to me. She was at the top of her game, reaching for the brass ring with a couple of self-important fools clutching her ankles. The Midnight Suns wanted to snatch her prize away, but the ring's metal was already in reach, shining and cool and aching for Satana to claim it.

○————————○

CARETAKER had worked with Stephen Strange since he'd become the Sorcerer Supreme, as she'd worked with the Ancient

One before him. The young man lacked the humility of his predecessor but was much better organized and, as protector of Earth's magical defenses, had done a fine job of preparing for the celestial alignment. For the last decade he'd been strengthening wards and meeting with various dimensional beings to strike up peace treaties, researching methods to lessen the alignment's effects, training young adepts to develop their skills. Nico had been at Strange's school when Caretaker and Agatha had invited her to join the Midnight Suns. It had been many years since they'd actually met in person, which she preferred. She respected Stephen but he simply talked too much, which she was far too old to put up with.

Caretaker lay on a training mat in the forge chamber, arms relaxed at her sides, her eyes closed. The Sorcerer Supreme's physical body was at the Sanctum Sanctorum, but he was traveling along the astral plane, most of him far from home. She could disrupt him—she certainly had reason—but a physical conversation would lack the nuance of an astral one. She needed him to understand what was at stake, immediately, and be able to reflect on her impressions of the Triumvirate's strength. Talking was inaccurate.

Caretaker set her thoughts aside and breathed from her center, then rose from her physical form. She floated through the Abbey's roof, gaining speed, and arrowed into the clouds, finally grasping the mists of the astral plane, soft and shining, a rippling dimension of consciousness. Caretaker considered the Sorcerer Supreme's essence—bright, sharp, masculine, a kind of dry and studious flavor, ever curious.

She sensed him at a vast distance, through many layers of matter and space. His signature was like a candle's light from across a great dark field.

Caretaker went to him, speeding through the plane's mists, and arrived at his side in seconds. As she'd expected, he was deep in concentration. Her image was of his physical body floating in black space, perfectly still, the Cloak of Levitation attending him in a slow waving motion. Next to him, a plume of deep green smoke roiled and spun, keeping a roughly pine-tree shape. The silver at his temples had broadened since she'd last seen him, but otherwise he looked as he always did—neatly groomed, his expression intense even in stillness.

She waited. Finding Strange was easy, but knowing when to break into his concentration was more complex. He was communing with the top sorcerer of a dimension with an unpronounceable name that existed in alignment with Dormammu's realm. Caretaker couldn't hear them, and they weren't aware of her presence; alerting them might be a breach of etiquette for the alien sorcerer, and she wouldn't interrupt a negotiation that might be important.

Time passed, but Caretaker's thread back to her body marked it in minutes rather than hours. The smoke of the celestial tree billowed within its borders, and Strange maintained his perfect stillness.

Robbie is awake by now. The Suns were working to find the Triumvirate, but watching Zarathos's spell eat through her best shield had changed her estimations. The degradation of magic was already farther along than she had believed, still half a year from the alignment. The Varkath Star was too valuable to risk without alerting Earth's Sorcerer Supreme.

Strange's companion disappeared abruptly, and Caretaker let herself be known.

Sara. His attention was tightly focused, analytical.

She didn't allow herself to be annoyed, only acknowledged him in turn, and explained as concisely as she could, feeding him her assessment as she showed him the tapestry of her awareness. Soulless and gamma shields, leading to Satana Hellstrom. The Triumvirate. The Varkath Star. The concealed vault, and Zarathos, and the human machine-maker. The unspelling, and the attacks. She didn't need to tell him about the conditions on Earth as the alignment drew closer; he was fully aware.

When she'd finished, she could feel his consideration.

And? His expectation for what she was asking surprised her.

And the Varkath Star. She projected the value of such an amulet, and the strength of the shield spell that had failed.

Current conditions will hold another month. Midnight Suns seem capable. The Avengers can assist. If you need help, speak with Captain America.

Caretaker pursed her lips. She hadn't come for advice or a referral, she'd come to alert him to what was happening, and had expected…

What had she expected? That he would send in the cavalry, she supposed, or offer to attend the vault's opening, releasing the Suns from responsibility. And that he would grasp how vital the Varkath Star was to their cause and would share her worry about the deterioration of magic's constancy, and what that was going to mean for the Midnight Suns in the days ahead.

He waited for more from her, attentive, but she could feel his slight impatience, too. He had others to meet, and she realized that she had what she'd come for. The Sorcerer Supreme understood the situation and expected her to handle it.

Caretaker thanked him for his time and withdrew promptly, following her silver thread back through the mist, back to the Abbey. She settled into the weight of her body and opened her eyes, sighing. She stayed where she was for a moment, assessing how much time had passed. Little more than an hour, but the Midnight Suns were working on a timer now and every minute counted. They had to find the Triumvirate and stop them from getting to Transia, if they could, and they'd all need to rest and be ready for the vault's opening either way.

She had doubts. Since she'd released them to fight they'd left themselves open to attack, underestimated their enemy, acted recklessly… but they had also been resourceful, quick.

The mistakes don't matter anymore, Agatha said.

Mistakes always matter, Caretaker protested. *A mistake can mean death!*

And they are as inevitable as death. Fighters change course and recover, as the Suns have. As they will. You regained your purpose. Hold to it now. Stand with them, invest them with the confidence they need to prevail.

I miss you so, Caretaker thought, and felt her grief try to rise, putting a stone in her throat, but Agatha had withdrawn. She wasn't even real, and she was still Caretaker's best counsel.

Another minute had passed. Caretaker stamped on her feelings and stood up. The Suns were in the war room, waiting.

○━━━━━━━━━━━━━○

MAGIK stood at the mirror table with Blade and Nico, searching New York City for patterns in psychic movement, dead spaces in the light as before. Robbie studied their evolving image, working his way through a box of protein bars. He'd already made two trips to the kitchen. Magik was relieved to see him back to himself.

They'd followed a dozen false leads and Magik watched the changing Eye with growing dissatisfaction. Zarathos and Satana were nowhere to be seen. She should have paid closer attention to the shield box's energies when she'd had the chance. Its magic had been obscure, understated, hidden by the gamma radiation… yet enlaced with it, and hiding the radiation in turn. The effect was a null, strong enough to cover demonic signatures and soulless beneath its effect. If Magik had better studied the machine, she might be able to find one herself, rather than rely on the table.

Caretaker joined them, nodding at Robbie.

"How are you feeling?"

Robbie swallowed. "Fine, thanks to you. I ate an entire pot of spaghetti when I woke up."

Caretaker smiled, though it didn't touch her eyes. "I'm glad you're well."

She turned to the table, looking into Ereshkigal's Eye. "Any progress?"

"Not yet," Blade said. "They may not be in the state anymore. Or they've moved somewhere more populated, and we're just not seeing the draw."

Caretaker put her hands on the table. "I'll look for Zarathos."

Magik was compelled to speak. "He is not where we're looking, or the shield still hides him. Satana, too."

Caretaker lifted her hands. "Perhaps we should consider a different approach. All of you have felt the effect of these shields. What can you tell me about them?"

"They're hybrids," Blade said. "The radiation blocked me from sensing their magic. The magic hides the radiation. Up close I got a sense of it, but it was unfamiliar."

"The magic is ancient," Nico said. "And it's got kind of a bitter flavor. Like unsweetened licorice."

"It's demonic," Magik agreed. "I didn't know the energy either. It was simple but potent."

Robbie shook his head. "Sorry, I got nothing. They shoot green light and hide demons."

"A few words of making in an ancient tongue, that can hide radiation," Caretaker said slowly. "Nico, can you recreate the scent?"

Nico took her hands off the table, and the Eye closed. She centered herself and waved her hands, speaking in Latin. A tangy smell occurred in the room, and she frowned, spoke a few more words.

Magik and Blade both nodded as the scent refined, almost a taste. The experience lacked the texture of the real thing, but it was very close: dark, old, secretive.

Caretaker breathed deeply and frowned. "Are you certain?"

"What is it?" Blade asked.

"It's similar to… There's a spell in the Darkhold that holds such a flavor. When Hiram Shaw attacked the Abbey in the New World, he carried that page. It's an intention enhancement."

Magik's heart beat faster. Chthon's Darkhold was cursed. "It did not seem so strong."

"The radiation is cloaking it," Blade said.

"We can find it," Caretaker said. "I can find it."

She put her hands back to the table and the Eye opened, but instead of lights or city streets, the image was of vapors, in every imaginable color. The sphere was like a bubble filled with a mosaic of smoke.

Caretaker cleared all the light colors from the Eye, then the deeper shades, and changed the view to outline what remained against a field of pale gray—a handful of tiny wisps of dull black. A few were grouped together.

"Energies of Chthon's enhancement spell currently in use in the area," Caretaker said. The image changed, a background of busy streets and buildings rising through the gray. The wisps gained context, became places. Homes, two vehicles, a warehouse. The Eye would not look into them but could finally see them. Robbie took out his phone and snapped pictures.

Blade smiled, a tight, small thing. "No more hiding. Those shields just got worthless."

"The spell will reinforce intention," Caretaker said. "I wonder that the Triumvirate hasn't used it against the vault."

"Or us," Blade said. "We're assuming John Doe built the machines. Maybe he didn't tell Zarathos or Satana how he did it."

"He can't have," Caretaker said. "If either of them had access to a Darkhold page, we would know it by now."

"Maybe John Doe doesn't even know," Robbie said. "Maybe it's just a copy of the spell. Maybe somebody else helped him."

"We'll go now," Magik said. They needed to wipe out every trace. The Elder God was a disease, an abomination.

Nico pointed at the densest concentration of vapors, an ugly smudge across the Eye on the island of Manhattan that extended east, a very crowded area.

"That's Laurelton," Blade said, as the Eye refocused. A tall, narrow house tucked among many.

"This has got to be them, right?" Nico asked. "That's, like, four or five shields running, at least. Everywhere else just has one."

They all nodded.

"Here's what we're going to do," Caretaker said. The table's image changed to a bird's-eye view. "Magik will take us to the alley behind the building, here. We will stay in Limbo while Nico freezes the activity inside."

"Zarathos can break a stasis," Magik said. She wasn't sure about Satana Hellstrom. Nico's blood-magic was powerful, but the succubus had undoubtedly been feeding heavily.

"We will assess the situation from Otherplace," Caretaker said. "I'll make a shield to block Zarathos from our position. He may be able to break through again, but we'll have enough time to retreat, and we will re-evaluate from the safety of Limbo. We'll do the same for each of these locations until we find them."

"And what's the plan when we do?" Nico asked.

"The Midnight Suns will see to it that the Triumvirate doesn't cause any further trouble," Caretaker said. "Whatever it takes. We'll collect the Varkath Star and the other items in the vault at the appointed hour."

"And we'll destroy the machines," Magik said.

"We should preserve one of them to—" Blade began.

Magik interrupted to clarify. "We will destroy them."

The others looked uncertain, but Caretaker understood—Magik saw it in her eyes. Chthon's works could not be tolerated to exist in any realm. Whatever might be gained from studying the machines was not worth it; even an indirect line to the Elder God's will was an existential threat. The tiniest seed of his poison would always take root, a fast-growing, thorny black weed spreading a thousand corrupt offshoots toward the black sun of his evil. Chthon slept but was ever dreaming of ways to return to form, probing at the cracks and crevices of his veil. Words from the Darkhold would draw his notice.

"Magik is right," Caretaker said. "They're toxic. Trigger their destruct mechanisms and get them away from us, from people."

"We should take my ride," Robbie said. "Lotta trunk space."

Ghost Rider's Hell Charger would be useful. There was a portal in its trunk that opened to a desolate wasteland of Hell, the Spirits' favorite dumping ground. Magik had her own place in Limbo where an explosion would do no harm, but Robbie would also be able to dispose of any soulless they found.

"Not yet," Caretaker said. "Finding and stopping the Triumvirate is our primary aim. Investigation and clean-up can wait until they're out of the picture. Any questions?"

There were none. Caretaker raised her hands and moved them out to the portal dais. In the Abbey's dimension, Caretaker's intentions were like her Soulsword, a concentration of her essence that she could manifest into reality. The dimension's stability was an ongoing testament to Caretaker's power and resolve.

Magik drew her own sword, armor rippling up across her torso and shoulders. Its weight was a comfort. Magik feared nothing like she feared the Elder Gods. A demon could be defeated, even the most powerful of them. An entity like Chthon could only be held at bay, eternally, and never be allowed to wake. The Elder Gods were chaos incarnate.

13

CARETAKER began her shielding spell as soon as they were in Limbo. Robbie called the Spirit and Nico cut her hand, the salt of her blood zipping through Otherplace's thin air. Blade waited for Caretaker to nod, for Magik to open a disc onto a shaded alleyway in Queens. The portal faced a dirty painted aluminum door at the top of three pitted concrete steps. The once-white paint had chipped and was covered in dents and dirt smudges.

Nico held up the Staff of One, her expression fierce and slightly haunted. "Beku!"

"Praesidio," Caretaker breathed, and projected her shield through the portal, a thousand winding ropes of white light twining into a wall that touched the base of the steps and extended nearly ten feet into the air.

Blade smelled soulless, and demon, and John Doe, but

none of it was fresh. If there were hearts beating inside, Nico had paused them.

"It's working," Nico said.

"Let me check for trip wires," Blade said, and glanced at Caretaker.

"You can walk through it. Just don't come back the same way."

Blade darted out of Limbo and up the steps, feeling the tug of Caretaker's shield as he passed through, like multiple blasting air vents of vibration. He crouched in front of the door, his senses open, and touched the dingy metal. He went quickly around the sides and top. The deadbolt was thrown. He smelled chemicals inside, metal, sweat, death… and now that he knew its signature stench, the very faintest whiff of the Darkhold spell that powered John Doe's gamma shields. Nico had codified it back in the war room.

He looked back at the Suns, blurry through the thick white light. He pointed at the door, held up three fingers. The Suns were ready. The women floated at the edge of the disc, Ghost Rider grinning and crouched to run.

Blade backed up a step, counted himself down, and kicked the deadbolt. The hollow door crunched, the door frame's inset squealing as the thin metal tore around the bolt, and it flew wide open.

Absolute silence and stillness inside. A filthy kitchen littered with food wrappers and cake pans, broken dishes by the sink. The room glowed by the ugly green light of a small gamma box in the corner.

Caretaker released her shield as the Suns followed, its light fading behind them. Blade led the team into a shabby, used rental, two stories of thickly layered paint and cracked linoleum. The kitchen opened to a hall with two bedrooms and a half bath. The doors stood open, revealing more gamma shields. The smaller room had been used for storage, but was empty now. From lines in the dust, it was clear that a number of boxes had recently been moved out, and from the smell, at least a half-dozen dead bodies. More. There were fluids. The larger room was thick with Zarathos's stink. A wide cot had been smashed against one wall.

Nobody home. The Triumvirate had cleared out.

"Recon," Blade said, and left the Suns to run upstairs, noticing a hundred signs that the house had been full of people, recently—clutter, body odor, oily smears on walls and furniture. Upstairs he found an overdecorated room, strewn with clothes and mirrors, that smelled like sex and brimstone. A smaller room with another cot, neatly made, only the faintest scent of John Doe and no personal items, no papers, no evidence that anyone had slept there. A final room looked like a frat house after a kegger and smelled like a gym locker. Blankets and dirty clothes on the bare floor, testosterone, crusts of food. There were three more gamma shields in all, stilled by Nico's spell but operating. Now that he knew what they were, Blade was repulsed by the vague, seemingly harmless scent.

He met the Suns back downstairs. Nico was looking at Robbie's phone, at the pictures he'd taken of the spell's signature over the city streets. Magik knelt by the gamma shield in the sparse living room, scowling at it.

"Nobody," Blade said.

"We'll check all of the signature sites," Caretaker said, and the Suns nodded, but Blade could feel their collective disappointment at the anticlimax. Yes, they'd check, and maybe learn more about John Doe and the extent of the Triumvirate's resources, but Blade thought it was pretty likely that the threesome was already at the vault, waiting for the Midnight Suns to show. The background wasn't as important as keeping them from the amulet.

We should hit 'em before they get dug in.

Caretaker seemed to know what he was thinking. She made eye contact and shook her head ever so slightly, then addressed all of them. "If they're not in the city, we'll return to the Abbey for a few hours' rest and then go on to Transia."

"We should go now," Ghost Rider said, and Magik nodded.

Caretaker was firm. "We still have a full day, and we're not at strength."

Blade couldn't disagree. They'd already had an eventful day, and they might be in for a siege at the vault. The younger Suns needed to sleep, and an extra dose of serum was called for before he went up against Zarathos again.

"She's right," Blade said. "They might still surprise us at one of the other sites. Don't get complacent. But if tomorrow's the big game, we need to rest up so we can get there early."

"One moment," Magik said, and turned off the gamma machine, the sound flat in the frozen air. She slashed open a small portal and the sound of a howling wind rose into the silence. Magik tossed the heavy machine up like a softball, striking it with her sword, her lean muscles flexing. The machine exploded into a thousand glittering pieces on its way through the portal, Limbo hungrily sucking in the flying debris.

"Keep it open," Nico said, and the other boxes from downstairs floated into the room, moving like they were on an invisible conveyer belt. The motion was slow and level, their static green beams thickening the air.

"Three upstairs," Blade said, and the boxes appeared a few seconds later, casting murky splashes on the wall behind the stairs as they floated down. They all watched Magik smash them to bits with short, powerful strikes of her sword, watched her portal vacuum in the shattered bits. Blade wished they could keep one to study, the technology was important, but Magik and Caretaker were right about how poisonous the Darkhold was. It was better this way. Once the Triumvirate were handled, he'd conduct a more thorough investigation of John Doe's safe houses. There had to be schematics and parts to find.

When Magik destroyed the last one, she looked deeply satisfied. Nico showed her a picture off Robbie's phone and Magik cut a new portal, the smaller one popping out of sight.

They left the empty rental behind, stepping onto the Limbo bridge.

"Same as before," Caretaker said, and Magik raised her glowing sword. Blade cleared his mind of expectations and then thoughts, ready to respond to whatever came next.

○————————————○

TWO more rental houses, both empty. Two panel vans, empty. A warehouse that Blade said had been divested of its contents very recently, perhaps only minutes before the Suns' arrival, but of course that meant it was also *empty*, no Triumvirate, no secret compound of military guys, no slavering demonic guard beasts. Nico was disappointed and angsty. Now they had less than twenty-four hours. She got that they needed to be bright-eyed when they faced off with the baddies, but time seemed to be speeding along and she resented having to stop to take a nap.

"At least we know they're not fronting a major operation," Robbie said, stepping off the portal dais. The Abbey was already deeply in shadow. The last rays of daylight skipped off the gray ocean waves, painted a fiery trail to nowhere. "All of those places were dumps."

"And that they await us in Transia," Magik said. "We should not linger here."

"We will eat and then rest," Caretaker said, leading them toward the Abbey's east entrance. Its many windows glowed with warm candlelight, lit by the chandeliers and lamps that flickered to life whenever it got dark outside. The torches that flanked the door cut through the gathering shadows, lighting their path. For a gothic pile, it was super homey.

"Nico, do you know the spell for healing sleep?" Caretaker asked. The heavy door at the top of the Abbey's steps opened for them.

"No, but I know the deep-meditation one, from the Sartorius." Nico said. The receptive, thoughtless state lasted about an hour and a half, and coming out fully rested happened to be a side-effect. She used it all the time when she stayed up too late watching movies or reading.

"Good, that's fine," Caretaker said, leading them toward the kitchen. "After dinner, you and Robbie will use it. We'll leave for Transia when you wake."

Charlie trotted in, panting, and Blade flashed off to his room. Nico cooed over the good girl, who allowed herself to be petted but kept her eye on Caretaker, who was looking through the cabinets.

"What shall it be?" Caretaker asked. Blade reappeared, *sans* weapons and coat, and pulled a chair out from the table.

"Supreme pizza," Robbie said.

"Think *fortifying*, King," Nico said.

"Extra pepperoni and sausage, then."

"You'll destroy the Triumvirate with your breath," Nico said.

"Burn out their eyes," he agreed.

"Chef salad and miso soup," Nico said, and Magik nodded.

Caretaker took out a platter and carried it to the table, a loaded, steaming pizza appearing as she set it down. She waved her hand and there were plates and bowls and napkins, a pitcher of ice water and glasses.

Nico lifted the pitcher with a thought and poured, rubbing the soft skin around Charlie's horns. "Do you want any help?" she asked.

"No, I've got it," Caretaker said, setting an empty pot on the table, the rich scent of miso steaming out when the flat bottom touched the wood. A giant bowl of salad was next, full of cheese and deli meat and egg, and a plate of warm rolls. Silverware appeared next to each plate, along with a glass bottle of vinaigrette.

Caretaker looked the table over and sat down. When she picked up her spoon, the bowl in front of her filled. Everyone but Blade loaded their dishes, and though they discussed tactics and spells while they ate, the atmosphere was anything but grim. Robbie kept talking trash about the Triumvirate. Nico fed Charlie slivers of meat under the table, and the hellhound had the good sense to be discreet. Magik recounted a little of Zarathos's history, about how Mephisto had defeated him. There was a feeling like Christmas Eve, an anticipation that had everyone interested and alert.

And Caretaker's here. Caretaker had mostly stopped eating with them after Agatha died. Nico hadn't realized how much she'd missed it until now, tonight, with all of them in the same room and talking and there was no horrible tension or cold silence. Blade was leaned back, legs crossed. Magik and Caretaker both smiled at Robbie's crack about Zarathos having a skull for a head.

Caretaker stood up finally. "We'll meet at the forge

in two hours. We'll want light body armor in case they've armed their soulless. I meant to have new armor forged, but I'm afraid time got away from me."

"We'll manage," Nico said. They weren't even going to need it. They were going to show up the same way they'd hit John Doe's shield sites—magic forward, careful. Whatever happened, they'd be ready. Magik and Robbie would open some Hell portals and the Suns would shove the villains through. When the seal finally expired, they'd bring the vault to the Abbey, where it would be safe.

"I know you will," Caretaker said. "There's no alternative. But regardless of the outcome, I will be there to fight alongside you."

Nico wanted to say something as powerful, to let the old woman know that her support was appreciated. "I'm proud to be in the Midnight Suns," she blurted instead.

"Same," Blade said, the others nodding.

"It's an honor," Robbie said. "The Spirits of Vengeance think so, too."

"I have faith that we will serve the Balance well, now and in future days," Magik said.

Caretaker nodded. "And so we shall. Two hours."

She blinked out of the kitchen before anyone had a chance to thank her for dinner.

"Anyone else getting a last-supper kind of vibe?" Robbie asked.

"Last supper before we dominate," Nico said, and Robbie leaned in for a fist bump.

All the Suns stood, Blade flashing off to his room, Magik saying she wanted to take a walk. Charlie trotted after her. Nico and Robbie were left meandering toward their rooms. Nico felt a sharp tug in her guts, a low internal heaviness, and sighed. Her period was due. The Staff of One responded to her cycles; for six days a month she didn't have to cut herself to call it up, but she probably wouldn't start for another day.

Figures. It would show up too late to be useful, but just in time to give her cramps for the big showdown. She'd have to wear a pad, too. Fun.

"I don't even feel tired," Robbie said, opening his door. He kicked off his boots and dropped his jeans, keeping his T-shirt and boxers on as he flopped on his bed.

"Doesn't matter," Nico said. "You won't sleep, exactly, just… like, extremely zone out. You can wake yourself up if you try hard enough, but you won't want to—it's chill. The spell will wear off on its own, and you'll just be awake all of a sudden, feeling like you got a solid ten hours."

"*That's* how you get away with all the late-night movies," Robbie said. "Man, I could have used some of that when I was in school. You've been holding out on me."

"Witch's advantage," Nico said. "Get comfy."

Robbie lay down, pulling his blanket up to mid-chest.

"No Sleeping Beauty moves when I'm out," he said, and batted his mismatched eyes at her.

"In your dreams, loser."

Robbie chuckled. Nico recited the familiar words of the

spell, changing the pronouns, and Robbie's eyelids drifted closed, his body relaxing completely. Nico closed his door on the way out and headed for her room. She wanted to take a shower but decided she'd have time when she woke up.

The dim halls were silent, and it felt late, though in fact it wasn't even full night. Nico was wide awake, excited and nervous to go back to Transia. She wished Wanda was coming with them. The Scarlet Witch was as strong as Magik, stronger probably; Agatha had said that neither Wanda nor Nico had fully tapped their potential. Wanda was doing okay: the last time they'd texted she'd been settling in at the Sanctum Sanctorum, busy, still not ready to talk about the accident.

Poor Agatha. That was the only thing missing tonight, Nico thought, opening her door: Agatha's wizened smile, her calm humor. She'd been the glue that had held the Suns together, she'd been their biggest cheerleader, and Nico's real, true friend.

Ebony was curled and asleep on the folded quilt at the foot of Nico's bed, and Nico's eyes prickled again. Agatha wasn't really gone, not really.

"Yeah, I'm PMS all over," she said, sniffling, and Ebony raised her soft head, blinking at her.

"Sorry to wake you, gorgeous," Nico said, sitting on the bed. "I'm going to have to pet you a little, too."

Ebony allowed the trespass, even rubbing her cheek against Nico's fingers. Nico kicked her pillow off the bed so she could lie with her face near the sleek cat and keep stroking her.

"You can stay as long as you like," she whispered, and Ebony started licking one paw, purring.

Nico recited her spell and Ebony's soft rumbling contentment followed her into the warm dark. When she opened her eyes again, the cat was gone, and it was time to get ready to go.

ZARATHOS sat in contemplation of the vault for many hours, observing the seal, learning its magic. Only time would open it, but if he could find the exact vibration the seal was looking for, he believed he might be able to mimic the condition. Satana and Fenn were busy setting up a defense above ground, mostly, but they appeared at the edge of Zarathos's focus several times, dropping into the vault's chamber to take measurements or seed the ground. Zarathos ignored them, concentrating deeply.

When he had memorized the patterns of the complicated lock, it came to him what he might do... but he needed more power—a lot of it.

Zarathos stood and willed himself to the nearest large collection of mortals, finding them north of Transia at the edge of a small town. A rickety wooden stadium of several hundred souls watched a handful of men kick a ball across a wide green field. Ideally there would be more, but he would take what he could get. When Zarathos manifested near one of the big nets, there were shouts and laughter, although the humans nearest to him screamed and tried to get away, stampeding up the tiers of creaking stairs that encircled the field.

He didn't wait for their terror; he wanted to return to the vault immediately. Zarathos raised his arms and breathed in, letting his hunger be known—

—and countless souls flowed into him, ripped from their vessels, pouring across the field. He felt himself grow, expand. The transference lifted him off the ground, the torrent of souls like a fountain, pushing him high into the air.

Zarathos waited until the last straggling souls joined his essence and then roared, triumphant, and the ground shook so hard that the walls of the arena crumpled, crushing many of the empty vessels. Their pain was sweet and he brought what was left of the stadium down on top of the screaming survivors with a wave of one hand, the rich scent of gore and splinters following him back to the vault's chamber. Every particle of his being was spinning with power and purpose. He sat on the ground and rocketed through the astral plane, through the dimensions that would soon align, tasting the air, changing his essence to recreate it. When he returned to his body, he was ready.

The succubus appeared before him, her gaze crawling over his form. "My lord, you have fed again, and traveled far."

"I understand what the seal seeks," Zarathos said. "Watch."

He spoke the words of his intention, but it was his increased power that gave them direction. The air in the chamber changed, the flavors of a dozen dimensions whirling into being.

Zarathos listened to the seal, and felt it was changing, too.

Satana disappeared, returning with Fenn seconds later. The man had his device and he mumbled to himself, turning the dials. When he spoke, his voice was high, excited.

"The seal is starting to give! At this rate, it will dissolve in less than an hour!"

The succubus clapped her hands, and immediately started gushing at Zarathos's brilliance and strength. Fenn's eyes were wide and he went over his measurements again, showing all of his tiny square teeth.

Zarathos was gratified, but also impatient. He was bursting with power and barely half full.

I can eat so much more. In an hour's time he could swallow a whole city and wouldn't even need the Varkath Star to challenge Mephisto. He could—

"The Midnight Suns are here," Satana said, and smiled, her eyes sparkling. "To the east."

"Release the fire-demons," Zarathos said, and Satana popped away.

The air in the chamber was already changed; the seal would continue to unravel quickly. Zarathos decided that it would amuse him to see their enemies fall. Watching the Midnight Suns die would whet his appetite for the coming chaos. Zarathos reached for the dimensional rift that Satana had created and left the vault's chamber.

14

MAGIK'S portal to the Transian hills didn't open the way it should, the rip slow, the disc's shining edges traveling outward at half speed as it followed the clean slice.

"Close it," Caretaker said, immediately. A demonic ward was in place, a resistance to dimensional changes. The image of the sun-dappled trees and rocks flashed closed. They could easily force their way through, dispel it, but the spell-caster would already be aware of the attempted incursion.

How far does it extend? And what else is in place?

"We need to appear outside their wards, so that I can see what they've set up," Caretaker said.

"There's a ridge east about half a klick," Blade said. "Lots of cover."

Caretaker nodded, and Magik cut again. This time the portal opened easily, and Nico used her staff to shield and warn, speaking in what sounded like Somali.

The Suns exited the portal, stepping into a flat, rocky field surrounded by thick woods. The day was sunny, warm. Boulders as big as houses blocked them from seeing the area of the vault, west, but the raw power of multiple demonic spells was palpable, concentrated. Zarathos had grown, his signature dominant, but there were dimensional protections, glamours, gathered soulless, and—

Caretaker sensed it just as Nico spoke, her young brow furrowed. "The seal is breaking!"

Minutes. The ward keeping the vault hidden was all but gone and its lock was crumbling fast. They needed to—

A fire-demon dropped from the sky, landing in a splash across a boulder behind them, immediately growing into a towering humanoid tornado of flame. Its eyes were blackened red pits, its long limbs rippling, melting the rock beneath its hissing form.

A burning portal had split the sky sixty feet above and another demon, then a third, hit the field like rockets, more of them splashing over the forest surrounding them, roaring to life. Trees burst into flame as the creatures rose and walked, all headed for the Suns.

"Magik, a portal in front of theirs!" Blade shouted, and Magik flew high.

The Suns were instantly enveloped in searing heat and Caretaker condensed the moisture in the air, blasting the demon behind them with a sheet of water as its flaming arms reached out.

The force of the splash knocked it back, but the demon didn't diminish. If anything, it grew, spreading wide. Smoke boiled from the flash forest fire, rocks cracking and liquefying all around them.

"Non noceamur, coagmentatio!" Caretaker threw up a dome around herself and the other Suns, filled it with her dimension's cool air, fixing it to the ground. Three demons leapt on it at once, their amorphic bodies pouring over the sparking half-bubble, and Caretaker strained to keep the shield whole, to keep the air inside from roasting the Suns. High overhead, Magik floated next to her portal, flames pouring into Limbo from the rift above. The formless monsters tried to escape their new destination, sent long droplets of liquid fire out from between the portals. Everything the demonic fire touched burned.

Magik rained blasts of energy down at the fire-demons, knocking them out of shape, but they instantly reformed. Eight had come through, and they raged toward the gathered Suns. Magik hit the hill north of them and an avalanche of dirt and stone swallowed two of the creatures, but they burned through in clouds of hissing smoke.

"I can hold it a minute," Caretaker managed. "Water won't stop them. They're Koth's children, Sumerian."

"Nico," Blade and Robbie both said.

"How?" Nico cried, the Staff of One tight in her bloody fist—

—and she disappeared in a flash of purple light.

Magik couldn't leave her portal—they'd be buried in fire, and all of Caretaker's energies were invested in the shield, the only thing keeping them from incineration. Robbie and Blade both stood ready but there was nothing they could do against an inferno.

Caretaker sensed Zarathos near, his presence a foul stain, but the rocks were crumbling and melting around them. She had to pour more of herself into the shield, to increase its coverage where it touched the ground. A blast from Zarathos might end them. Wherever Nico had gone, Caretaker prayed the young witch would be back in time to help.

○————————○

NICO hit what felt like a brick wall, the impact dazing her for a second. She was standing in front of the forge at the Abbey. The demon that lived inside was awake, filling the giant glass wall, a roaring sphere set against the worn stones. The chamber was like a sauna.

I got through. The Staff of One had punched into Caretaker's dimension, *impossible*, but the thought was background; it didn't matter. Nico had to get back.

With an answer.

Nico concentrated her will, held up the Staff. "Let's talk."

Light blasted from the Staff's eye, but she still stood in front of the roaring forge. Nothing had physically changed.

WHAT

The voice was sexless, annoyed, as loud as a scream in her mind. The flames of the demon's body beat against the glass.

"The Suns are being attacked by your kind. How do we stop them?" Nico asked.

The silence was sullen. Nico could feel its irritation at being commanded by a mortal.

"*Please!*" Nico's desperate shout echoed from the high, shadowy ceiling.

EXTINGUISH FiRE

The forge demon's tone was patronizing to the extreme.

"How? Chemicals, sand, what?"

There was a sound like roaring flames, a clatter like embers, and Nico felt its disdain. It was laughing.

THEY WILL GROW

Time time time! Her friends were going to burn to death and the vault's seal was breaking!

"Please tell me," Nico said, because *please* had worked before and she had nothing at all to bargain with, except that the demon had no interest at all in continuing their conversation. Nico seized on the idea.

"I promise I won't ever bother you again if you'll tell me how to extinguish their fire. I'll leave you alone and never force you into a conversation that you don't want to—"

WE EAT AIR GO AWAY NOW

"Thank you, thank you!" Nico raised the Staff of One and didn't consider how to return to Transia, only visualized the faces of her friends and willed herself to them. "Go!"

The Staff protected her entrance back to the scene, floating her high above the burning ridge, above Magik and the sandwiched portals. Bitter smoke roiled up from the fiery ground, the demons dancing through the flames, converging on Caretaker's tiny bubble. There were eight demons in all, slipping through the burning trees, pounding at the invisible umbrella above the rocks.

"Magik, hold on to something!" Nico screamed, and saw Limbo's energy shoot from Magik's portal and envelop her.

Nico didn't stop to think, she thrust the Staff out. "Deep space!"

A crack opened in the sky and the world flew upward, fire, trees, boulders, everything loose sucked to the icy vacuum. The eight fire-demons stretched and thinned, clawing at the passing debris as they whirled upward in streaming sheets of smoke.

Yes! It was working, she just had to—

"Nico!" Magik's cry was faint in the rushing air. Nico turned—

—and saw Zarathos hovering in the sky above the pit west of them, saw the ball of lightning hurtling at her head.

Nico brought the Staff around and split the demonic light shooting toward her, streams of power crackling away to either side, but the energy blasted her backward, spinning wildly, and she felt herself sucked toward the crack in space above.

"Blue sky!" she shouted, the Staff drawing from her panic, and the gaping, icy void zipped closed, along with both portals. The few clouds floating around disappeared.

A ton of smoking rock and flaming trees that had been hurtling for the rift fell, raining down like bombs on the ridge below. Magik flew into the destructive chaos, blasting pieces away from where the other Suns were still gathered. Nico shoved the majority of the flaming rain against a cliff farther east, the debris dropping harmlessly into a stony crevasse.

Zarathos hit the Caretaker's shield with another lightning ball. With a twist of her hand, Caretaker wrapped what was left of the shield up and around the incoming blast, hurling it back at him.

The Suns broke apart, Blade and Robbie joining Magik in knocking the last flaming chunks out of the air, Caretaker sending a bolt of white at Zarathos's hovering form. Nico got her bearings and threw a disruption spell at the musclebound demon, the tight beam of energy rocking his horrible face back.

"Get to the vault!" Caretaker shouted, and Magik scooped up Blade as Ghost Rider portaled across to the hill where the vault was buried. Nico darted after them, over a narrow gorge that separated the blocky hills. The air was thick with magic—dark spells, dark ether, wards like webs clinging to Nico's skin as she swooped down to join her team at the edge of the pit, where—

"Gotcha," a seductive voice drawled, and Nico went deaf and blind, the Staff of One knocked from her hand. She was paralyzed and falling, lost.

GHOST Rider ran for the well, alert for their enemies. Caretaker appeared at the rim of the pit, ducking another lightning strike from Zarathos. Blade and Magik were running with Robbie, Blade darting ahead.

"We don't have much time," Caretaker shouted. "We—"

She disappeared. All the Suns were gone. Ghost Rider stood alone… and the ground trembled and came to life.

Rock creatures sat up from the broken ground, demonic forms wrenching out of the soil, cracking free of the earth. They stirred and climbed to their blocky feet, joints crumbling dust, blind, featureless heads turning toward Ghost Rider. A dozen at least, each seven feet tall with rough-hewn limbs, and the first few were stomping in his direction.

Robbie dove for the closest, spinning before he tackled the thing to land face up, the creature's solid body pressed to the ground beneath him. He slung his chains at the next two closing in, the flaming links knocking them together with a thundering crash. A jerk of his hands and they went down in a heap. Robbie turned, wrapped his chain around another and whipped him into two more, turned again—

—and the monsters he'd flattened had disappeared. More were wrenching themselves free of the stone, the sound like shattering ceramic, like pebbles in a blender, but there weren't any bodies on the ground.

Glamour? The Suns could still be there. He could be attacking them now, like he'd gone after Magik before.

"Nico!" he shouted, and whipped his chains at the

stumbling, relentless onslaught, afraid to hurt them, not sure what was happening.

BLADE sensed the thick magic slamming down and then he was alone.

Glamour. Rock demons sat up all around him, conjured from the ground. They pulled stumpy limbs out of the Earth and staggered toward Blade, rattling the ground, joints forming in cracks and puffs of dust.

The rock monsters plodded forward, and Blade reflexively dodged when the closest one swung its block of an arm, driving his heel into its rough thigh. It was like kicking a house, but the thing was unbalanced and fell backward, crashing to the ground.

I kicked something. A glamour but something more. He could smell the Suns, hear many hearts beating, but the data was diffuse, blurred by the heavy spell that thrummed in the deceitful air.

"Nico!" he called, dancing back from the clumsy attacks, turning to slip between another pair of looming monsters, ducking another swing. He couldn't *see.*

CARETAKER felt a glamour envelop them and she was alone at the empty pit.

"Revelare," she commanded, and she saw soulless soldiers with guns dropping into the open crater, pointing their weapons in all directions, several trained on her. She sensed the other Suns, close by.

"Revelare omnia!"

The soldiers disappeared. Ghost Rider flicked in and out of view. She saw a handful of small rock demons knocked down by his chains—

—and she was alone again. Small puffs of dust rose from the ground, painting shafts of sunlight, and there was a sound like heavy rocks being smashed.

"Diluere lux," she said, and spread her hands, and the pale light that should have illuminated movement appeared and settled to the trembling ground like powdered chalk.

Layered glamour. She needed more power to cut through it. Caretaker tried to open a channel to her dimension but it was blocked, the effort like opening a jar that was glued shut. Magik might be cut off from Limbo. Caretaker couldn't feel the vault's seal anymore. She couldn't find the Suns or their enemies. The Triumvirate had the upper hand.

The Staff of One. Without dimensional access, the Staff was the Suns' strongest magical asset.

"*Nico!*" Caretaker called, weighting the word with intention for the girl to hear her, reaching out with her mind to find her—

—and a fist-sized chunk of rock slammed into Caretaker's shoulder. She stumbled, startled and enraged by the pain, and forced her attention back to finding Nico, sending the intention to the other Suns: *Nico, find Nico.* If they couldn't fix this fast, they were all dead.

15

THE witch child hit the rocks and Satana threw a blanket of gravel over her, even as she manifested her own perfect spell, dropping it over the Midnight Suns like a sopping blanket. The girl's blood-magic staff had vanished when she'd knocked it loose, but Satana wasn't worried, the little witch was frozen; it was costly power-wise, but so worth it. Her enemies were at her mercy.

Zarathos immediately swooped in and blasted the old Blood witch with lightning, but Satana's glamour protected itself and his lightshow skipped off like a flat rock on water, blowing up a tree to the south. Flaming splinters flew.

"Only watch, Dark Lord, and see how they dance for you," Satana said. She lifted a handful of rocks from the piles of them and started throwing, flipping them into the crater with a thought.

Together, they watched the "heroes" fight imaginary soldiers as the Triumvirate's real army took up positions around the pit, Satana's soulless dressed in camouflage she'd designed herself to match the dull colors of Transia's rocks and trees. Fenn had been able to procure weapons—*Glox*, he called them—and her soldiers looked handsome and lethal. They wouldn't fire until Satana commanded, and she was having too much fun to interrupt. She'd wasted hours transporting Fenn's things around and planting his bombs in the chamber, making a deal with the fire-demons on Zarathos's behalf, widening her channels to home. The stupid Suns had showed up early, too. She hadn't had time to set up more than one good spell.

But this one is sooo good.

The vampire and the Ghost Rider were a special joy to behold. The vampire moved like a bat, fast and fluttering, his stylish coat whipping against the ground. He ducked and jumped with the precision of a ballet dancer. The Ghost Rider was a lean mean machine, shoulder-rolling and chain-flinging, the Spirit of Vengeance riding with abandon and lethal power. Magik was fine, Satana supposed, very athletic, but she didn't look so bright slashing and kicking at the air. The old witch was eating through layers of design, but the beauty of Satana's spell was that it filled in its own holes. Satana chucked a rock at her, and Zarathos laughed when blood dripped from the old woman's wound.

Like a merry-go-round. Just as she'd intended, the Suns were stuck on a ride that wouldn't let go. Satana had drenched the rocks in dimensional magic, and drew from them now to feed the complicated web of deceit, pushing the fighters closer together. The rock creatures would turn to soldiers, then demons, each dumb hero convinced they were fighting alone, and Satana had a lockout on portals. None of them would escape.

Zarathos laughed again when Magik tripped over the frozen witch. He preferred to break things, but had to enjoy getting a flush of energy from his enemies' confusion and distress.

Fenn's voice trembled up through the well of the vault. "Just a few more minutes!"

Satana grinned and threw another rock at Magik.

○———————○

THE ugly feel of Satana's spell cloaked Magik's senses. The ground stank of her, like brimstone and synthetic roses, entrails and cheap sparkling wine. The Suns were hidden, and glamours rose from the soil and stalked her.

Magik slashed a portal and it wouldn't open, the slice sealing behind her blade. She spoke a line of revelation and it died in the tainted ether. She was alarmed when one of the stone monsters slammed into her armored shoulder— they were more than illusion—but she slashed at it and her sword touched nothing, kicked another and her boot passed through air.

Even as she opened her mouth to call for Nico, she felt Caretaker seeking the young witch, calling for her. Nico was close but something was wrong. She would have dispelled the glamour otherwise.

Magik focused on the girl's signature, the sharp pulse of her energy, and thought she caught a glimmer, buried in the demonic miasma. She moved toward it—and tripped on the air, stumbling. Another of the semi-solid apparitions hit her. Magik swung her sword at the creature to no effect. She searched for the glimmer again.

There. The sense of Nico was on the ground where she'd tripped, where there were only a few stones.

Magik crouched and put out her hand, touched loose rock, invisible, and pushed her awareness through. Nico was frozen by Satana's dimensional magic, and Magik forced a crack, shouting with her whole self for the witch to wake, lending the girl awareness by her dwindling energies. Cut off from dimensional power, Nico was their best chance.

○―――――――――○

NICO heard Magik, a distant cry in the dark, and grabbed on. Her thoughts stumbled but she knew she was alive, awake, stuck. Stress flushed her; she couldn't move, couldn't see, but she had awareness of her body at least, the Staff of One back inside her, sharp rocks digging into her back and side. Her uterus clenched, and she felt the Staff tingle in her marrow. She was bleeding.

Nico concentrated, making her need manifest, and felt

the Staff rise out of her body. Her fingers were numb but she felt the Staff touch them, sliding against her palm. She formed a word in her mind, wrapped it in anxiety and force, investing her entire will into shouting it.

Espresso!

The staff's energy shot through her, defined her form. Nico was back in her body and wide awake.

Nico leapt into the air, shedding rocks, aiming her fury at the demons that floated just east of the empty pit, aiming it at the trashy demoness who just now noticed that she was in trouble. Her eyes went wide, and she reached for the hulking Zarathos.

"Eat it!" Nico screamed, with her whole heart, and Satana's black power was blasted from the rocks and soil, leached out and lifted into a swarm of pulsing atoms that arrowed back into their creator and pummeled the brute Zarathos at her side.

Satana shrieked, overloaded, and was knocked into the trees south of the pit. The staff kept the torrent going, hammering her with the power that she'd created. Without form, without will, the dark energy was only force, and it smacked that trash down and shook her good. Zarathos roared, shielding himself from the onslaught with a wave of one meaty hand.

The Suns appeared suddenly in the open pit, surrounded by men in camo holding big semi-automatics. The soldiers weren't shooting but had their guns pointed at the Suns.

Soulless.

Zarathos's giant, fanged lower jaw dropped open like it was unhinged, impossibly wide, and he exhaled. A swarm of chittering locusts poured from his black throat, a seemingly endless stream of whirring, flying insects. They spread out like a fan. In a second, the pit was thick with them, and they went after the Suns, trying to sting or bite—but Caretaker brushed them aside with a wave of her hand, sent them in a cloud toward the melted, smoking rock of the ridge to the east.

Magik cut a portal and floated up on the wave of power that poured out. She flung her hands at Zarathos and a burst of brilliant, pale-blue light shut his mouth and turned him sideways. She hit him again, while Caretaker began a powerful spell of binding.

Ghost Rider and Blade attacked the soldiers, Ghost Rider taking out a half dozen with a flick of his wrist, a bladed chain slapping across their chests, knocking them off their feet. Blade had his sword out and was hamstringing more of them, slashing weapons to the ground, whirling around them like they were standing still. There were a few shots fired but not on purpose, the soulless waiting on a command that Satana wasn't giving. The succubus was still wrapped in a cloud of pulsing darkness.

Nico could feel the seal on the vault underground, still holding, but it wouldn't be long. The air was different. It was—

Zarathos bellowed and a tidal wave of black energy crashed over the Suns, the ground under their feet rising, wrenched from its stasis by raw force. Caretaker shouted in a language Nico had never heard before as the world flipped, spun, the sky disappearing. Nico hugged the Staff and ducked as explosion after explosion ripped through the air, as tons of rocks slammed down and buried her.

○——————————○

SATANA had been slapped from the air by the young witch. Magik and the old Blood resisted Zarathos's attacks, Limbo's Mistress daring to strike him with her not inconsiderable power, the hag dispelling his locusts. The Ghost Rider and the vampire went after Satana's useless soldiers.

Enough. He was Zarathos, a god, and he was finished with these games.

He opened the sky and absorbed the force of every storm, every charged atom, and channeled the turbulence, speaking the words of power that were his due. He broke the earth deep, just over the vessel's chamber, overwhelming the hag's stasis by brute force. He lifted and turned the massive sheaf of collapsing rock upside down, then slammed it back to the earth on top of the meddlesome Suns. They were crushed, along with most of the worthless empty men.

Much of the vault's chamber collapsed, and the stones rumbled and shook as Fenn's bombs discharged deep underground. Zarathos reached for the space he'd secured around the vault and found the Triumvirate's mortal huddled there, faithfully waiting for the seal to break, to claim his pitiful vengeance.

Zarathos gouged a path to the vault, tossing the tons of rock and clay aside. His ascension was at hand.

16

THE blood-magic staff's relentless force cut off suddenly as Zarathos picked up a warehouse-sized chunk of earth and flipped it like a pancake, dropping it on the scurrying Suns and a dozen faithful servants. The chamber below mostly collapsed with a shuddering *crunch*, and Satana heard a half-dozen explosions through the ground. Fenn's carefully placed bombs rattled the stones on the surface, useless now to the Triumvirate's purpose.

Satana shook herself, half-drained and battered, saw Zarathos part the massive heap of rocks, arcs of breaking stone and splintering clay rising on either side of his new path like cresting waves, landing in a crashing hailstorm across the ruined earth. A deep crevice peeled open, angling straight to the vault. It was too dark at the bottom to see, the sun's angle was wrong, but Satana could sense that Fenn was down there, still alive.

She floated up from where she'd been mercilessly thrown, furious at the little witch, furious that Zarathos had robbed Satana of the chance to retaliate.

And my soldiers! Nothing stirred beneath the fresh heaps of damp stone. There were only a handful still alive, those who'd been missed by the big Z's tantrum. They stared around with blank eyes, holding their Glox, most of them bleeding from various cuts and scratches. Their uniforms were stained and rumpled.

It doesn't matter. None of this matters. The Varkath Star was what she'd come for, and Zarathos wasn't going to lay his sausage fingers on it before her.

Satana could feel a few magical signatures buried in the rocks and called to her servants. If the Suns were alive, they'd still be digging themselves out by the time the vault opened, but better safe than sorry.

Seven empty vessels climbed onto the broken heaps, knocking stones into the narrow opening that led to the vault.

"Anything comes out of these rocks, you shoot it," Satana said. "Keep them busy."

Her faithful servants nodded. Any one of the Suns could wipe them out without much effort, but she only needed a few more minutes and then all of this would be over.

Satana floated down into the deep crevasse, saw light at the bottom—Zarathos's big dumb head, burning, and Fenn's tiny blinking lights, green and red and white, like fireflies in what was left of the shadowy chamber.

Satana called a light of her own when she reached the boys, crowded around the metal vault. Zarathos was exhaling heavy air, tinged with the scents of faraway worlds. Fenn had his shirt over his mouth against the fog of dust, his eyes red and watering. How he'd avoided getting blown up or crushed was nothing short of a miracle. He had some new device out, another dumb blinking box.

Satana cleared the air, glancing up at the huge crack of blue sky overhead. Zarathos's impulsive smackdown had left them open to attack, should the Suns manage to crawl free of the mountain he'd dropped on them.

"Dark Lord, a spell to protect us as we wait, should more enemies come..." Satana did her best to make it sound sexy and obvious.

"Do so," Zarathos rumbled, not looking away from the metal box.

"My power is diminished," she said, careful to keep her voice even. Not that Zarathos cared, but holding off the blood stick's assault had cost her. Satana had invested a healthy portion of her dimension's energy into the stones, and the witch child had managed to extract it, separate it from Satana's essence, and then pound her with the raw power. A despicable trick, and Satana sincerely hoped that the girl was now so much warm jelly.

Zarathos threw up one hand, grated out a few words, and the rocks around them shifted. They were in a new room, smaller than the original, the air suddenly thick with the giant demon's murky signature. The sharply angled tunnel leading back to the surface widened and darkened, humming with gathering power. A screen of mist raised up to block their new room from sight of the broadened corridor, solidifying into rock that was Zarathos's will made manifest; the fresh stone radiated deflection.

Satana moved to stand behind Zarathos, opening herself to his throbbing aura, drafting off the strength of his intention. If need be, she'd "borrow" some of his strength to touch the Star before him.

Let's not jump the gun on that one. The second she took from him, Zarathos would mark her as an enemy. Dealing with the Suns had depleted him slightly, but he could still stomp her out if he chose.

"Any minute," Fenn breathed, his red eyes glittering, and the Triumvirate waited.

o———————o

BLADE had ducked and covered, sensing Caretaker's spell as the force of the rocks drove him into the earth. His body was compressed, buried, but a thin, pliable shield had been thrown over him, a bubble that extended a handspan around his entire body.

All he could smell was dank soil and dark magic. Blade opened his mouth and let a thread of drool hang off his lip, orienting himself by its direction. He was on his side, the sky to his left.

He pushed at the stones over his head, then all around

him, but a hundred tons of compressed rock wasn't about to be muscled aside.

A sense of the other Suns opened into his awareness, and Caretaker's voice spoke clearly in his mind. *The Triumvirate are with the vault. We will assemble at once atop the rocks and break their barrier. There are more soulless. Beware.*

Got it, Blade thought, and heard Robbie echoing him before the brief connection went dead. Blade felt the shield's pliable energy stretch and extend, crunching new space out of the compacted stone, his skin tingling—

—and then he was standing on top of the devastation. He picked the closest soulless and rushed him, just as the creature raised its weapon and fired, spraying rounds.

Bam bam bam bam! A scattering of soulless fired brand-new Glock 22s, loaded with .40 ammo. The ragged hills echoed back the booming cracks, but none of them could shoot at all—fifteen rounds per mag and they wasted shots left and right. Blade's coat caught a hole entirely by chance and then he was tossing the soldier into the guy next to him, both falling into a deep crevasse that had opened in the broken ground, that led straight to the vault.

The vault's magic was faint, a bare whisper. Blade could feel Zarathos down there, he could smell Satana and John Doe, but they weren't in sight. The observations occurred in a split second.

Blade spun and flipped a knife at a cleft-chinned soulless who was firing at Nico, neatly slashing the semi out of his hand, along with two fingers. The empty man howled but picked up a rock with his good hand. He still wanted to fight.

Blade flashed past Ghost Rider, who was stomping a pair of luckless soldiers and blasting the last two with a torrent of Hellfire. The Spirit laughed, and Robbie with it. Blade heard them just as he drove his elbow into the rock wielder's temple and knocked him cold. The soulless dropped and didn't come back up.

He turned, ready for more, but the Triumvirate's victims were all down. Robbie kicked the last one twitching a couple more times, hungry to continue. Magik had cut a portal to Limbo and was glimmering with power, standing with Nico and Caretaker at the edge of the deep new tunnel, a sixty-degree angled slide to a block of shielded magic where the vault lay. The soulless that Blade had dropped in had slid to the edge of the demonic shield at the very bottom.

Caretaker opened her hands, breathing deeply. Blade could feel the old woman's dimensional power pouring through the open portal, Magik floating easily on a wave of her own. Nico had stripped the area of Satana's workings, blown it away like dust, and the Suns' dimensional players were getting a boost. Nico's staff had pulled her three feet into the air, enveloping her in purple swirls. All three women were focused on Zarathos's shield, their eyes narrowed, their jaws tight.

Caretaker started murmuring in Latin, Nico's voice falling in with hers on the third word.

Blade and Ghost Rider both fell back as the expanding urgency and creation around the women blossomed into a fierce and powerful intention, the weighted air bending to their shared will. Blade could only just get a sense of how vast the hit was going to be.

Blade flashed over to Robbie and backed them both up to a rocky rise in the trees west of the site. They had a clear view of the trio's powers joining, Caretaker's brilliant white river, Magik's electric tinge of pale blue, the ropy thick twists of deep purple pouring from the Staff of One blending with them into an arrowing, explosive blast.

BOOM! The crash of imploding rock was nothing next to the terrific hiss of violently clashing magics, a roar that Blade felt rather than heard. The edges of the blasted pit crumpled inwards, and Caretaker promptly hurled a few tons of rock out of the way, tossing them aside. The deep ditch east of them thundered clattering echoes through the stony hills.

This time Robbie grabbed Blade, portaled them back to where the rest of their team stared down into the blasted pit. Caretaker had ripped rough, uneven steps down the length of the rocky slope. The vault was hidden by a demon-grown wall of rock, but the mega-shield had been obliterated. There was nothing left… except for the energies of a furious arch-demon and his sidekicks, and the delicate sliver of magic still holding the vault closed.

○————————○

ZARATHOS pushed at the last of the seal's magic, but it refused to give. Fenn sweated and fiddled with his toys.

Satana stood at Zarathos's right hand, silent, working not to betray her excitement. Who wouldn't be excited, to witness his becoming? Songs and stories would be written about this moment for—

BOOM!

The air around them flared, a bomb dropped on them from above. Zarathos felt his shield melting and screamed with rage as the ground shook and shifted, boulders crashing into their new space.

No no no! He threw energy at the dissolving spell but there was nothing to save, his powerful ward sizzling away.

"HOW *DARE* YOU!" He roared, and phased through the outcropping that protected his vault, opening his bottomless need, expending his power to destroy these interlopers in all ways. He summoned the high air to create a storm, and the day instantly blackened to night, the crackling air rising to his call. He revealed his hunger to suck in their light and let it snatch for their souls. They would be obliterated, now. The Varkath Star was his!

17

CARETAKER was ready when Zarathos appeared at the bottom of the pit. She felt him expose the abyss of famine at his core, as she'd expected he would, and opened herself in turn, letting the Abbey's dimensional energies pour into the howling empty space. The light magic was anathema to the demon, burning, painful, eating tiny holes through his essence. Zarathos tried to close himself, but Caretaker kept him pried open, drawing a thousand layers of magic from the Abbey's stones and driving it into his fathomless guts. The steady power whittled at him, forced him into a defense that would drain his resources.

The shrieking demon crashed into a rough wall at the side of the new pit and Caretaker pushed him into the rock, levitating down into the giant misshapen new cavern to keep up the pressure.

Lightning struck the trees just south of the pit, and Magik called that she had it. Caretaker felt Limbo's energy open overhead, a crash of lightning, a blast of heat, and the smell of Limbo's smoky air. She heard the other Suns following her down into the rocky opening, fanning out around the hidden vault, but her full attention stayed on keeping Zarathos pinned. The demon writhed and spat as she pushed him another three feet into the crumbling rock. He beat holes in the stone, jagged cracks rippling outward from his giant fists, but he couldn't keep her out.

Caretaker sensed the wisp of seal left and renewed her intention. She would keep Zarathos at bay for long enough, whatever the cost—

A demonic portal opened above her and chaos spilled through.

○———————○

SATANA felt the shield give and Zarathos charged out to fight, furious at the interruption, leaving her and Fenn alone with the vault.

"How much longer?" she asked, wincing when she felt Zarathos open up and then get hit with a torrent of flavorless old energy, a thousand intricate designs of power channeled like a firehose. One of the Suns was giving the demon a thorough thrashing, and the rest of the team was moving in.

"Two, maybe three minutes," Fenn said.

Dammit! Two or three minutes too late. She didn't mind the Suns taking Zarathos out of the picture, but she needed to stay *in*, and she had about two seconds to come up with something. She could portal out but the Varkath Star would fall to the Suns, and that wasn't an acceptable outcome.

The eternity pits.

It would drain her almost completely, but she could eat when the Star was in her hand. If she didn't do something big, the Triumvirate was over.

Satana opened herself to home and tore a hole to the deepest, oldest pit in her realm, where she'd thrown the ugliest, most vile, violent creatures that had ever walked her slice of Hell, her enemies and former friends, her mistakes, her exes.

She had to step away from the vault to open a rift in the chamber, and she shielded herself and moved before she could overthink it. She was hidden right in front of the glowering Suns, all of them alive and well, the old witch off to her right, driving Zarathos into the wall like a reluctant nail. Magik and the child floated next to the Ghost Rider, the handsome vampire leading them with a sword in his hand. His nostrils flared, and as close as he was, she wouldn't stay hidden for long.

Go go go! Satana channeled her essence and ripped a wide portal in the low roof of the new chamber, between the Blood hag and the wriggling Zarathos. Killers and beasts, powerful demons and dumb actresses spilled out onto the rocks along with a load of picked and splintered bones. The soulless prisoners were starving, bloodstained, raving, and they knocked the crone down and went after the Suns, more falling into the chamber, screaming and moaning. The stench of blood and decay exploded over all of them.

Satana turned back to the vault, exhausted but satisfied that she'd bought enough time—

—and was knocked off her feet by a whipping chain. She landed on the rocks, banging her precious elbow. Pain shot up her arm.

A charging screech demon ran for the Ghost Rider, its piercing cry deafening, teeth-rattling, and Satana had to roll out of the way, farther from the vault. The vampire dashed past her, swinging his sword at a scuttling jackal spider, its fangs dripping poison, and Satana ducked from his shining backswing, barely able to hold her glamour.

She inched back to the partly shielded chamber where Fenn huddled and the vault waited, while all around her chaos reigned.

○————————○

GHOST Rider danced, the Spirit delighted by the variety of damned things that fell into the vault's chamber. Demons, soulless, monsters that crawled and stumbled, flew and oozed, tumbled out of Hell and into his path, and he let loose. A kick to the throat of a gabbling blood angel, a punch to knock the head off a shrieking scarecrow, a swinging chain sweeping all six legs from under some kind of matted tiger thing. Robbie and the Spirit engaged in a spectacular beatdown of the wicked, fire singing in his veins.

Blade dashed back and forth through the motley army

of the damned, slashing throats, spilling guts, rotten blood slinging off the shining blade. Magik had Zarathos against the wall, but the demon was screaming spells, pulses of darkness blasting through the dirty air like indiscriminate punches. Nico and Caretaker were chanting together, zipping the open rift closed, amputating limbs off a dozen dropping monsters.

Robbie put his back to the vault and took on all incoming: a pair of one-horned bruisers, another squatting, leaping screech demon, a madman with a pair of bone spears. Ghost Rider cut them with his chains, knocked them screaming with Hellfire, whipped them into the walls, the ceiling, each other.

Zarathos shouted another spell and a bolt of lightning slashed through the room, zapping Magik. She fell out of the air and Blade flashed to her side, lifting her away from a trio of monstrous obsidian spiders that had dropped from the Hell portal. The flying spiders ejected streams of smoking poison, shooting through the whirling dust in inky jets, but Blade and Magik were gone before the liquid hit the stones.

Don't mind if I do. Ghost Rider whipped a chain at the nasty threesome, the shining blade at its tip plunging through their bloated black bodies. He slung them at Zarathos, cackling when the nasty things splattered across his ugly face.

Magik shook off the hit while Nico blasted a half dozen of the soulless creatures with the Staff, fiery purple light gathering around her in a radiant burst and arrowing out of its eye, disintegrating the corrupt flesh of the attacking monsters.

Robbie tackled a sinister-looking dog-faced beast, the demon's jaws snapping and sliding off his leather. He pounded its snarling mug and chucked it at a thing that looked like a ball made out of fangs and bloody wax.

"Protect the vault!" Caretaker shouted. She was back at the arch-demon, binding his jaws closed with a web of white magic. Zarathos ripped it away and reanimated half the corpses of the soulless, mortal and monster alike, throwing their maimed bodies back into the fight.

The Spirit of Vengeance caught the familiar, rich, good smell of the succubus suddenly, the same one who'd stabbed its Rider, and locked on. A shadow against the wall behind him, close to the vault, a blur between the stumbling damned. Robbie slashed at the open, empty space with both chains.

Satana Hellstrom flickered into view, shrieking, batting at the chains that had wrapped around her upper arms, and Robbie grinned, jerked her away from the vault's chamber.

"Nooo!" She tried to shake off the links, but she was barely stronger than a mortal and he held her easily. She smelled like sex and food and victory, but her expression was agonized.

"I got the succubus!" Robbie called.

"Blade, get John Doe. He's at the vault!" Nico shouted, the Staff's eye arrowing light at something that looked like a pink pterodactyl. "Hurry, the seal's about to go!"

"On it!" Blade called, and the Spirit of Vengeance felt something change in the air, a snap of Hell energy flashing through the gore-streaked stones.

Zarathos and Satana both screamed and broke free.

WHEN Fenn was alone, he tapped at his signature copier, mimicking the dying seal on the vault. His newest device projected the mystical "scent" of the magic holding the vault closed; his sensor couldn't distinguish between the real magic and the false scent—exactly as he'd planned. The mystics he'd worked with were all new, still training, but they'd performed marvelously throughout his work with the Triumvirate, getting him to Satana, charging his gamma shields, setting up alarms. The quality of the spells they were working with surely had something to do with it.

And all credit is down to me.

Outside the stone barrier that mostly hid him from the chaos, unseen monsters shrieked and spat, the Midnight Suns beating down Satana's minions, Zarathos lashing out at the witches and getting lashed in turn. Satana was howling.

Fenn waited for the vault's seal to expire, anxiously watching his sensor tick down the real time. He sat the projector next to the vault, between the vessel and the violent ruckus taking place just past the thin wall that Zarathos had erected, and wedged pieces of rock under the suspended box. Now was the worst moment, the final crawling seconds. Fenn held his breath, his thoughts on repeat.

Grab it push the button grab it push the button—

The seal on the vault failed a half second after his sensor told him it would, and the top of the metal box dissipated all at once, not even a flash of light or a puff of dust. The loose rock beneath crunched, angling the vault a few degrees.

The contents lay across a roughly tanned hide, radiating power that even he could feel.

The spell was written on a flat sheet of parchment, inked in blood. The shield was a rough hammered circle of shining metal, an amalgam of steel and copper with a broad X etched across the top in blackened lines. And the amulet, the Varkath Star, was a deep blue stone set in a cage of silver, a shining chain coiled around the egg-shaped pendant. It was stunning, simple, the stone pulsing with hidden depths of power.

Fenn took the item of greatest value, slid it into his jacket's inner pocket, and punched the button on his bracelet, which did two things at once: black chemical smoke poured from the signature projector, and his exact coordinates were sent to a trio of mystics at a farm in Romania. They'd been preparing for days. If they pulled it off, his would be their first successful transport. If they didn't, he was dead. But they would succeed. He'd dreamed it.

A gloved fist punched a hole in the barrier, and Fenn saw a flash of red eyes through the ragged opening and ducked into the billow of smoke.

Come on, come on—

Fenn's skin tingled all over and he just had time to grin before he was carried safely away, the screams of demons following him into the dark.

18

IN spite of the terrible Suns, Zarathos stayed in tune with the vault's seal, listening for its end. The Blood witch was strong but she couldn't hold him alone; Magik was powerful but flinched from his blows. The rest were fighting a score of decrepit soulless, Satana's damned dragged to Earth to fight for his reign, and he was losing strength but had more than enough to end the Suns, if he could just—

A black portal flickered in and out of existence at the vault, a door quickly opening and closing, and Zarathos screamed, his rage swelling him, lending him a burst of great strength. He slapped the Blood witch's dimensional beam aside and flew for the vault's chamber, his limbs slashed by swords and chains as he barreled through the rock shield that hid the precious vessel. *How? How?* The seal was at the edge of breaking, but it was still there, he could taste it.

And something new. The Varkath Star.

A cloud of noxious smoke spilled out of the chamber, and the vampire was on Zarathos like a storm, cutting him with a narrow blade, but Zarathos didn't feel it. He only saw and felt the power of the Varkath Star, its rich energy pulsing like a beacon in the black mist. He'd feared that Mephisto or another had come to claim it, that Fenn had stolen it, but the amulet lay glittering in its iron cradle, the vault open in spite of Zarathos's senses telling him it was still closed.

At last! I have—

A chain wrapped his ankle, jerking him backward. Zarathos turned and saw the Ghost Rider, Satana struggling against one of his chains, screaming for help, the lanky fighter's other cursed chain steadily pulling at Zarathos. The Rider's tiny skull grinned at him, fire dancing in its eyes.

Zarathos blasted the Ghost Rider off his feet with soul power, a concentrated blow, and pulled his boot loose from the Spirit's enchanted links. He landed a clumsy blow against the fluttering vampire and knocked him to the broken stones.

Released, Satana ran to Zarathos's side, grabbed his bleeding arm—and drew threads of power from his essence, using it to portal to the vault in front of him, her greedy fingers reaching for the amulet. Fenn was nowhere to be seen.

Traitors! Zarathos grabbed the lesser demon with his mind and tossed her at the vampire just as the trained fighter charged forward, both of them going down.

Spells arrowed at his flesh, ichor dripped from his wounds,

but the Varkath Star gleamed through the choking smoke and then Zarathos was reaching for it, the thin chain icy to the touch, the incredible power of the stone radiant and depthless. He lifted the Varkath Star from where it had lain untouched for so many centuries, laughing, *Victory! Victory!*

"Blade!" someone shrieked, as Zarathos raised the amulet—

—and a shimmering, hissing whisper whisked by his skull, and his mighty right hand with the amulet in it was sliced off at the wrist. Fiery pain exploded. The vampire's blood-spattered sword clattered to the stone floor next to Zarathos's clenching, disembodied fingers, the amulet's chain dripping between the quivering digits.

○━━━━━━━━━○

HELD by the Ghost Rider's chains, Satana felt a window to Hell open and close, a split second of black at the vault where Fenn waited. She screamed, fighting harder against the clinging links, but she'd put everything she had into opening the eternity pit, she was running on empty.

Zarathos felt it too, his shriek of rage and disappointment louder than her own. He broke from the energies pushing him to the wall and flew for the vault. Satana watched helplessly as he smashed the barrier to the vault's chamber, watched his eyes flare with pleasure at whatever he saw there. Black smoke poured into the larger space, and the Ghost Rider loosed one of Satana's chains to sling it at Zarathos, catching his left ankle. The Spirit pulled, cackling, and Zarathos turned and blasted him with a pulse of dark energy.

When the Ghost Rider's chain loosened from around her shoulders, Satana didn't hesitate. She ran to Zarathos, leaping over the slain bodies of soulless, and reached for one bulbous, bleeding arm, opening her empty reserves. She only had a second, but it was enough. A bolt of black power shot into her, soul energy twisted to his signature, thick and heady.

As soon as she had it, she pushed herself through the smoky, screaming air to stand at the vault. It was open, the top gone, the Varkath Star a shining knot of silver and blue inside, *beautiful*, and she grabbed for the chain—

—and Zarathos lifted her, threw her before she could touch the amulet.

No!

She crashed into the hybrid vampire and they both went down in a tangle of limbs, the handsome fighter cursing, slamming her off with arms like pistons.

"Blade!" the old witch shouted, pointing at the vault, at Zarathos, who was lifting the priceless Star from its cradle—

—and the vampire dropped into a half crouch, pulled his arm back impossibly fast, and launched his sword at a slight upward angle, following through with his whole body.

The blade sliced through Zarathos's thieving hand and lopped it off. The sword, the demon's right hand, and the Star all clattered to the ground, the amulet's chain still touching the disembodied fingers that spasmed and twitched.

Mine!

Satana pushed herself back into the smoky chamber and fell to her knees in front of the roaring demon, black blood oozing from the clean slice at his wrist. She snatched the amulet's chain from Zarathos's disembodied hand, laughing. The Varkath Star dangled from her perfect fingers—*mine!*—and she raised it to slip it over her head.

○——————————○

NICO had put a dozen slobbering monsters down with the Staff of One, soulless mortals, weird spiders and reptilian birds, starving demons driven mad in whatever prison they'd poured from. Robbie and Blade were taking down the rest, Caretaker and Magik keeping Zarathos busy and away from the vault.

When Nico felt the flash of a black spell flicker behind the vault's stone blind, everything happened fast. The vault's seal still held, barely, but Zarathos and Satana both screamed, and the giant grinning demon got a second wind from somewhere. He jetted across the chamber for the vault.

The Suns were on him like white on rice, Magik and Blade both slashing at him as he rocketed past, opening wounds across his limbs and torso. Ghost Rider whipped a chain across his back, but the demon didn't seem to notice, crashing through his blind. Black smoke poured from the small chamber and whirled around the few soulless fighters still standing.

Robbie got a chain around the demon's ankle and pulled, Satana held by his other chain. Blade was all over Zarathos, delivering cut after cut to the monster's heavily muscled body, crisscrossing lines of black appearing like magic across his chest and back.

Zarathos blasted Robbie with a powerful slap of energy

and Ghost Rider flew backward, losing his grip on both demons. The wannabe ruler of Hell swung his arm at the darting Daywalker and knocked him away. Satana ran to Zarathos, touched him, and then portaled herself into the choking black billows that poured from the smaller chamber.

Zarathos gestured and Satana was tossed over his shoulder and into Blade, who was coming in for another attack. The succubus squawked, flailing, knocking him backward.

"Blade!" Caretaker shouted, as Zarathos disappeared into the smoke, grinning.

Blade pushed Satana away and threw his katana, the bloody blade flying in a smooth arc through the smoky air, and Zarathos shrieked. The movement of the sword cut through the smoke and Nico saw Zarathos's hand fall, still clutching the shining silver amulet.

Satana Hellstrom flashed into the vault and grabbed for the Varkath Star, her wild grin shining through the clouds of black, her greedy eyes glittering like dark jewels.

"Nico!" Blade shouted, and Nico held up the Staff and poured all her energy into the words that formed in her mind, that were the truth, that exploded in power as she shouted them aloud.

"IT'S NOT *YOURS!*" Nico cried, and the Staff of One lit up, a purple tornado of light spinning from its eye, blasting away the choking air. She felt the violently powerful energy narrow and focus to a penlight's beam, concentrated and swift, pouring through her and into the Varkath Star that Satana held up in one slender fist.

Nico could feel the amulet's blue ocean of energies, complex and vast, could feel its resistance to change—and then it exploded, the Staff's energy bursting through the stone's integrity all at once.

Released, the amulet's potential radiated outward in a shock wave, blasting everyone in the chamber off their feet. Streams of dark and light magic swept the rocky room, the few soulless left alive dashed to the rocks. Nico was blown backward, slamming into one stony wall.

Zarathos and Satana both screamed again, wordless cries of rage. Zarathos snatched up a small machine that was dumping out the black smoke and hurled it at Nico.

Robbie whipped it out of the air and into the ceiling. The device shattered, bits of metal and plastic flying, and Nico's sense that the seal still held was gone, cut off like someone had flipped a switch.

John Doe, she thought, and nothing else, because Satana and Zarathos were both blasting her, unleashing a torrent of black spite and hate and power that drove her into the wall again, knocking her thoughts free.

○────────────○

MAGIK was bounced into a backflip by the storm of energy that burst from the amulet, saw the other Suns react. Caretaker fell against the wall, her face ashen. Robbie and Blade both shoulder-rolled to their feet, Robbie lashing a chain at a wounded six-legged big cat that tried to launch at him, Blade coming up with knives in his hands.

Zarathos hurled a smoking machine at Nico with his remaining hand and Ghost Rider flipped it out of the air before it could hit her, but the arch-demon and Satana had both turned their rage on Nico, a river of darkness slamming her against the stones.

"You *brat!*" Satana screamed, the furious cry turning to a shriek as Blade's knives were suddenly sticking out of her generous chest, dark blood running into the valley between.

"Hunc puerum custodire ab horror noctis!" Caretaker shouted, and threw one hand toward Nico, visible light pouring from her fingers. The light smashed against the torrent of demonic power and turned it, like Caretaker had thrust a mirror into the vicious beam, deflecting it to the bare stones past the girl. Released from the river of darkness, Nico dropped to the ground, stumbled, her eyes dazed.

Satana jerked one of Blade's knives out of her flesh and threw it at Caretaker, using her energies to make it fly true, but Ghost Rider again flicked it out of the air with a chain. The polished steel hit the ceiling and landed on one of the many soulless corpses that mounded the floor, Satana's inmates finally at rest.

Enraged, darkness spit from Zarathos's every pore, crackled around him like a fine net of negative sparks. He started chanting, words of power in the demonic tongue, a spell to steal strength from his enemies. Blade and Robbie both charged for him, but Satana threw a glamour and suddenly the chamber was filled with hulking, bloody copies of Zarathos, all moving, all chanting.

Ghost Rider and Blade weren't fooled—no one was. Zarathos's signature was a beating pulse of evil. The two fighters tackled the demon as one, Blade jerking him off balance, Robbie stopping the ancient words with a roundhouse that knocked a handful of Zarathos's pointed teeth out. They rattled across the rocky floor.

Caretaker pointed at the succubus, pinning her to the wall at her back. The demoness's face was a mask of impotent rage. The copies of Zarathos popped like soap bubbles.

Zarathos planted a boot in Robbie's belly and kicked him away. He tried to hit Blade with his remaining hand but missed, the Daywalker dodging the strike in a blur of movement.

"Magik!" Blade shouted, Robbie echoing the call.

"Magik, take the ball!" Nico said at the same time, and Magik contemplated her action for a fraction of a second as she flew forward, stopping six feet in front of the raging demon. She brought the sword down, the embodiment of her will cutting a portal in the hazy, wretched air.

The smells of sulfur and lava filled the broken cavern, the red darkness of Mephisto's Hell spilling out of the portal in a pall of black intention and bloody light.

"No!" Zarathos shrieked, and Mephisto's realm heard him, felt and knew the demon's blood, tasted his signature, and reached for him.

Magik grimaced at the awful darkness, the familiar smell of Mephisto's essence burning her senses as tendrils of crimson and black reached out of the portal, enveloped the screaming demon, and pulled him in. He clawed at the portal's pale edges, strained against Mephisto's hungry will, but the ruler of Hell wanted him and would have him.

As soon as Zarathos was through, Magik closed the portal, slamming it against Mephisto's curious eye before he could examine where his gift had come from.

○────────○

MEPHISTO'S realm, his manifest will, closed around Zarathos and pulled him inexorably, steadily, through the portal, back into the stench of Hell.

Zarathos was still strong and he broke free of the winding energies that spun out of the choking air to imprison him, but there were more and more. For every bond he severed, two more appeared, dragging him down through the blood-red sky, into the burning ground.

"I will have my vengeance!" Zarathos screamed, aware of Mephisto's interest and glee, and he babbled his spell again, to take the strength of his enemies but in his tormentor's realm, Zarathos's words were empty, meaningless.

The Triumvirate had betrayed him. He'd tasted life and freedom and paid for it with his right hand, stabbed in the back by the treacherous Satana and the worthless Fenn, tossed back into torture and servitude by the Midnight Suns.

Burning with impotent rage, Zarathos was unceremo-niously dumped back into the tiny cell where he'd been held prisoner for so long. He shrieked and beat at the walls, Mephisto's uproarious laughter drumming at his ears, shaking the very foundations of Hell.

ZARATHOS was gone, Fenn was gone, the Varkath Star was gone. Satana's rage dropped a few notches as she realized her exact situation. The old witch held Satana pinned against the rock wall, blocking her glamours, containing her in a mesh of pale, prickly light. The Midnight Suns were all staring at her, their grim faces spattered with blood, only the Ghost Rider grinning, ever grinning.

Alone in a cave with five supernaturals she'd tried her best to murder. She couldn't even break the old woman's web. She didn't stand a snowball's chance of winning anything.

And there's nothing to win. The Triumvirate was a bust, her visions of ultimate leadership snuffed out by incompetent men and a smug little group of goodies who weren't even interesting enough to invite to a party. The Varkath Star was a handful of broken silver threads and a few shards of rock.

Satana swallowed her fury, forced it down with a winning smile.

"Can't blame a girl for trying," she said, making it light and friendly, doing what she could to fluff up her chemistry. The Blood crone was holding her tightly, limiting her options.

"Would you follow Zarathos?" Magik asked, floating in front of her, her dumb little face haughty and judgmental.

"I was thinking I might go home," Satana said, sincerely. Elder Gods, she was tired. She'd drained a hefty chunk of her dimension to make this thing happen, invested *herself,* and all that energy was just gone. Zarathos had been sucked back to his prison, and Fenn… *Where did he even go?*

She assessed herself and realized she didn't care even a tiny bit. She was over this.

"You will return to your realm now and stay there for a hundred years," Magik commanded.

Satana couldn't keep smiling, not while being directed by this pixie mutant, but she managed not to choke. "*Fine.*"

"You'll swear it by blood," Magik added.

Don't even think; just do it. Instead of punching that smarmy face as she *deeply* wished to do, Satana held up her left hand, stabbed it with the middle finger of her right, deliberately, and gave herself a healthy scratch.

"I will go home now and stay there for a hundred years," she spat, her willing offer of blood binding her to her words. She could break the promise, but Magik would know about it the second she did.

Magik nodded, stepping back, and the Blood hag let Satana go, the mesh of white containment evaporating into the air. The other Suns stood ready, tensed to rush her if she tried anything. The child witch grinned at her and waggled her fingers, *bye-bye.*

Fuming, Satana opened a hole to her realm and pushed through, glad to rid her sight of the ugly Suns and their ugly expressions of satisfaction, glad that Zarathos was suffering, glad to be going home, where things were exactly as she liked them. Fenn was a loser, he'd wasted her time, and Earth was just stupid.

GHOST Rider surveyed the wreckage of corpses and rocks, Blade flashing around to double-check there was no more threat. The Spirit of Vengeance was satisfied, in high humor since Zarathos had been pulled through Magik's portal, but there was nothing left to fight. The Triumvirate was gone; the soulless were dead.

We killed some of them twice, Robbie thought, and the Spirit cackled.

Caretaker brushed the foul air away as Magik stepped to the vault, lifting a small round shield of hammered metal. She picked up the crushed remains of the Varkath Star, looking all around the floor.

"There's no summoning spell," she said.

All of the Suns started looking, and Robbie let the Spirit go, the better to see low contrast. The Spirit was eager to take off, to share the news of Zarathos's comeuppance with its brethren. Robbie counted twenty-six dead creatures, mostly demons, all soulless—beasts and flying things and a few mortals were tucked in among the Hellspawn. From the look of them, the Suns had put them out of their misery.

Caretaker was shaking out a ratty piece of leather at the vault, and Blade dashed around again, checking, but the spell wasn't anywhere.

"It's no big, is it?" Nico asked. "Aren't Mephisto spells like a dime a dozen?"

"It's a loose end," Blade said. "Just like John Doe. I'll follow up on a few of those shield sites when we get home."

"I'm sorry about the Varkath Star," Nico said, addressing Caretaker. "I didn't mean to kill it."

"It wasn't any of ours," Magik offered, when the old witch didn't answer. "Better that it's gone, than for it to fall into demon hands."

The Suns looked tired and frankly disgusting, every one of them spattered with a dozen kinds of blood, a real mélange of stink, but Robbie couldn't handle their serious expressions.

"Hey, team, we beat the Triumvirate," he announced. "We brought the pain, am I right?"

"Damn straight," Nico said, nodding her filthy face. She was caked in dirt.

"Zarathos is in pain," Magik said, honestly, and Blade smiled, a tiny quirk of his lips.

Robbie raised his hands, gesturing for more.

"We smacked the crap out of them," Nico said.

"Tossed 'em like trash," Blade agreed, and Magik nodded.

Caretaker still looked pale, but she finally got on board. "You all fought very well."

Still not a jubilee, but Robbie would take it. He nodded, satisfied, while Caretaker and Blade discussed clean-up. They would collapse the chamber, bury all the bodies, and Caretaker would transplant trees over the ruined ground. The empty vault would stay hidden and secret, the metal free to oxidize and rot alongside the bones of their enemies.

All in a day's work for the Midnight Suns, Robbie thought, and felt pretty near perfectly happy. A shower and a fat breakfast, he'd be golden.

19

IT was late when they got back to the Abbey, or early, depending on how you looked at things. Nico decided late. Her body was worn out, crampy, but she felt wide awake. She couldn't stop replaying the look on Satana Hellstrom's face when Nico had told her to eat it. The succubus had gotten off easy considering all the harm she'd done, but at least she wouldn't do any more for a while.

Charlie was super interested in all of them when they stepped out of the pale moonlight and into the dim foyer—they absolutely stank out loud—and by silent agreement everybody hit the showers. Nico exfoliated and triple-washed her hair, grateful to be clean as she pulled on her comfiest sweats and a clean tee. She headed for the kitchen, hoping the other Suns were in the same mood as her, relaxed, awake. Maybe a little bit proud.

Blade and Robbie were already there, Robbie boiling a big pot of ramen and recounting his favorite parts of kicking soulless ass. Magik wandered in and sat down, Nico conjuring a plate of cheese and crackers for them to share while Robbie cooked.

"I say we've got tomorrow off," Robbie said, stirring the noodles. "All-day party in the common, video games, board games, movies. And we should have a cake."

"We can write *the triumvirate eats poo* right across the top," Nico said. "In cursive white icing."

"I like the board game with the paper money," Magik said. "I like to be the tiny boot."

For Magik, volunteering such information was uncharacteristically chatty, and Nico smiled at her, sincerely warmed by her participation. "I like the little dog."

Magik smiled back at her, pleased.

"I want to go back to a couple of John Doe's spots first thing, do some digging," Blade said. "But count me in for the afternoon."

"We can all go," Nico said, but Blade shook his head.

"Nah, take a break," Blade said. "A little detective work is all. If I can track him, I'll call in the team."

The team. The Midnight Suns had successfully worked together to foil the Triumvirate's nefarious goals, and Nico felt like they all understood each other at a new level, as colleagues. She felt closer to all of them than she ever had. Knowing that your friends had your back felt amazing, and watching them prove it was…

Well, icing on the cake.

"Where's Caretaker?" Robbie asked, carrying the steaming pot to the table. Nico sniffed and added a few things to the noodles. Robbie never got the spices right. She grabbed three bowls and a handful of spoons with a thought and moved them to the table, along with a roll of paper towels.

"In her study," Blade said. "I think she's following up on that loose thread."

The spell to summon Mephisto. "You think John Doe took it?" Nico asked.

"Maybe," Blade said. "Did anyone see him leave? I know he was there, and then he wasn't."

"A window opened and closed," Magik said, and Nico nodded. She'd felt a flash of something down in that chamber, a dark, alien something that had strobed once and fallen still. She had to wonder if it was another spell from the Darkhold.

"I'll find him," Blade said. "We know how to locate the shields now, and without his demon friends he won't be able to hide for long."

There were fierce smiles and nods all around. The Midnight Suns were ready for anything, ready for *the* Midnight Sun. They had kicked demon butt and could look forward to kicking a lot more in the days ahead.

Nico ate her ramen, memorizing the warm good feeling in her chest. She was with her excellent friends, her team, and tomorrow they would have cake.

CARETAKER showered and changed, the uneasiness she'd felt when she'd realized the summoning spell was missing growing all the while. She told herself that she regretted the loss of the Varkath Star, the destruction of such a useful tool, but by the time she'd sat down at her desk, she knew it was more. Something about a spell to summon Mephisto, a memory that she couldn't place but that nagged at her like a toothache.

She brought books to her study, titles she hadn't considered when she'd searched for the amulet, titles she *should* have considered. Why hadn't she bothered looking up the other items in the collection? She'd just decided that the Triumvirate would only care about the Varkath Star and hadn't given it a second thought.

Time passed, the piles of books around her desk multiplying as Caretaker searched for the reference she couldn't remember. She called up everything the library had about Mephisto, and found nothing. The young Suns gathered in the kitchen for a while and then split apart to their rooms, and Caretaker was still reading, scanning pages. She told herself to set it aside, she was tired and very likely it didn't matter. Nico was right: spells to call up Hell rulers were commonplace.

As the earliest birds began their songs, Caretaker found a hint exactly where she'd hoped not to find one—a handwritten tome about the Knights of Wundagore. The book was filled with battle stories and only mentioned in passing the brave group that had buried a powerful demoness, hidden her tomb from the "eyes of the Earth and the sky, light and dark." The book named the knights who'd participated in the burial, all long dead, and Caretaker's eye caught on the cleric Sedilos, who had accompanied them.

Sedilos. She remembered the name. Caretaker retrieved the cleric's dusty memoir from Agatha's desk and skimmed, her heart heavy in her chest, beating like a funeral drum by the time she reached the story.

...whereupon I was Entrusted to Record the Lay of her Unholy rest, the Knight's Leader providing me the Parchment of a Spell to Call Forth the King of Hell, a Final Recourse should the Knights' Best Defenses fail against the Prophecies of the Foretold. This Sole Record of her Resting Place was Sealed with Magical Items to Tame the Awful King and Ensure that the Dark Mother will Keep to her Eternal Grave.

Caretaker re-read the words, hardly aware that her heart ached like a knife had been thrust into it. The story was about her sister. Lilith had been a girl with a laugh that lit up the air, and they'd sometimes held hands walking through the woods, as sisters did. Pain and regret, self-pity and self-loathing swept Caretaker's old soul, overridden by the pure hatred she harbored for Lilith, for what she'd willingly become.

She laid her head across the pages and wept, memories like wounds clouding her mind, stress and grief and sorrow and fear wrenching her insides. The past oppressed her, her mistakes unforgiveable, and the future promised violence and loss. And in the middle, she was so alone...

Let it go, Agatha whispered, and Caretaker felt a cool hand touch her forehead, smoothing her hair away from her brow. *Let it go so you can rest now, you're so tired, you've been so brave.*

Caretaker let herself believe that Agatha soothed her even as she grieved the old witch's loss, and she finally fell asleep, a blissfully empty darkness that welcomed her in.

○————————○

"DOCTOR Faustus to speak to Lieutenant Pruitt."

The voice on the line was new. "Who?"

"Doctor Faustus." Faustus sighed. "Johann Fennhoff. For Lieutenant Marcus Pruitt."

"Hold, please."

Faustus checked his watch, his eye on the airstrip outside. The cargo jet he'd chartered was overdue. He wished he'd had Satana move more of his equipment, but of course she might have suspected something. Zarathos had never had a clue, but the succubus had been quite a bit sharper.

Not sharp enough. She'd never doubted his motives, or asked any real questions about how he'd known about the vault of the Varkath Star. Hydra had been collating information for millennia. When the dreams had begun, Faustus had known exactly what to look for.

A gruff voice barked into his ear. "Pruitt."

Faustus couldn't help smiling. "I have it."

"You have what, Doctor," Pruitt said, already sounding bored.

"The map to Mother's tomb," Faustus said, and the silence on the other end of the connection was glorious. Marcus Pruitt was barely thirty and he was a suit. All of Faustus' "superiors" were suits these days, more interested in stockholdings than in fulfilling Hydra's true purpose.

"And?" Pruitt said finally, and now he was only trying to seem uninterested. The lieutenant was the latest in a long line of Hydra's frontrunners who had sidelined Dr. Faustus, who'd turned their backs to dimensional realities. They'd slashed his budget to a sliver of what was needed while they paid millions to politicians and influencers, trying to legislate and manipulate their way to totalitarianism. Faustus knew what they all thought of him, their jokes about "Dr. Flaky," but he'd stayed the course. The Midnight Sun approached; he had the majority of the Darkhold pages, meticulously collected by Hydra in the centuries since it had last been assembled; and he had just recovered the only map to Lilith's tomb ever drawn. The prophecy of the Midnight Sun was unfolding exactly as it should, as Power Incarnate had whispered to Faustus in his sleep.

"*And*, I'll need better equipment, and soldiers," Faustus said. "I'll also expect your approval on my recruitment plan for additional mystics, and full funding for my workshop."

"Hydra doesn't need more mystics, Doctor," Pruitt said, latching on to his favorite argument. "I'm not convinced the ones we've got are worth the cost. And how do we know we can control her? We've got a lot of investments that are paying off right now, without the hocus pocus. Our soldiers are training for the new world order. They need to know how to fight, not dance around cauldrons."

"You misunderstand," Faustus said. "I will be at Lilith's tomb in a few hours to begin excavation, and Hydra's mystics will raise her as soon as its possible. A few days, I expect, a week at most. Whether or not Hydra's current leadership chooses to serve in the new world or join the ashes of the unworthy billions, well, that's up to men like you, isn't it, Lieutenant?"

Another long pause. Dr. Faustus waited, fully aware of who had the high card. Hydra had strayed from its roots, but even Pruitt knew better than to turn away from real power.

"I suppose I could spare a few men to protect the dig site," Pruitt said. Grudgingly.

"And?" Dr. Faustus smiled again.

Pruitt sighed. "I'll send someone to take a look, assess the situation."

"Who?"

"Crossbones, if he's willing," Pruitt said, and Faustus frowned. Crossbones was a mercenary, he didn't understand or like magic, as Pruitt was perfectly aware.

On the other hand... Wouldn't it be fine, to raise Lilith in front of *Crossbones*? The thug had more pull than he deserved; once he was on board, the full breadth of Hydra's resources would be at Dr. Faustus's disposal.

At Mother's disposal.

"I'll ask him myself," Faustus said.

"You do that," Pruitt said. "Have *him* call me, and I'll consider your requests. If that's all, Doctor..."

Outside, a small cargo plane was landing, its whining rumble and the shrieking of its brakes filling the tiny waiting room. Inside was excavation equipment, and a marvelous device that had taken Faustus years to develop, which would lend great power to Hydra's small "trial" group of mystics. Once Mother was awake, Pruitt and his colleagues would regret their blindness, curse their own narrow minds.

But not for long. The alignment was barely six months away. They would believe, embrace the prophecy, or they would die. Perhaps they'd die anyway.

"Yes, that's all," Dr. Faustus said, and hung up on the lieutenant before Pruitt could disconnect, chuckling to himself. He walked out to meet the plane, the handful of workers he'd hired standing by the empty rental trailers, ready to unload the jet's cargo. Mother was waiting. *Hail Hydra!*

○————————○

AT dawn, Blade and Magik went to New York and Blade spent a couple of hours investigating the dust that John Doe had left behind. He found a few odds and ends—part of a receipt for a box of flip switches, a broken phone that had belonged to one of the soulless, an uncompleted shipping order that had slipped under a desk at the warehouse. Nothing apparently useful. For a man reckless enough to team up with demons, to work with a Darkhold spell, Doe had been careful.

Blade was back at the Abbey in time to sit with the kids over a very late breakfast. They were still riding high, feeling good about their showdown with the Triumvirate. Blade felt good, too. Their first mission as a team had been a success, the kind of confidence builder that no amount of training could provide.

Caretaker stopped in for about two seconds to say she wasn't feeling well, but she hoped they'd enjoy their day of celebration, that they deserved it. The old woman looked under the weather, low energy and pale, but she'd also been crying, in Blade's opinion. Maybe she was finally letting herself experience some of what she'd been putting off since Agatha died, which could only help her in the long run. Hiding from feelings always ended up costing a lot more than letting them in... but that was also his opinion, and her philosophy was her own business. Not his dog, not his fight.

He followed the younger Suns to the common room, which Nico had decked out with black balloons and red streamers. As promised, there was a mildly vulgar sheet cake on the bar. Robbie and Nico set up a group shooting game, pushing controllers at Magik and Blade, but Magik said she'd prefer to watch and Blade still had digging to do. He agreed to come back for movies in the evening and retired to his room with a laptop.

He ran searches on the rentals, vehicles and homes, and came up with new names—Mario Rossi, Josef Novak, Jan Kowalski.

Now we're getting somewhere. All of John Doe's aliases were placeholder names, like Mustermann, which was roughly equivalent to *Exampleperson.* Men like Doe always thought they were so witty, hiding their jokes in plain sight because they were convinced no one would catch on. Their arrogance was something else.

Blade tapped out some new search parameters for rental records in and around New York and followed up on the switch receipt—paid in cash, the clerk didn't remember. He found the missing-persons report on the broken phone's owner, and spent a couple of hours coming up with IDs on a number of the local soulless. Young men just hitting their prime, mostly. He also read a series of news releases about a town on the Serbian border grieving a stadium collapse, apparently the result of an extremely localized, unrecorded earthquake. A few hundred people had died and local geologists were baffled, but Blade thought he knew where Zarathos had filled up before the fight. The Triumvirate had caused a lot of grief.

It was late afternoon by the time Blade started digging into the empty warehouse's history, adding in a search on the abandoned machine shop. He wasn't really expecting much—he didn't *have* much—but he wouldn't feel right about things until he'd found all there was to find. John Doe was a menace. He'd been staring at the screen for so long that when the connection finally came up, he almost didn't catch it.

The empty warehouse was for rent, and was owned by a company called Strucker & Sons; it was their only holding. Strucker & Sons was a subsidiary of a shadow group, ECI. The machine shop had been owned by Nutechsolutions, which was run by one Fulan AlFulani, another placeholder name, and he was listed as the head of technical development for Keystop Incorporated… which was also owned by ECI.

Oh hell. Blade found the acronym in the Avengers' database in about two seconds, now that he knew where to look. Echidna Capitol Investment. The Von Struckers had led Hydra through their Nazi years, and Echidna Capitol Investment was a subsidiary of Hydra. The bag they'd found in John Doe's storage unit had been the real thing.

He went to Caretaker's rooms, stopping in the foyer when he realized she wasn't in the house. Nico called out from the common that they'd be starting movies in an hour, but Blade was already through the door, sunset painting the cliffs to the east in shades of orange and red. She'd be in the gardens around Hunter's tomb or at Agatha's memorial, he figured, but she was sitting on the stone steps that led down to the grotto.

Blade joined her, deliberately crunching the dry grass underfoot for the last few steps so she wouldn't be surprised.

"John Doe has a definite connection to Hydra," he said. "I don't know if it's current, but the Triumvirate could be theirs. We need to tell the Avengers."

Caretaker was leaned back on her elbows, face turned to the shadows of the trees overhead, her eyes closed. "Yes, let them know."

Her tone was indifferent. Blade sat down next to her.

"How are you feeling?"

"Old," she said.

"Did you find anything about the missing spell?"

Caretaker finally opened her eyes, turning her head to look at him. "This grotto was one of Hunter's favorite places, you know."

Blade wasn't going to take a deflection. "If you're not up for it, I'd be happy to research for you."

"No," Caretaker said. "It's not important."

She closed her eyes again, but Blade had heard the lie in her voice. In the two years he'd been at the Abbey, he'd noted that Caretaker often worded things extremely carefully, too carefully not to be suspect, but he couldn't remember an outright lie.

"What is it?" he asked. "What is it that you're not telling me? Something about the spell? About the Midnight Sun?"

Caretaker wouldn't look at him. "I came here for a few moments alone."

"Whatever the truth is, I won't judge. Tell me. Let me help you."

She didn't answer, didn't look at him, but he could feel hesitation. Blade waited patiently, listening to the eternal crash of the ocean. She'd tell him or she wouldn't, there was no point in pushing… but he hoped she would. The alignment meant a lot more craziness was ahead of the Midnight Suns, and he liked to think he'd earned Caretaker's trust, or at least her respect.

The air went silent. The sound of the waves, the wind in the trees, the life in the woods froze for a millisecond, and Caretaker sat up abruptly, her expression deeply unhappy. At the same time, Blade felt a tiny shift in the dimension's reality, a darkness that hadn't been present a second before. The difference was so subtle that Blade would have been hard pressed to describe what had changed, exactly, only that something had. There was a stain in the air, so faint, like the end of an echo, the last particle of a scent...

The three younger Suns spilled out of the Abbey's west entrance, just off the grotto. Blade raised a hand.

"What was that?" Nico asked, leading the group. "You feel that, right?"

"Bad news," Robbie said.

"We should check the mirror table," Magik said. "A dimensional rift, perhaps."

Blade shook his head, but Caretaker spoke up.

"The Shalidas Collective has touched the alignment," she said. "As expected, we're only feeling it now. We've been so busy, I hadn't prepared for the change."

Blade was watching her, watched her body language, her eyes... and concluded that she was lying again.

Twice in one night. Maybe she didn't trust any of them, maybe it was a personal matter, somehow... or maybe he should respect her enough to leave it alone, trust her to tell him if she saw fit. If it was important, if it mattered to the Midnight Suns, she would let them know.

Or she won't, and we'll find out when it happens.
Blade didn't know and couldn't predict. He'd keep ready,
like always.

○────────────────○

BLADE waited. He wanted her to talk, and part of
Caretaker wanted to tell him, about the map, the prophecy,
her connection to it all. But she was tired, and if her worst
fears came into view, all of the Suns would know soon
enough. And she truly might be worried for no reason at all.
There were a number of elements that had to be perfectly in
place before she was willing to consider the prophecy of the
Midnight Sun's viability, and there was no reason for the
young team to know of it prior.

She opened her mouth to tell him that she needed a few
days, and felt the shift.

For a second, she couldn't breathe. The Abbey's stability
flickered.

Blade was watching her, but he looked away when the
Suns came out. All of them had felt it.

Talk to them, Agatha said, but Caretaker wasn't ready.
She just wasn't. She'd slept for a few hours at her desk and
then lain on her bed all day, detached, numb, trying to come
to terms with what had happened, what could be happening
now. The Knights of Wundagore had entombed her sister
and left behind an emergency kit to halt her resurrection,
set to open before the alignment. Mephisto hated Lilith, she
threatened his reign; with the tools in the vault, the Knights

had created a failsafe, to keep the prophecy of the Midnight Sun from becoming a reality. And she'd led her team of eager children to victory against the Triumvirate, inadvertently giving the prophecy a path to one of its key elements, and destroying an artifact that might have prevented it.

The lie came out like she meant it. "The Shalidas Collective has touched the alignment, as expected. We've been so busy, I hadn't prepared for the change."

It was the truth, partly.

"Wow," Nico said. "It's… yuck." She shivered.

"I did not think we would feel the Collective," Magik said. "The dimension is vast but contains very little substance."

"Size matters," Robbie said, and both he and Nico laughed, but not easily. The palpable taint of dark creation had seeped back into existence in every dimension.

Blade knew she wasn't saying something, and she raised her chin and stared him down. They would talk—they would *have* to talk—but not now, not today.

She thought about the foxglove on her desk, still vibrant, and stood up to address them all. Blade rose too, barely masking his suspicion.

"The days will get darker. The air will keep getting thicker, and many immutable laws will falter as the Balance keeps shifting toward chaos. But each of you is a light, and I know you'll do your best for each other, and for Earth, now and throughout the alignment. I have faith in the Midnight Suns, in all of you, and am satisfied that the legacy's worth is upheld."

Nico bowed her head. Robbie grinned, and Magik

nodded, but Blade shot her a look that said they'd be speaking again later. Soon.

"You should watch a movie with us," Nico said, smiling at her. "Or at least come have some cake."

Caretaker nodded. "In a bit."

"What's the first movie?" Blade asked, leading the team back inside to enjoy their day of rest, Nico and Robbie bantering up an argument, and Caretaker sat down again, making herself remember to breathe.

The sense was quite faint. Caretaker's sister still slept, but the signature of the Mother of Demons was specific and powerful, her ability to create children unique. Even a whisper of her was enough to taint the air. It had been stripped from perception for centuries, muted, the flavor lost... but somewhere on Earth, Lilith's mark had just sprung back into existence. Chaos had claimed ground.

The tomb. Lilith's place of rest had been found, and Caretaker's own failures had led to the discovery.

She can't be resurrected. They'd have to have whole chapters of the Darkhold. And say they do, even she can't find all of the Darkhold pages, there's no reason to assume—

No point in lying to yourself, dear.

"Thank you, Agatha," Caretaker said, and exhaled deeply, letting go of what she wanted to believe. She was too tired to construct anything. Darker days *were* coming, the darkest, and the Midnight Suns were brave and would fight, and she had made many, many mistakes. All of it was what it was. Tomorrow, she'd figure out what came next.

She closed her eyes again, listening to the waves, to the gentle wind rustling leaves. She smelled the roses at the altar, and the threads of magic always wafting through the Abbey's grounds. The stones were cool against her back. Caretaker let herself be, and for just a moment, she was at peace.

ACKNOWLEDGMENTS

THIS book would have been impossible without the enthusiastic participation of the game developers and their team of excellent associates. If you enjoyed this book and want to be involved in the sequel, play *Marvel's Midnight Suns*, where the story picks up right after this one ends. If you didn't like the book, you should still try the game, because, I mean: have you seen the graphics? The story is solid, too. I'm not trying to sell anything, only to acknowledge the amazing work by Rocco, Jake, and the teams at Firaxis and Marvel. Thank you for letting me play around in your universe.

Thanks also to Davi Lancett, for his tireless efforts to hook me up to resources on a very tight deadline, and his keen eye toward making the story stronger. Thanks to Sarah Singer and Peter Rosas, for their decisive comments, and my agent Jennifer Weltz at JVNLA for her advocacy on my behalf in all things business.

On a personal note, please let me express my appreciation to Myk, for environmental support, and Cyrus and Dexter, for being who they are. Appreciation also to the following lovely people, for not minding overly that I drop out of sight for extended periods: Rachel, Sara, Scott, Leslie, Tamara, Mattiey, and Marcus (you're in Hydra, Marcus!). Also thank you for reading. People who read are the best people.

ABOUT THE AUTHOR

S.D. PERRY has been writing novelizations and tie-ins for most of her adult life. Best known for her work in the shared multiverses of Resident Evil, Star Trek, and Aliens, S.D. is a horror nerd and an introvert. Her father is acclaimed science fiction author Steve Perry. S.D. lives with her family in Portland, Oregon. SD tweets @sdp668.

For more fantastic fiction, author events,
exclusive excerpts, competitions, limited editions and more

VISIT OUR WEBSITE
titanbooks.com

LIKE US ON FACEBOOK
facebook.com/titanbooks

FOLLOW US ON TWITTER AND INSTAGRAM
@TitanBooks

EMAIL US
readerfeedback@titanemail.com